CROSS YOUR

HEART

An Emerson Novel

K L Finalley

Published by Copper Penny Press

Copyright © 2016 K L Finalley

All rights reserved.

ISBN-10: 0692673237

ISBN-13: 978-0692673232

For ARIELLE, JACOB, and GANNON...

The fireworks that dance in your eyes light my soul.

Chapter 1

Jacqueline Emerson had been startled in the night. But, she would have denied it if anyone had asked; and, her denial wouldn't have been a lie. She didn't know that her old self-defense methods were still in use. In her mind, the second Friday night in late September had been the same as any other Friday night in the last few months. She had left work on time, picked up Zoe Russell, her girlfriend's daughter, from her elementary school, and headed to her penthouse. In her story, she would have mentioned cooking dinner and helping Zoe with her homework. She would have told anyone who asked that dinner was served when Mallory Cummings, her girlfriend and Zoe's mother, joined them around six. After dessert, Zoe was ushered off to bath time while Jacqueline and Mallory cozied on the couch and watched the final game of the Tampa Bay Ray's season. To her, nothing was out of the ordinary. She would've explained that she had adapted to life with a girlfriend and a second grader; however, it wouldn't have been completely honest.

It was the sound of the bedroom door opening that disrupted Jacqueline's sleep, but she did not awaken. Her mind dispatched her senses to evaluate the situation. Having lived alone all of her adult life, it had not yet adjusted to the constant presence of others. Its alerts remained in place; in turn, her responses to those alerts remained in place. Her mind commanded her long, brown legs to be straightened beneath the warm, teal sheet. Then, it ordered that she relocate from her back onto her side to improve her hearing. Immediately, her ears began reporting sounds while her nose recorded any foreign scents. Even her mouth, which had dried in the night, began to fill with saliva as it might be called upon to speak, or worse, scream.

After all the data was gathered, her subconscious security system disengaged. It was not needed this early Saturday morning. While it had been fine-tuned over the last thirty-four years to guard and protect, in the past five months, it was being retooled to listen and observe. The sounds had been identified as that of pint-sized barefeet shuffling across the bedroom's laminate flooring. The scents captured by her nose were the smell of citrus shampoo. These details were the evidence her mind needed to end its investigation. Neither her home nor her body was under siege. The evidence proved that Zoe had opened the bedroom door and was in the room. And, she was of no threat to anything but Jacqueline's heart.

Yet, Jacqueline's mind wondered why Zoe had entered the room. Wanting more information, it was, then, that Jacqueline was calmly awakened. Complying with her mind's request, her eyes opened slowly. In the darkness of the room and without the aid of her Wayfarer glasses, she could see only the outline of a small face hovering over her own. In a voice that only existed after the witching hour, Jacqueline forced out, "Zoe? What's wrong, honey?"

As she rolled to her side, the height of the bed placed her face to face with the small person standing in barefeet beside her. Whispering, Zoe leaned forward and said, "Jax," a nickname that Mallory had given her and Zoe had adopted as well, "My stomach hurts."

Jacqueline furrowed her brow. In the last few months, she had encountered a number of childhood complaints, but she had not experienced a child's middle of the night stomach pain. She crept forward in the bed hoping not to awaken Mallory. Made uncomfortable by Jacqueline's change in position, Mallory rolled to her left side - away from Jacqueline, the door, and her daughter. Free from her, Jacqueline swung her legs from under the cozy sheet and sat upright in the bed. Zoe stepped back when she perceived what Jacqueline aimed to do. Once she was upright, the girl stepped between her legs. As she retrieved for her glasses from the nightstand, Zoe placed her head against Jacqueline's body. Trying to assess the situation, she asked, "Do you think you have to poop?" Zoe did not answer. Instead, she thrashed her head from side to side, as children often do. Jacqueline stroked her head and tried, "Do you think you need to throw up?" Again, there was no audible response from Zoe. However, this time, she swept her head up and, then, back down against Jacqueline's body. Jacqueline responded, "Oh," and snatched the young girl into her arms.

In a t-shirt and a pair of boxers, she darted from her bedside with Zoe. Racing from the bedroom, she closed the door behind her and headed across the dark penthouse to the main bathroom. In her haste, she never thought to enter her own bathroom, which sat unoccupied only a few yards away on the other side of the room. When they entered the main bathroom, the sensors perceived movement and the recessed lighting brought a natural, sunlit glow to the bathroom. The cold ceramic tile made Jacqueline curl her toes. She caught a glimpse of herself in the bathroom mirror as she proceeded to the toilet closet, as Zoe called it. There was no time to cringe at the unsightly image of herself. She flung open the door that kept the toilet out of sight. Gently, she placed Zoe on the floor and stood behind her.

3

Acting as Zoe's vomit coach, she placed her hands on her hips and said, "Okay, Zoe. We made it. You'll feel better if you just let it out."

Zoe leaned forward and clutched the toilet seat. For a few moments, they both stood quietly in the bathroom waiting. Jacqueline had begun to think that it may have been a false alarm. She wondered if young children were aware of the true signs of vomiting. She thought that she may need only to reassure the child and return her to bed. But, this thought was interrupted by the sound of a cough. It was a puny cough. Perplexed, Jacqueline thought she might be faking it. Before she could inquire, the hiccups began. Surprised by this turn of events, Jacqueline cocked her head. She started to snicker, but quickly, she stopped. She had never before encountered this progression of bodily responses. Curious, she folded her arms and leaned against the wall. The hiccups continued for some time. Sleepy, her mind drifted off, but her attention returned when the hiccups became belches. Jacqueline stood against the cold, cream colored wall in the toilet closet and watched as Zoe began to make awful faces and shake her head from side to side, as if an exorcism was underway. But, this was a sign she recognized. Finally, something signified an impending regurgitation. She returned to her post behind Zoe. Using one had as a ponytail holder and the other as a back massager, she presided over the small child awaiting the unwelcomed return of dinner. Then, the eruption began. She tried to comfort the girl by saying reassuring phrases like, "It's almost over," and "It's going to be okay." Standing in that bathroom, she meant every word of what she said. She was more than willing to change places with Zoe. Her heart broke when the sounds of vomiting were no longer louder than the sounds of Zoe's sobbing. Jacqueline wanted to cry herself. Instead, she bent down beside Zoe and said, "Honey, I think it's all out now." Then, she bent forward and with a swoosh all the contents were sent downstairs and underground.

Once again, she leaned down and scooped Zoe up in her arms. They proceeded out of the toilet closet and into the bathroom. Holding her close, Jacqueline retrieved her wash cloth. Lying on the side of the whirlpool tub, it had not dried from being used hours earlier. She walked to the bathroom counter, which was perpendicular to the glass enclosed shower and tile pedestal on which the tub sat. She placed Zoe there next to the sink. The cold marble countertop caused a shiver to run through Zoe. Jacqueline could see it in her face. She leaned over and touched the panel to activate the sink lights. Tucking the girl's blond ringlets behind her ears, Jacqueline looked into Zoe's tear-stained face. Her blue eyes were brimming with misery rather than full of the mischief that normally filled them. Jacqueline began to warm the water. She said, "It's gonna be okay now, my big girl."

She stuck her hand into the water that had pooled in the sink to check its temperature. Making all the necessary adjustments to be certain the young girl was not placed under any additional duress, she checked and rechecked the water. Once it was at an acceptable temperature, she soaked Zoe's washcloth, rung it, and proceeded to clean her face and hairline. She smiled as a sad and silent Zoe started to show signs of a little smile emerging. She dipped the daisy-decorated toothbrush in the pool of warm water and applied a bit of toothpaste to it. "I think we should brush that taste out of your mouth. Okay?" Jacqueline said as she began to brush Zoe's teeth.

At almost eight, no one had brushed her teeth for her in years, but sitting in the bathroom in the middle of the night with Jacqueline, Zoe did not mention this fact. Jacqueline released the pool of water, so Zoe could emit the toothpaste-vomit combination from her mouth. Then, she passed her a cup of warm water and Zoe rinsed and spat a few times as Jacqueline noticed that the pink nightgown was speckled with things she didn't care to investigate. Once Zoe's feet were firmly back on the tile floor, Jacqueline helped her to remove it. Wanting to erase this entire episode, she thought of discarding the nightgown completely but feared that Mallory would not agree. Instead, she turned and flung it towards the hamper under the counter. When she returned her attention back to Zoe, she lunged into Jacqueline's waiting arms.

Wearing only panties that had the incorrect day of the week on them, Zoe began to tremble. Holding her close, Jacqueline hurried the cold child into the spare room that she had made her own. The room was dimly lit by the recessed lighting that should have turned off hours ago. Jacqueline walked to the dresser and removed a white t-shirt and a pair of cotton shorts. She sat Zoe upon the dresser and slipped the shorts as far up the girl's body as she could while she sat atop the furniture. Sensing what needed to be done, Zoe pressed against Jacqueline's back to lift herself into the air. Once suspended, Jacqueline pulled the shorts onto the girl's waist. Had the two been on ice the move would have garnered a roar of applause. In the absence of an audience, their dance went uncelebrated. Jacqueline stood upright as Zoe lifted her thin arms into the air. In a quick move, Jacqueline slid the t-shirt over her head. Now, dressed like twins, in t-shirts and cotton bottoms, Jacqueline delivered Zoe back to the cold queen sized bed where Zoe had begun her night.

Confident that Zoe had been tucked back into bed, she said, "I think the worst is over now. I'm sure that you still don't feel great, but I bet you'll be okay in the morning." Jacqueline smiled and stroked her sandy blond hair.

As Jacqueline leaned forward to kiss her forehead, Zoe spoke, "Lie down with me." Her little voice was scratchy from her throat's early morning endeavors.

Still standing over her, Jacqueline could not deny her. In fact, she did rarely. She knew it and Zoe knew it. As Jacqueline lifted the blanket and sheet, Zoe moved from the center of the bed. Bargaining, Jacqueline promised, "I'll stay until you doze off. Deal?"

"Deal," the girl said.

Jacqueline slid her brown form into bed. The mocha color of her skin was in distinct contrast to Zoe's rosy complexion, but that observation did not matter to either of them. Jacqueline folded her hands behind her head. All of this activity had energized her. She had enough adrenalin rushing through her veins that she considered turning on the flat screen television. Mounted on the wall facing the bed, it beckoned her attention, but, as quickly as that thought came to her, she rejected it. Instead, she became aware that Zoe needed to sleep some. She was uncertain how long she'd been awake alone before she came to rouse her. And, although this was the wee hours of Saturday morning and there would be no school, there was a birthday party and sleepover later that Zoe wanted to attend. One of the few things that Jacqueline had learned in these recent months of being a backup parent was that children cannot shake off fatigue.

Turning her eyes from the ceiling to Zoe, Jacqueline said, "Do you feel any better?"

"A little. It doesn't hurt as bad now."

Smiling at her, Jacqueline confirmed, "Yeah, things always get better once you get it out." Then, Jacqueline's mind thought of the things that might help. Ginger ale. Medicines. Cold compresses. She reached out and placed her hand on Zoe's forehead.

Zoe asked, "What was that for?"

"I just realized that I should've checked to see if you had a temperature. Maybe, this is more than just overeating. Maybe you're getting sick." While

7

Zoe did not feel warm, Jacqueline thought that her hand was no true medical instrument. She thought how she had not known for certain if Zoe had a fever or not. Then, she realized that she did not even own a thermometer or any children's medicine. Hell, she didn't even have ginger ale.

As she was becoming increasing disappointed in her efforts to make her home a welcoming place for the most important people in her life, Zoe declared, "I'm pretty sure I don't have a fever."

"How do you know?"

"Cuz, a bunch of other stuff feels bad when you've got a fever." Zoe's voice was returning to its normal timber. She rolled into a small ball and placed her head upon Jacqueline's chest. As Zoe was snuggling closer to her, Jacqueline was making mental notes to go to the drugstore in the afternoon and purchase medications specific to the treatment of childhood ailments as well as a thermometer and, possibly, a humidifier. Then, without a thought, her left arm abandoned its post under her head and repositioned itself around Zoe's body.

Jacqueline cast her gaze around the bedroom. The furniture had been selected by an interior designer when she purchased the penthouse. The pieces selected for this room and the other spare bedroom were perfect for rooms without occupants. The designer had chosen articles that she said would pay homage to the West Indies. It contained a double dresser, nightstand, bench, and queen sized bed made of palm but decorated in a herringbone pattern of Lampakanay rope, native to the Philippines. Underneath the bed, a matching rope rug lay atop the cork flooring. The bed covers and linens were cream and tan with sheets that resembled bamboo patterns. Jacqueline never mentioned to the designed that Lampakanay rope and bamboo were not native to the West Indies. She realized that the room

8

was well-decorated as the spare room for a single person inhabiting a bayfront penthouse. At the time, the room felt very international. Now, the thought was laughable. Lying in it, with a sick seven-year-old, Jacqueline realized how out of sync it was.

Months ago, when Jacqueline and Mallory were no more than friends and colleagues, Jacqueline had offered to babysit Zoe on those occasional evenings when Mallory had to work late or attend business events. Soon, she discovered that, occasionally, a room was needed for the girl to complete her homework, watch television, or sleep. Hoping to make her feel at ease, Jacqueline did not select a room for her. Instead, she had allowed the girl to make her own choice. Of course, this room, with its floor to ceiling windows that overlooked Tampa Bay, was chosen. As the Earth rotated about the Sun, the room was ablaze with crimson, scarlet, pumpkin, and salamander rays of light. The visual display was stunning. Despite all of its great features, it had become the part-time bedroom of a second grader and it felt wrong.

Glancing around, Jacqueline said, "Maybe we should see about getting you a new bed set or something."

"A new bed set?" Zoe muttered. She had started to doze off, but the sudden conversation had stirred her.

"Yeah, this room is too mature for you. Maybe, we should redecorate it with something you'd like. A cartoon character or princess stuff or something."

Yawning, Zoe reminded her, "Jax, I'm almost eight."

"Oh yeah. The grown-up age of eight."

"Eight year olds don't have princess bedrooms."

"What do eight-year olds have?"

"Beach stuff."

"Beach stuff?" Jacqueline repeated. She was not sure how to decorate for that. She thought of blue walls. She thought of installing curtains to match that theme. "I guess this bed could still work with that kinda theme. This is tropical."

"Uh huh," Zoe agreed.

"Maybe, we should take out that bench and find the twin size model of this bed." Jacqueline continued to think aloud.

Cognizant enough to disagree, Zoe rebuked, "I don't want another small bed. I'm big now."

"Twin size beds are what kids sleep in," Jacqueline responded with authority. "I had one until I got my own place. You even sleep in a twin bed in college."

"Not me. I like this one. It's soft. And...and Abbie was so jealous when she saw that I had this big bed and a TV on the wall. She said my room was better than her mom and dad's room." Abigail Goto was Zoe's schoolmate, a fellow Sunshine Girl cheerleader, and a member of her Girl Scout troop. If asked, Zoe would say that they had been best friends since they were little. In truth, it had been about two years of sleepovers, theme parks, skating, birthday parties, and camping trips. A few weeks ago, Abbie and Zoe had had a sleepover. While Mallory and Jacqueline agreed that the girls would sleep at Mallory's house, the four had to make a trip to the penthouse to retrieve Jacqueline's picnic basket on their way to the beach. While cleaning and loading the basket, the girls ran about the penthouse. Zoe was excited to show Abbie everything from the closets, to the lights, to the bathroom, to the anteroom. Mallory had denied them the chance to venture onto the wraparound balcony that Zoe loved, but every other inch had been explored that afternoon.

"Well, I guess that's settled. We will look for something more...beachy," Jacqueline exclaimed.

"Why?" Zoe asked.

Jacqueline hesitated. She was not sure how to answer. She and Mallory had many conversations about Zoe's adjustment to a life in which her mother had a girlfriend, rather than a boyfriend. On the surface, Zoe had seemed very well adapted, but, often, Jacqueline felt that she was waiting for signs of upheaval. Nervous that this may be the moment, she proceeded with caution, "I guess I just wanted you to feel at home when you're here."

"I do," Zoe said without hesitation.

Calmed, Jacqueline went on, "Well, good. So, we should make this room look more like the room of a soon to be eight-year-old than a soon to be eighty-year-old."

"I don't wanna have three rooms."

"Huh," Jacqueline was perplexed again.

"I have a room at my dad's house and my mom's house and one with you."

Trying to be considerate of the reality of divorced children, Jacqueline said, "I guess a lot of people have that when their parents are divorced."

She explained, "I'm fine with them being divorced. I just don't want to decorate this room. I don't want to have to pick what to throw away when we move in."

That moment had caught Jacqueline off guard. She thought, *How'd we get here? When did I mention moving in?* Attempting to be cool, Jacqueline said, "When are you moving in?"

"I hope soon," Zoe said as she yawned again.

"Your mom and I have tried to be honest with you. So, I have to let you know that she and I haven't talked about moving in."

11

"You should," Zoe suggested.

"Oh, I should?"

"Yeah, you're either with us at our house or we're here with you. We should just all stay together here."

Hesitant, Jacqueline said, "I don't know if your mom wants that."

"Of course, she does. Don't you want us to be together all the time?"

Jacqueline had never been asked that. While she had thoughts about moving in together, Mallory had never mentioned it. Honestly, she was unsure about the future, but there was a tiny cherub pressing her to answer questions that she had only mulled over when she was alone. Realizing that she was thinking rather than responding, hurriedly, she began to explain, "Of course, I do. Of course, I want you and your mom around all the time, but your mom may still want things to be just the two of you. She may like to have a place where she can go and it be all her own. A place to entertain her friends, visit with your family, or just be with you."

"That doesn't happen. When you aren't there, she just talks to you on the phone or texts you. We should all just move in here together and be a family all of the time."

Jacqueline's heart warmed. Her mind repeated Zoe's words over and over again 'be a family all the time.' She liked the sound of that. She leaned down and kissed the top of Zoe's head. When she did, her nose filled with the smell of citrus shampoo. She readjusted the covers over their bodies and caught a glimpse of them in matching white t-shirts in the dresser's mirror. She smiled knowing that Mallory would be upset that neither were wearing the pajamas that she had purchased them. In a soft voice, Jacqueline said, "Get some rest or you can't go to Abbie's cousin's birthday party this afternoon."

Zoe nodded her head against Jacqueline's chest.

Talking to herself more than expecting to be heard, Jacqueline said, "I love you, little one."

In a whisper, Zoe said, "I love you too, Jax." Jacqueline smiled and they both dozed off.

Chapter 2

Slightly after eight, Mallory's eyes fluttered open. Lying on her side of the massive koa-carved bed, she rubbed her face, hoping to separate her eyelashes. She stretched her arms and legs out from under the covers and yawned the kind of yawn that she did only when she was alone. With her mouth open and her fingers and toes stretched separate from one another, she was at ease. The world was quiet. Lying beneath the bed's canopy, she imagined herself under a real tree. She turned sideways in the bed and allowed her long, red waves of curls to drape over the mattress. As the curtains strained to hold the outside world at bay, a beautiful day seeped into the room and rays of sunlight danced in her hair.

Abandoning the notion of leaving this cocoon, she returned to a vertical position and settled back under the white duvet. She wasn't quite certain that she was ready to leave the comfort of a quiet room with an empty king size bed. Repositioning the bed covers, she rolled onto her other side to avoid the beckoning day. As she laid there, she thought of how Jacqueline's bedroom had become their bedroom. Originally, she had thought Jacqueline's penthouse was classically decorated but felt cold and uninviting. While she had not moved in officially, she had added a sense of color, a sense of life to the place. The window shades had been replaced with blush colored curtains. The bed linens had been updated. With changes here and changes there, the room started to feel more like a home.

With her back to the window, she closed her eyes and released a long, slow sigh when she realized that sleep would not return. Instead, her mind filled with its own conversations. *Where's Jax? I wonder if she's working in the office. Why don't I hear Zoe talking? Hmm, maybe they went to pick-up donuts or croissants. I bet that's it. I bet there's a note out there telling me that they'd be right back with breakfast. Maybe, I should get up and start a pot of coffee to go with whatever they bring back.*

Convinced that she had determined why she was all alone in an empty bed in a quiet penthouse on a Saturday morning, she sat upright in the bed. With a grumble, her ivory shoulders went slack and she allowed her head to hang low. She began to rotate it around from one side to the other as though she was a boxer preparing for a fight. In a final huff, she committed herself to getting out of bed. She threw back the covers on her side and slid her thin body to the floor. Still rotating her head, she walked into the master bathroom. The sensor on the vanity light was triggered by her presence and, instantly, her face was illuminated in the mirror. She leaned forward into the reflection and inspected herself. Recognizing that there were no new changes to her face since last night, she began to brush her teeth. She hated to see her face in the mirror while she brushed. To her, she seemed transfigured by all the little facial muscles activated by the violent motions inside her skull. Rather than watch, she turned from the mirror and leaned against the sink. She stared at the phenomenal size of the bathroom. It was larger than her bedroom at home. With two sinks, two medicine cabinets, a whirlpool tub, a double shower stall, and a small room for the toilet, the room was huge - almost too big; yet, she admired her decorative skills. The rugs and towels had been bought to match other embellishments that had been added to the bedroom. Working to add color to the penthouse without alienating Jacqueline, the bathroom complimented the bedroom with a blush color overload. She had added bright printed teal and blush towels to the bathroom. From washcloths to rugs to vanity accessories, Mallory had achieved a mini redecoration that was far better and far cheaper than Jacqueline's interior designer. After rinsing her mouth and drying her face and hands, she smiled to herself and left the room that darkened upon her exit.

Outside the master bedroom, things were untouched. The curtains were still drawn. The living room, kitchen, and dining room sat still and dark. She was perplexed. Jacqueline was an early riser. Most mornings, she slipped out of bed and into the penthouse while Mallory slept. However, once up, Jacqueline would open the curtains. She would start the household around sleeping Mallory. If she had decided to leave, there'd have been evidence of her having been up and a note. Walking into all the rooms where notes would be left, Mallory was confused that there was not one. She scurried back to the bedroom hoping to discover that she had overlooked it. Standing at the doorway to the master bedroom, she glanced around. She looked on the dresser, on the nightstands, and in front of the television. There was no note. Fear set in. This wasn't like Jacqueline. No longer did she want to understand, now she just wanted to know where Jacqueline was.

She hurried back across the penthouse. This time, anxiety drove her to the opposite end of the penthouse. She passed through the living room and headed to the other bedrooms. As she entered the hallway, she knew that Jacqueline hadn't been in her office. The office door was open and the light was off. Unable to resist looking in, Mallory stopped in front of the dark room and turned on the light. Like everywhere else, the room sat cold and quiet. It was obvious that it had not been entered this morning. Her stomach fell; she felt light-headed. She had no idea where Jacqueline was, but she noticed that Zoe's door was still closed. Fearing she might wake her, she hesitated to open it, but she was desperate to be comforted by normalcy. She needed to see someone where she was supposed to be. She stood in front of Zoe's door and gently placed her hand on the knob. Turning it slowly, she did not open it until she heard the latch retract into the door. Gently, she pushed the barrier away and slipped inside.

As she peered towards the bed, her nausea was quelled at the sight of Jacqueline's boundless brown body cradling her pocket-sized daughter. The sight of them lying safe and at peace rendered her thoughtless. She stood staring at them and became overcome with emotion. Her eyes began to tear up; she felt flush as a smile etched over her face. In the five months that she and Jacqueline had been dating, she loved most how Jacqueline loved Zoe. Standing in the room at that moment seeing the two of them sleeping soundly, she couldn't love anyone or anything more. She glided out the door and back to the living room to locate her purse.

Desperate to savor the moment, she snatched her phone from her purse and dashed back to the room. Easing around the room, she thought of many angles. She stood beside the bed, she stood at the foot of the bed. She placed the camera over them. She placed it at their feet. Finally, when she had selected the optimum pose, she engaged the shutter. It was quick, but not quiet. The shutter sound, coupled with the burst of light created by the flash, disrupted the moment, but not before the scene had been frozen in time. Zoe squinted her eyes and rolled away; but, Jacqueline opened hers.

Looking down into her confused face, Mallory whispered, "Did we have an argument I forgot?"

Jacqueline smiled. Slowly, she crept out of the bed. She stood up, reached for Mallory's hand, and led her out of the room. Once they were in the hallway, she spoke, "What time is it?"

"Eight, eight-thirty. When'd you go in there? Did she have a dream or something?"

Jacqueline was rubbing her hand over her face as she led Mallory through the penthouse. When they arrived back at the master bedroom, Jacqueline climbed back into bed. Mallory stood beside her waiting on the story, but all Jacqueline said was, "Come lie next to me."

"I just got out of bed."

"Come on, just for a few minutes," Jacqueline pleaded and patted Mallory's side of the bed. Mallory complied. As Mallory slid down beside her, Jacqueline explained, "Zoe came in here in the middle of the night with a stomach ache."

"Why didn't she wake me up?"

Jacqueline scooted up beside her and placed her arm around her. "I don't know. She came to my side. She told me that her stomach hurt."

"Did she have to poop?"

"Nope. The other one."

Mallory chuckled. "Well, you've been fully initiated, then."

"No joke. Puke came spewing out of her. I cleaned her up and took her back to her bed, but she didn't want me to leave. We talked for a little bit, then she started to doze off. I told myself that I was just gonna lie there until she was asleep. But, I guess I fell asleep, too."

"I woke up all alone and I thought you'd gone for donuts or croissants or something. But, things didn't look right. I went looking for you. Oh my God, I was freaking out. I had no idea where you went."

Jacqueline interrupted, "Without my keys?" and pointed to them sitting on her nightstand. "Besides, who runs off from her own place in the middle of the night?"

Mallory was silent. She didn't care for Jacqueline's teasing. In truth, it wasn't the sarcasm in her voice that stung. She could handle sarcasm. What unsettled her was how easily Jacqueline said *her own place*. They had been together for the past five months. They had keys to one another's homes. They had alternated sleeping in one place or the other, but they hadn't talked about next steps. Mallory was ready to talk about it. She wasn't sure that she was ready to make the transition to a unified life, but she was anxious to know if Jacqueline ever saw it as a possibility.

Jacqueline noticed Mallory's silence. Her eyes had opened as she thought of how best to get out of the hole she had dug. In the end, she thought a simple apology was the best course of action, "I'm sorry. That was rude." Mallory smiled. "I shouldn't have been sarcastic. You were obviously scared when you couldn't find me."

Mallory stopped smiling when she realized that Jacqueline had missed the point of her silence. She thought against discussing it today. Things were going great between them. She and Zoe were happy with Jacqueline in their life. She thought that was what mattered most. "It's okay. Anyhow, I found you lying in bed with Zoe." Mallory rolled over inside Jacqueline's arms. Face to face, she went on, "It was so sweet to see the two of you lying there together. See, I'm crying, again, just talking about it." And, she was. There were tears in her eyes. Jacqueline smiled at her, but didn't speak. "So, I had to run and get my phone and take a picture."

Jacqueline yawned. "You know what I realized last night?"

"What?"

"There's no kid medicine or kid stuff here. I need kid stuff here."

"Kid stuff?"

"Yeah, a thermometer or medicine or a humidifier?"

Mallory laughed, "A humidifier? She'll be eight in two months, honey. We're past the age of a humidifier."

"Well, the other stuff. I couldn't even take her temperature last night," Jacqueline was serious.

"I'm sure that she didn't have a fever," Mallory countered.

"Yeah, well, why'd she throw up?"

"Kids throw up. I'm sure she's fine." Mallory dismissed the entire event, but Jacqueline laid there still making a mental list of all the supplies she would purchase by afternoon. Again, Mallory rolled inside of Jacqueline's arms. She faced the window and waited for Jacqueline to scoot closer.

Jacqueline was in heaven with Mallory lying in bed with her. The sun was trying hard to steal this moment, but the curtains were holding it bay. With just enough light for things to be aglow, she was warm both inside and out. She thought it was very close to perfect, so she said, "You know that room isn't great for a kid."

Mallory's eyes opened. "What's wrong with it?"

"It's all wrong. You know, it's too...grown-up. I asked Zoe if she would rather have something more for little girls..."

Mallory interrupted, "What'd she say?"

Jacqueline laughed, "That she wasn't a little girl. I tried to explain what I meant, but she told me that she didn't really want a third room."

"A third room?"

"Yeah, one here, one at her dad's, and one at your place. I was bummed out."

Mallory said, "I guess that does suck to have so many bedrooms. I didn't want that for her."

Mallory seemed to deflate a little bit. Jacqueline regretted bringing up this topic. In an attempt to lighten the moment, she said, "Better than one bad room, though."

"Yeah, I would've loved a bedroom in a penthouse overlooking Tampa Bay when I was growing up." Mallory regretted saying that as soon as it came from her lips. The last thing she wanted to do was pressure Jacqueline into thinking that she wanted she and Zoe to move in. Hoping the comment would float away into the place where poorly chosen phrases go, she laid still waiting on Jacqueline to speak.

"You and me both," was the extent to which Jacqueline responded. She wanted to discuss moving in together, but she feared that Mallory was not ready. When Abbie spent the night, Mallory required that the sleepover be at her house. Jacqueline complied with the request despite the girls wanting to be in the penthouse. Since that weekend, Jacqueline wasn't sure if Mallory wanted to be in her home, because it was more conducive to children or if she wanted to be in her home because it was their life and should be in her place.

The silence was broken by the sound of Mallory's rumbling belly. Jacqueline said, "Sounds like you really would like some croissants."

"Oooh, that would be nice." Excited by the idea, Mallory flipped over and pushed Jacqueline onto her back. "I will trade you a kiss for a croissant." Then, she leaned down and pecked Jacqueline several times on her lips.

Almost cooing, Jacqueline announced, "Don't start this. There's no time to finish it before Zoe gets up. And, croissants are calling your name."

In the midst of her shower of kisses, Mallory said, "Rain check?"

"Definitely!" Jacqueline reciprocated with one long passionate kiss and, then, hopped out of bed. She closed the room door and began to undress. As she did, she continued, "So, let's recap today's events. You're leaving me and Zoe to go dress shopping with Alex. I am taking Zoe to Abbie's house for the sleepover. Right?"

"Right."

"What time are you leaving?"

"About eleven."

"About eleven? It's almost nine now."

"That's why you have to hurry up and feed me," Mallory teased.

Jacqueline headed for the bathroom. With the water running, she asked, "When does Zoe need to be at Abbie's?" She heard Mallory's response, but she still re-entered the room to talk. Toothbrush in mouth, she said, "I drop Zoe off at one, but then what do I do?"

"Honey, you do whatever you want to do. I'll be back later. I don't know when. Maybe, you should catch up with Elet. Surely, you have things to discuss."

Jacqueline didn't speak. Mallory's comments made her think of Elet. She hadn't spoken to him in nearly two weeks. She did need to talk to him.

~~~~~~~~~

It was a late on a Thursday afternoon last month when Elet Walden had called. Jacqueline was sitting in her office reviewing the upcoming edition of the paper when her cell phone vibrated. Surprised that he was calling, she answered quickly. The two exchanged pleasantries for a while before she asked, "What's up? You never just call me to talk anymore."

"I know, but I should."

"Well, of course, you should, I'm your only friend." She teased hoping to lighten his mood. He chuckled softly. However, she sensed that something was on his mind, so she said, "All right, spill it. What's bothering you? You're acting strange."

"No, I'm not."

"Yes, you are. You called me at work. You asked how my day was going, but you haven't said much else. So, out with whatever it is you want to talk about."

"Maybe, you could drive out here sometime."

"Aww, you miss me? Sure, I can come by this afternoon. What time will you be there?"

"I'm here, now."

"Okay, then I'm on my way." Without saying good-bye, he disconnected the line. That confirmed that something was suspicious. She gathered her belongings and placed them in her leather messenger bag. She stopped at Grant Kincaid, her assistant's, desk to tell him that she was leaving for the day, then she headed down the elevator to the news floor to explain to Mallory what had happened on the phone with Elet.

"What? You're going to see Elet? Why?" Mallory pretended to be puzzled.

"It's hard to explain. He called me and was acting weird. He asked if I would come over. I couldn't say no. So, I'm gonna swing by his place for a little bit, but I'll still pick up Zoe from school. Okay?"

"Okay. Just let me know if I need to get her. I can work late another night this week if you need to be with him."

"No, I got her. I'll call you later." And, Jacqueline turned to leave. As she walked away, she thought the hardest part of working with your girlfriend was pretending that she is not your girlfriend, even when the entire office knows. She had wanted to kiss her goodbye or speak in a less matter of fact way, but they had agreed to remain as professional as they could in the office. So, instead, she walked away with purpose. She didn't stop to make small talk with anyone who tried to lure her into a conversation. She headed to the elevators and out the building. Walking at a pace that exceeded her normal lumber, she arrived at the Laredo in blistering speed. She roared its engine and raced out of the parking garage and off to Seminole Heights.

Using pure muscle memory, she weaved in and out of traffic. In ten minutes, she was at the house Elet had been renovating. As she drew the Jeep onto the new driveway, she realized just how distracted she had been on the drive over. She hoped that she hadn't run a light or hit a pedestrian. She exited the Jeep and turned to face the street behind her to see if any angry driver might have followed. After a few moments of standing in the driveway, she heard her name.

"Jacqueline? Are you here?"

"Yeah, I was making sure no one followed me."

Confused, Elet asked, "Have you come to kill me?"

Jacqueline laughed, "No, you sounded so out of it that I raced over here. When I pulled up, I wondered how I got here. Then, I was scared that I might have been a part of a hit and run and people might be chasing me."

Elet laughed, "It's funny how that happens."

Jacqueline stood in the sun in front of him. He looked fine. His sandy blond hair was tussled as though he had been working. His skin had its usual outdoorsy tan. He was barefoot and his long toes were as speckled

24

with as much paint as there was on his overalls. Standing there in his driveway in overalls with no shirt and no shoes, this tanned man's look was wasted on her; but his neighbor, Betsy, from across the street was enjoying the view. Jacqueline noticed that she had stopped sweeping her porch and was very obviously staring at him. Using her head to point in Betsy's direction, Jacqueline said, "Nice outfit."

Unaware of Jacqueline's teasing or Betsy's leering, he responded blankly, "I was working on a new piece out in my studio."

"Elet, are you okay? You seem distant."

"Actually, I'm great."

"Really?" She asked.

"Really. The house has turned out great. You haven't had a chance to see it, have you?"

"No, I'm sorry. I haven't. Why don't you give me the grand tour?" He held his hand out in the direction of the front porch. Jacqueline complied and walked towards the house.

His brick bungalow house was built in 1922. He had purchased the house to act both as a home and a studio. With the help of his brothers, most of the home's renovations had been completed without a professional.

"I like the new driveway," she said.

"It's not new at all. This baby has secrets in her." He stopped and crossed his arms. Jacqueline thought of how Betsy was enjoying the flexing of his bronzed arms. "Do you remember what it used to be like? It was just grass. I mean, it had been driven on so long that people had made it a drive way, but it looked like it was just grass. Well, I was gonna pull it all up, dig down, and have concrete laid. Silas got to digging with the backhoe and hit something. BANG." Pleased to see that she had found something to warm him up, she listened as he went on. "Reese and I stopped planting the shrubs and came to see what he hit. Turns out there was a driveway down there. A damn brick driveway."

"Was it intact?" She asked

"Hell no. Some of the original bricks were broken. Some of them were missing. We had to dig out all the original bricks by hand, and, then level the damn thing. We laid the original ones in the middle and found some pavers that would work with a nice pattern. It turned out really well." He unfolded his arms, stuck his hands in his pockets, and raised his body onto his tiptoes. Standing by his side, she looked back at it as well. "You never know what you're gonna get," he said and jogged onto the porch. Following behind him on the paver path that matched the driveway, Jacqueline caught up to him on the blue front steps onto the porch.

He raced ahead to open the door and led her inside. She was overcome by the beauty of it. The front door opened into a sitting room. It had been painted a light turquoise color that was accented in white trim.

"You've outdone yourself."

"My dad would have been proud of his boys. We got in here and planned to gut this thing. I mean, we removed layer after layer of paint and wallpaper. We got down to what I thought would be nothing but studs. Then, underneath all the garbage there was these tall baseboards and thick window casings. I was gonna add a new ceiling, and then we discovered the damn thing had coffered ceilings all along. This fireplace was sitting behind wood panels with a kerosene heater in front of it. Amazing."

He led her from room to room pointing out tidbits that he had found. The chandelier that was in the dining room was found in the loft. That the bookcase in the fourth bedroom had books on it as if someone had left them for him.

When the two entered the master bedroom, Jacqueline teased, "Um, this is obviously Alex's pick."

"Yeah, a dark red bedroom. How'd you know it wasn't me?" He laughed. "I traded the wall color to make this old fireplace work again."

Looking around, she responded, "The red works, though."

"Yeah, I really do like how it's all turned out."

As they passed through the modernized kitchen with green-tiled floors, she leaned against the ceramic counter and asked, "You know, if you just wanted me to come out and see the house, all you had to do was invite me."

He ran his hands through his hair. His mood darkened to where it was when she arrived. "No, I need to talk to you about something." In the middle of that thought, he opened the backdoor and exited onto the back deck.

"This place gets nicer and nicer," she remarked as she stood outside on the deck that overlooked the landscaped backyard. As she inhaled the ginger that surrounded her, she noticed that he was crossing the yard towards a detached garage. She stared at him for a moment, not sure why she was here or what was going on with him. She wondered if the source of his apprehension was in the garage, so she followed him.

She scurried across the yard and into the garage - which was not a garage at all. It was a studio. With an overhead LED lighting system, there was printmaking machinery, two computers, a 3D printer, paint, canvases, photos, and a darkroom. While the inside of the house might have been a mix between an old world and a new world, this space was all modern. She was glancing around the room at his machinery and his visual art. The two art forms wove together the collage that best reflected him. After absorbing the contrast of this place from the hipster vibe of the house, her eyes found him seated in a metal chair twirling from side to side. His toes gripped the bottom rung of the metal stool like crow's feet clutching a branch.

He said, "I've been trying to figure this out for a while and there's no right way to say this, so I'm just gonna say it.... will you stand up for me?"

She squinted her eyes. "Huh? Stand up for you? Like in a fight?"

He pulled his lips tight as if he was disappointed. "No, Jacqueline, will you stand beside me?" She still looked puzzled. He tried again. "At my wedding. Will you stand beside me? Will you stand up for me?"

Slowly, she was coming to understand what he was asking. "You want me to be your best...."

"Person," he filled in her quest for the right term.

Laughing, she said, "Hmm, I guess convention failed us. Wait, what about your brothers?"

"How could I chose between them? Reese isn't thrilled at the idea of me getting married and Silas is only thrilled about getting drunk in a tux in a room full of single women. My options aren't great. Besides, you're the one. I mean when I want to talk, we talk. It used to be you and I who were close. You introduced me to Alex. You helped orchestrate the first date and the proposal. You are my person."

She thought against asking about Reese's problem with him getting married. It would be a conversation that the two of them could have later. Right then, she walked over to him, stood in front of him, and said, "I'd be honored to be your best...person." They said person in unison.

He rose from the stool and drew her in close. In her ear, he whispered, "Thank you."

~~~~~~~~~

"Honey? Honey? Stop daydreaming and go get the croissants!" Mallory snapped Jacqueline back.

"Okay. Okay." Jacqueline spat out the toothpaste that had pooled in her mouth. She rinsed, found her shoes, and left to pick up breakfast.

Chapter 3

After breakfast, Mallory excused herself from the table. As she entered the kitchen, she looked back into the dining room at Zoe and Jacqueline who remained at the table. Jacqueline teased her with the final croissant and Zoe leapt from her seat and tried to reach it as Jacqueline held it over her head. Smiling, Mallory went to the bedroom, leaving the two to play at the table. As she closed the door behind her, she rested upon it. She wasn't sleepy. She had slept peacefully throughout the night. She wasn't unhappy. She had found someone who had made her and her daughter happy. Instead, she was overcome with panic. Try as hard as she might, she couldn't shake it. Recently, in the moments when she experienced a happiness she had never before, it was interrupted with pangs of terror. Rubbing her forehead, she wanted to both laugh and cry. She wished that she had the same abandon, the same freedom that Jacqueline and Zoe enjoyed. She wished that she didn't fear tomorrow or the next day or six months from now, but she did fear it. She had raised Zoe as a single mother for the past six years. She knew that finding someone to share her life with meant also finding someone who would share Zoe's life. While she had stumbled before and picked men who had failed her, failed Zoe, or failed them both, Jacqueline was different - in every way possible. The potential loss of this kind of bliss frightened her. As she stopped rubbing her head, she overheard Jacqueline say, "I'm gonna get you." The declaration was followed by the giggling pleads of her daughter. And, then, just like that, the panic passed. Relieved, she sighed, and walked into the bathroom.

Months ago, when she entered this bathroom for the first time, the left side of the counter top was bare. Now, the other side was Mallory's side and it was filled with makeup, makeup remover, perfume, hair accessories and so much more. As she stood in front of the mirror, she wondered what face to apply today. Tapping her fingers against the counter, she thought of eye color and lip stain. She thought of combinations that would suit daytime shopping. She wondered if she and Jacqueline had evening plans. In time, she chose a palate and a style based upon today's events rather than any additional travels. Knowing that she, Olive, and Paige were accompanying Alex to a boutique to search for her wedding dress, the day was certain to be fun; therefore, she determined her hair, makeup, and outfit should match the sentiment.

She exited the bedroom after an hour to silence. The sun had overtaken the living room and kitchen. It had forced Jacqueline and Zoe out of those rooms. Unlike earlier that morning, Mallory heard the sound of the television. The noise came from Zoe's bedroom as Mallory had expected.

Sitting on the bed still dressed in a t-shirt and shorts, Zoe said, "Are you leaving now?"

"Yes, baby. Where's Jax?"

Down the hall, she heard Jacqueline respond, "I'm in here."

"Be good tonight. Try not to fight with Abbie or any of the other girls."

Zoe stood on the bed to explain, "But, Mom, I told you. It wasn't me who started it. Nikki said that it was her turn and it wasn't..."

31

Fearing that Zoe might regurgitate the entirety of the last sleepover confrontation, Mallory interrupted, "I know, Zoe. I know. Let's just all be friends this time, okay?"

A flustered Zoe gave up and plopped down on the bed, "Yes, Mom." With that, Mallory leaned forward and kissed her tangled curls, then she walked down to the office.

"Look at you," Jacqueline said.

"What? Do you think my makeup is wrong?"

"Not at all. You look great." Jacqueline rose from her large mahogany desk and walked towards her. Mallory was posing as if Jacqueline was going to take her picture. Jacqueline reached to hug her mid-pose. "Will you call me when you're done?"

"Of course, I will, but I want you to call Elet after you drop off Zoe."

"I know. I will," Jacqueline mumbled as she kissed Mallory's neck.

"And make sure that she packs a nightgown or real pajamas in her sleepover bag. If I could get the two of you to wear pajamas, I would get a Nobel Prize."

"Pajamas are itchy," Zoe announced from her room.

"Whatever, I'm outta here. You two be good," She kissed Jacqueline and headed for the door.

~~~~~~~~

As she exited the high rise building, Eduardo, the night doorman, was leaving for the day. With his gray coat undone, he exposed his wrinkled white button-up shirt. He said, "Good afternoon, Miss Cummings. It's a nice day out."

"It looks beautiful. Warm and breezy. Just how I like it."

"Have a nice day. I'll see you this evening."

"Have a good one," she replied without thinking. As she fished for her sunglasses in her purse, the conversation between her and Eduardo replayed in her mind. Her mind repeated over and over *I'll see you this evening.* The chances were very high that she would see Eduardo in the evening. He was neither incorrect nor presumptuous. Most Saturday nights were spent at the penthouse. But, the phrase haunted her.

Despite being an avid radio surfer, she did not listen to the radio on her drive to Alex's apartment. Instead, she drove in silence. All she heard was the sing-song tone of Eduardo's voice reminding her that he also presumed that she would return to the penthouse by the evening. Her arm rested on the window frame and, once again, she rubbed her forehead.

When she arrived at the apartment complex, she sat in her car and reapplied makeup to her forehead and checked her eyes. After the touch-up was complete, she looked into her own eyes. She saw the worry in her face, but she didn't want to succumb to it. Not today. Today was supposed to be about Alex. She gave herself a half smile and said, "Stop driving yourself crazy. Everything's going great."

~~~~~~~~

As she stepped out of her car and trudged up the three flights of stairs to Alex's apartment, she reconsidered that today may not have been the day for heels. But, as she knocked on the door, she discarded the idea. The blue heels complimented the white shorts and blue and white striped shirt far too well not to be worn.

Half-dressed in very short baby blue shorts and a bra, Alexandra Stevens opened the door without acknowledging Mallory. Shaking her head, Mallory entered the dimly lit apartment and made herself at home. She passed through the path that separated the red leather couch and its matching loveseat from the glass table. Tossing her blue hobo purse on the couch that appeared to contain Alex's entire wardrobe, she entered the kitchen. She stood for a second awaiting the automatic lights to sense her presence. Then, she thought, *this isn't home. Turn the lights on, dummy.* Running her fingers along the wall, she found the switch. Once the fluorescent bulbs illuminated the kitchen, she leaned into the black refrigerator and retrieved a bottle of water. Rather than go in search of Alex, Mallory sat on a bar stool at the breakfast nook fearing that moving to the couch would force her to fold Alex's laundry. Sitting there, she overheard Alex speaking softly and sweetly, it was the voice a woman only used for a person of romantic interest. She smiled and thought of how well things had been going for everyone in these last few months. Less than six months earlier, they had all gone on their annual girls' trip. Jacqueline had rented a villa on Seaborn Island. Days prior to leaving, Alex had accepted Elet's marriage proposal. Mallory and Jacqueline were friends, but they were skating the line of friendliness and flirtation. For all of them, the time spent in the villa had caused their emotions to run high. Fearing change, anxiety pushed Alex into the arms of another man, a secret they had all sworn to keep. At the same time, Mallory felt overwhelmed by her developing feelings for Jacqueline and lost the ability to conceal them. Since their return, Alex had maintained her fidelity to Elet; and, she and Jacqueline had become the public couple their friends had already assumed that they were. But, the surest sign of happiness was that she never realized that she had just thought of the penthouse as home.

Resting her head on the palm of her hand, Mallory was content. She sipped her water with thought of her lipstick. She replayed the image of

Jacqueline and Zoe resting peacefully in Zoe's bed when, from the back of the apartment, she heard Alex yell, "Mallory, get the door."

"Oh okay," she responded. She hadn't heard anyone at the door. She thought, *Jax's rubbing off on me.*

Upon opening the door, she found Olive Dean in a wispy peach sundress and canvas shoes with her signature crimped brown hair. She hugged Mallory and asked, "What's up?"

"Hey, Olive. How are you?" Olive's affection caught Mallory off guard and, she failed to return the hug.

Olive released her and walked in. "I'm good. I mean things are really good. Drew and I have been getting along so well. Things just couldn't be better."

"That's wonderful. I'm glad to hear it."

As Mallory trailed behind her, Olive inquired, "How are things with you and Jax?"

"Things're good. She's great. Everything's great."

"Uh huh. How's Zoe's responding?" Olive pressed.

"Zoe loves her. Hell, she may love her more than me."

"Is that cool?"

"Oh yeah. That's fine. I'm glad they have such a good relationship." Mallory returned to the stool and crossed her legs.

"Well, then, things sound great."

Fiddling with her nails, Mallory said, "They're great."

"Where's the bride to be?"

Mallory pointed towards the bedroom, "Still getting ready, of course."

Immediately, Olive headed towards Alex's bedroom. Talking to Alex as she walked, "Let's get this show on the road. Mama's got a date tonight."

Before Mallory could decide if she was going to follow Olive or stay in the kitchen, there was another knock at the door. This time, Mallory expected it. Before she opened the door, she was speaking, "Hey, Paige."

"Sorry, I'm late."

"There's no such thing when you're hanging out with Alex," Mallory teased.

"Don't you look nice?"

"Thanks. You look nice, too. Is this new?" Mallory said as she touched the decoration on her scoop necked white tank.

Paige Little blushed. "I thought about what you and Alex said the other weekend. I tried to get some of those styled things."

"What did Alex say?" Alex questioned as she entered the living room. She was fully dressed. Her baby blue shorts were coupled with gold heels and a matching baby blue and gold striped cutaway shirt.

"Don't you remember? You told me to get the right size and to get the right colors," Paige reminded her as Alex glanced aimlessly around the apartment.

"Oh, yeah. Yeah, I did say that." Finally, looking at Paige, she remarked, "And, look at you! This is better." Alex tugged on Paige's pants, "But, I'm not sure these were on the list. You're far too short for capri pants."

"The lady at the store said that I looked nice." Paige said disappointedly.

"Never take fashion advice from the girl who gets paid based on how much she sells. That bitch is not your friend," Alex wagged her finger in Paige's direction.

"You look great," Olive tried to reassure.

"We should do a makeover weekend. Clothes. Hair. Makeup. The whole thing. It'd be fun," Mallory said.

Paige did not seem excited but kept quiet. On her behalf, Olive said, "That doesn't sound fun at all. That sounds like you and Alex treating poor Paige like a little sister."

Ignoring the rebuke of this plan, Alex added, "We can go have breakfast first at the bakery Jacqueline likes."

"Oh, it's the best. She went and picked up croissants and pastries from there this morning." Mallory patted her stomach.

"Aw, she's so sweet," Paige cooed.

"Yeah, she's something," Mallory muttered.

Concerned, Paige inquired, "What's wrong? Did you have fight this morning?"

Before Mallory could answer, Alex added, "See, you guys think everyone's so sweet. Yeah, sweet isn't everything." Alex picked up her purse and headed for the door. "Are you bitches ready? Let's go find me a dress."

~~~~~~~~

The women loaded into Paige's minivan. With Alex sitting in the passenger's seat navigating, Olive and Mallory made themselves comfortable in the second row. As they headed to the shop, Paige asked, "What kinda dress are you looking for?"

"Something beautiful."

Wryly Mallory answered, "All wedding dresses are beautiful."

"No, the hell they aren't. When Jo's friend, Tina, got married her dress was horrible. It was huge. She was covered in lace. All you could see was this dark face peering out of whiteness. I don't want that."

"Mental note. No lace." Paige said.

"Okay, then. What do you want?" Olive asked.

"Something sexy. I want form fitted. I want to show off the goods." Alex wiggled in the seat.

"Like a mermaid dress?" Paige asked.

"Hell no! Not like a mermaid. I want something form fitted all the way down to the ground, but with a little bit of a train."

Quietly, Mallory said, "Well, this should be interesting."

Olive heard her and responded, "It always is." She elbowed Mallory and advised, "As maid of honor, I think I speak for the wedding party when I say that we don't want to be in some horrible dress just so you look better."

Paige added, "And, form fitted is out. There's not enough biscuits for all this jelly." The truck erupted in laughter.

Through her tears, Alex offered, "I promise that I'll get a dress that's good for y'all." Pointing at Paige, she said "One that's not form fitted," then to Olive, "And, one that's nice."

"Are there wedding colors yet?" Mallory asked.

Alex held her head back against the seat and said, "Nope. We still don't have any. Elet and I can't agree. The other night, we were having dinner with his mom who suggested black and yellow. Both of us hated that idea. Then, he goes on and on about how gray and white would be classy. So, I tell him that doesn't have the pop of wedding. That's like an old folk's prom."

"So, whaddaya want?" Olive asked.

"Red and white," Alex retorts.

"Red and white? That's the prom, for sure," Mallory chimed in.

"Uh, we aren't gonna look good standing next to you in red dresses. It'll look like a damn trauma scene." Olive added.

"I thought it'd work. The guys could wear..." Alex started to say.

Paige reminded her, "And Jacqueline."

Alex sighed, "Fuck. The guys and Jacqueline could wear..."

"Does that bother you? That Jacqueline is the best person for Elet?" Paige asked.

"I hate that phrase. Look, Mallory, I'm all for marriage equality and when you two get married we can do whatever..."

"Who said we were getting married?" Mallory asked.

Olive leaned toward Mallory and answered a soft tone, "It's probably a matter of time."

Looking out the window, Mallory said in a whisper, "Somehow, I doubt that."

Paige turned down the music and stared into the rearview mirror, "What's going on, Mallory?"

"Oh. Nothing." Mallory replied with her face in her lap.

"Doesn't sound like nothing," Paige pressed.

"Uh, she said it was nothing. Let's get back to me," Alex protested.

"Hush up, Alex. What's the problem, Mallory?" Olive asked as she turned towards Mallory on the bench seat.

"Nothing, really. It's been a great five months. Some of the best of my life. Jax and I get along great. Jax and Zoe get along great. I guess I'm scared of what happens next," Mallory said as she continued to look away from them.

"What do you want to happen next?" Olive asked.

"Here we go again." Alex posed, "Why can't we get together without someone needing a damn intervention?"

"I just want to know what she wants next. Are we going to live together? Are we having fun? What are we doing?" Mallory's eyes watered.

Still looking at Mallory in the rearview mirror, Paige reached to the back and placed her hand on her knee. Rubbing it, she said, "Honey, you're overthinking this. I know she loves you and you love her. I think you're just scared of being happy. You know, I don't think any of us have seen her this happy. Ever. I know she has a plan for a future, and I'm sure that you're in it."

Looking off in the distance, Mallory responded, "I know. I tell myself that every time I feel this way. I know that she hasn't had much experience with relationships. And, she has no experience being a parent. We've had a few bumps and I've found ways to make suggestions for what she should do in the future. And, she does it. I guess I'm scared that this may all be too much. What if now that she knows what she's getting into, she runs away." Quietly, the tears rolled down her face.

Olive scooted closer to her in the seat. She wrapped her arm around her. Paige handed Mallory a box of tissues. Mallory rested her head on Olive's shoulder. "I know what you mean. You've fallen in love. Your daughter has fallen in love and you're scared of getting hurt. Me too. When Drew leaves, I wonder if he'll come back. When he does, I get scared. When he's late, I get scared." Mallory nodded her head on Olive's shoulder. "But, you know, I think fearing that I could lose him makes me better at loving him. If he walks away, I'll be crushed. But, God, I've found out what I really want out of life because of that man. And, I'll always be thankful for that."

Sniffling, Mallory responded, "I guess you're right. It's just nerves."

Alex asked, "Are you better now?"

"Yes, I think so. Thanks guys," Mallory said, dabbing the corners of her eyes.

While the other women were consoling and reassuring Mallory, Alex returned to her plan, "All the guys and Jacqueline could wear white pants and white vests with red shirts."

"Listen, bitch, can we give Mallory a minute?" Olive said.

"What? She said she was fine." Alex turned and looked at Mallory. "Didn't you say you were fine?" Mallory did not respond. Paige pulled into the parking lot of the bridal shop.

"We aren't wearing red, Alex. We aren't. That's dumb." Olive resolved as she opened her door.

As Mallory collected herself and reapplied her makeup, she received a text from Jacqueline:

```
Hi, baby! I hope you have a blast. I miss you.
```

She smiled and responded:

```
Just got to the bridal shop. I hope this doesn't take
the rest of my life. I'd rather your face be the last
thing I see before I die and not Alex in some too tight
dress.
```

With that, her composure was regained and she caught up to the other women.

~~~~~~~~

After three hours in the bridal shop, desperation had begun. The attendant had delivered size four wedding dresses in varying styles. Alex had paraded around the store in A-line dresses, in ball gowns, and in the mermaid dresses that she had been opposed to in the van. She hadn't liked any of them.

"Maybe, we should go look at another store," Paige suggested.

"No, I want a boutique dress, not some dress that everyone has. This is the only boutique that comes recommended by national magazines in two hundred miles. I'm getting a damn dress from here," Alex snarled.

"Fine, then, pick one," Mallory said. She had removed her shoes over an hour ago. The heels were beautiful. She had received compliments from other women, but they were a horrible idea for wedding dress shopping.

Alex screamed, "I'm trying. It's not my fault that _this_ woman," and pointed to the attendant, "can't find me one incredible fucking dress in the whole damn store."

As Olive laid down on the bench, she offered, "Why don't you go look yourself instead of just sitting here waiting on her to bring you something that you aren't gonna like anyways."

"Ooh, good idea. Help me, Olive." Alex hiked up the gown she was wearing and yanked Olive from the bench. Inspired by activity, all of the women began searching through racks of dresses. Talking across the store, they discussed dresses, sizes, lengths, and prices. They talked about style and color. When there was a dress to be shown, the women would come to the end of the row and display it.

In the fifth hour, Olive announced, "I've found it." The women had heard the declaration before and did not respond swiftly. Standing at the end of her row, Olive became upset, "Uh, where are you guys? I found _the_ dress."

Paige appeared first. With Olive holding it, Paige ran her fingers across the dress, "Oh my God! That's beautiful!"

Curious about Paige's crooning, Mallory stopped searching and went to perform an inspection. She bit her fingernail, cocked her head sideways, and closed one eye. Then, she agreed, "Alex, this may really be the one. Paige's right. It's beautiful!"

Still wearing the last ball gown, Alex emerged from between two sets of racks. She walked to Olive and held out her hands. Olive handed the dress to Alex who placed the hanger over her head. With the ball gown on her body and the new dress around her neck, she fell silent. She turned to her right side. She turned to her left side. She leaned forward. She walked away from the women. She paced about the racks. Anxiously, the women stood beside the three-way full length mirror and waited for her to speak. But, she did not for some time. Then, after walking across the boutique away from them, Alex turned and looked back over her shoulder at herself in the mirror. With a smile, she began to mimic that she was having a conversation. Once the fake conversation was over, she announced, "Ladies, I think I want to see this dress on."

Having missed lunch, the hungry women staggered back to the benches to await the change. Paige yawned. "Who knew this was going to take all day?"

Olive responded, "Oh, I did. It took weeks to find the right prom dress. I think we put in fifteen hours of pure shopping for a dress she wore for three hours. Tops."

Paige's phone rang. "Oh no, it's Brett. I hope the kids are okay." She answered.

Olive and Mallory tried to talk quietly to one another to give Paige some privacy. "Feeling any better," Olive asked.

"Yeah, I just get scared. Things aren't bad. We're happy when we are together, but we never talk about the future. I have a kid, you know. And, I don't know if I can just casually date anymore. But, I'm too scared that's what she wants or is it too soon to even talk about any of that. I definitely don't wanna run her off."

"Girl, me too." Olive had removed her canvas shoes and was rubbing her right foot. "Drew has been good with the kids. All four of them. He's even good with my crazy momma. Everyone loves him, but I got four kids. I love them, but I know life with me's a lot. Next week, I'm supposed to go with him to visit his family. I mean, everything's all great, but I just can't help worrying the hell he's gonna haul ass."

"That's me, too! I can't even explain it. We don't have any big problems. We don't argue a lot and when we do, it's over pretty quick. I just worry all the time."

"Just don't ruin things..."

Before Olive could finish, Paige spoke, "Brett wants to invite everyone over to the house for dinner. He got his new grill assembled and he's eager to fire it up. Are you guys interested?"

"I'm sure Jacqueline won't mind. Count us in."

Paige winked and bumped her with her shoulder, "See, making plans for your girl is part of being a couple. What about you and Drew?"

"Oh, you want us to come?" Olive said with surprise in her voice.

"Well, of course, I do." Paige said.

"Lemme text him. He said he wanted to do something tonight, but I don't know if he made plans or something." Olive typed away.

Paige placed the phone back to her ear. She spoke only a few more words before ending the call. Then, she looked at them and said, "This'll be fun. I told him that I'd text him a head count."

Before they could discuss the details any further, Alex reappeared. Standing in front of them, she was wearing <u>the</u> dress. In a lace tank dress that weaved around her form until it flowed into a small train, she was as beautiful and elegant and as sexy as she had hoped. As she turned to show them the lace back that buttoned closed, she asked, "The head count for what?"

Barefoot, Olive jumped to her feet, "I told you this was <u>the</u> dress."

"You look amazing. Do you like it, Alex?" Paige asked as she walked towards her.

"I think I do. I really think I do." Alex was quieter than normal. She did not have a snappy comment. All sarcasm was lost. Standing in front of that mirror with her friends, she stared at herself. Then, she stared at them standing beside her. Quietly, she said, "I think this is the one."

Mallory straightened the train, so that they could see the dress as it would be in pictures. She said, "I don't know, Alex. Maybe, we should see if they have one in red." She giggled as Alex slapped her arm.

Chapter 4

When the long beep rang through the penthouse, Jacqueline stopped what she had been doing and looked up towards the ceiling. A smile etched across her face. The sun had started to descend. Day was gone; but, Mallory had returned. Without first returning her office to order, Jacqueline exited the room. She flung open the front doors of the penthouse and waited for the second, long beep, which signified that the elevator had reached her floor. Waiting anxiously, she began to rotate one hand over another. While the time between one beep and the next was less than a minute, it felt far longer. So long that Jacqueline abandoned the idea of waiting behind the doors. Instead, she emerged from the penthouse, closed the doors behind her, and rested her body against the right door. Dressed in camouflage cargo shorts and a black t-shirt, she leaned against her custom doors. She had had them carved out of the same koa as her bed. However, its relief carving was that over a large tree with its overhanging branches. Standing against them, she appeared to be waiting casually under a tree. Her fingers were intertwined and placed atop her head. W

When the second beep sounded, she shuffled her feet and all her cool faded away. Then, the elevator doors opened and revealed Mallory. Leaving the entrance, she placed her sweating hands into her pockets and proceeded into the anteroom to greet her.

"Hey, baby," she said and pecked Mallory's lips.

A smile drew across Mallory's face as she said, "How long have you been waiting on me?"

"A lifetime."

"That's a good one," Mallory responded and walked past her into the penthouse. She beelined to the couch. With her arm outstretched, she released her purse and plopped onto the cold, leather couch. Her purse crashed and its contents spewed about the floor. Immediately, Jacqueline crouched beside her and began to regain order. "Honey, you don't have to get it. I'll pick it all up. I just need a moment." Mallory said as she yawned.

"Maybe, you should take a little nap," Jacqueline suggested as she looked under the couch for the lipstick that had escaped.

"Oh, no. I'm fine. Nothing a margarita won't fix."

"Well, I'm sure that Paige'll have some made."

"Had you made plans for us tonight? I guess I should've asked if a cookout at Paige and Brett's was okay."

"No, it's fine. I mean, I did have a surprise for you. But, we can go to that sold-out concert anytime." Jacqueline said as she stood up and proceeded out of the room.

"Oh, no. Really? I'll call Paige and cancel. Who're we gonna see?"

Laughing in the kitchen, Jacqueline peered at an intrigued Mallory, "I'm only joking. I was only going to ask if you wanted to go to the game, but we can go another night."

"Are you sure?" Mallory confirmed.

"Yes, I'm very sure. We haven't all hung out together since...vacation? It'll be great to just hang out. What time do we have to be there?"

"I think I'm going to change into something more casual..."

"You own something casual?" Jacqueline teased.

"Be glad you're in the kitchen. As I was saying, I'm gonna change into something else and check my face. Then, we can go." Mallory stood up from the couch and walked to the bedroom. As she opened the bedroom door, she heard the bed whisper a plea to her. Desperately, she wanted to answer. She walked to Jacqueline's side of the bed and sat down. She removed her shoes and thought of falling back onto the plush pillow top. She thought of curling up beneath the feather comforter, skipping dinner, and inviting Jacqueline to share a movie night in bed. She thought that she could convince her to watch a romantic comedy. Unfortunately, all of her favorites were at her house, so she would have to convince Jacqueline to go rent one and pick up some dinner. Lying there devising this plan, she realized that there were too many components that had to fall into place in order for this to work. So, she pushed it aside.

Her mind chanted, *Get up. Get up.* And, up she got. Standing on her barefeet, rather than in her brown, strappy heels, she already felt better. She stretched her toes, cried a fake cry, and trudged towards the bathroom holding her shoes by their straps.

As she opened the bathroom door, her nose worked before her eyes. She smelled sweetness that made all the aches of her body melt away. Her eyes searched the room for the source of the scent. On her side of the bathroom counter, there sat a large assorted bouquet. She blushed at the sight of such a large arrangement; without counting, she suspected that there were more than thirty flowers. Dropping her shoes to the floor, she touched and sniffed the assortment of lilies, roses, cremons, mums, and carnations. Her heart swelled so much that she had to beat back the water filling her eyes. In a bathroom full of sweet smells and beautiful sights, she went deaf to all of her senses, except the sound of her pounding heart. Had she known Morse code, she would have known that the pattern of those beats spelled: *This is love*. But, she never took the time to learn a language. Instead, she felt overwhelmed and searched for something to settle her.

Using a tissue to dab her eyes, she reclined on the camel colored chaise that rested in the middle of the bathroom. The soft velvet gave her a place to reclaim the emotions that were running too freely. As she peered back at the bouquet, she noticed a card peeking from under the vase. Quickly, she returned to the sink to free it. It read:

```
I couldn't wait for Valentine's Day. I love you, now.
                        Jax
```

Reading the card had been a mistake. The emotions that she sought to wrangle were loose. She fell back upon the chaise as emotions filled the huge room. There was elation in the tub and tears in the sinks. The mirrors were decorated with bliss and the floor gleaned with enchantment. The bathroom had been transformed into the den of her soul, but the emotional ride had left her exhausted. She stood from the chaise to look at herself in the mirror.

As the mirror illuminated, she could see her heart beating full of life. But, the reflection reminded her that she stood with only plumes of flowers by her side. With fervor, she flung open the bathroom door and raced in search of Jacqueline. Glancing around the living room and kitchen, Mallory dashed to the other rooms. As she entered the hallway, she heard sounds from the office. She ran to Jacqueline who had her back turned to the door and clasped her arms around her.

Playfully, Jacqueline responded, "Well, hello! I guess we can skip this party." Mallory didn't respond. She cozied herself into Jacqueline's back as Jacqueline tried to turn to face her. Wiggling in her arms, she pleaded, "Honey, this would be better if I could turn around."

Mallory released her grip and spun Jacqueline to face her. "I love you," she said gleefully and kissed her. Still swirling with emotions, the kiss was too hard, too long, and tasted of salt.

Jacqueline began to laugh mid-kiss. Mumbling, she responded, "I love you, too. And, I want this reaction every evening at six-thirty."

Mallory pulled her head back and placed her head against Jacqueline's chest. "I got your flowers."

"What flowers?"

"You know what flowers."

"Oh, the flowers in the bathroom? Those aren't from me. They were here when I got back home."

"And the card? Who wrote the card and signed your name?"

"Beats me," Jacqueline responded as she held her tight.

"You know, things like this are gonna make it hard for you to get rid of me."

"Thanks for the heads up," she teased. As she released her grip, Mallory slide her limp body into the desk chair. She ran her hands through her long red waves. Jacqueline returned to loading her violin into its case.

"Were you playing when I got here?"

"I had been earlier, but I hadn't packed it up yet. I was just taking care of it before we left."

"One day, you'll have to play for me." Mallory mentioned as she had on many occasions. Jacqueline was closing the case as she continued, "Or, at the very least, play while I'm in the house."

Returning the case to the closet, Jacqueline responded, "I will. I promise." After she closed the closet doors, she extended her hand to Mallory who rested her hand in her palm. Gently, she pulled her from the chair and onto her feet. She ran her fingers through Mallory's hair and said, "I think this looks great just like it is. Don't do anything else to it."

"Okay, lemme change into a different outfit and we can go." As she turned to leave the office, Jacqueline swatted her on the butt.

~~~~~~~

As the two cruised over the Gandy Bridge into Tampa, Jacqueline drummed the steering wheel in unison with the Southern Rock CD that she'd made for Mallory. Riding beside her, with her hand on Jacqueline's thigh, Mallory smiled at the thought of how their worlds had mixed.

When the song ended, Mallory paused the CD and raised the windows. She said, "You know, people don't ride around in a new Mercedes with the windows down."

Jacqueline chuckled, "But, they should. You should have all the windows down all the time, so everyone can see all the gizmos this thing has."

"Yeah, that's not how this works."

"We could've taken the Laredo."

"Yeah, I know, but you wanted my hair down. You can't take Jeep hair to a party, baby."

"Oh, there's nothing better than Jeep hair. You should've seen how big Zoe's hair was this afternoon when I dropped her off." Jacqueline held her hands over her head to show the volume Zoe's hair had achieved.

"How was she when you dropped her off?"

51

"Zoe? Fine. She was the same chatterbox that she normally is."

"I sure hope she doesn't fight with Abbie tonight."

"You know; I don't know if they fight as much as they try to outdo one another. When she and I pulled up, Josh was in the yard working on that Indian." She paused and looked at Mallory. "Did you know he was back?" Mallory nodded and reclined her chair. "Anyhow, he was out there working on that Indian. So, as we pull up, Zoe tells me to hit the horn. I ask her why and she tells me that she wants Abbie to know she's here."

"Did you blow the horn?"

"Well, I did."

"Honey, don't let her do that." Embarrassed by the very idea, Mallory placed her hand over her eyes, "Good Lord. You two."

"That's not the point." Jacqueline continued, "So, I beep the horn and Josh comes out to the street to say hello. He thinks that the beep is for him. But, Zoe sits right there in the backseat," Jacqueline pointed to the place where Zoe would have been sitting. "She sits right there until Abbie comes outside. Then, she stands up on the floorboard, grabs the row bar, and pulls herself out from the side. She puts her feet on the top of the wheel and jumps off onto the ground. I was so busy talking to Josh about his deployment, being in Africa, and what's left to do on the Indian that I didn't even notice what she was doing until it was too late."

Mallory began to rub her forehead. "Dear Lord."

"That's not the worst of it. Abbie saw this entire spectacle. She looked a little jealous, but she wouldn't give Zoe the satisfaction. She was standing in the garage with her arms crossed. It's like she was saying - *Just wait until this idiot gets that motorcycle running.* I swear we're all in some circus and these two girls are the ringleaders."

"Did Lauren speak to you?"

"She always speaks to me. She isn't very friendly, but she speaks to me. Abbie ran and gave me a hug as Zoe was hugging Josh. So, he and I were standing there with the girls when Lauren walked out from the kitchen door into the garage. I'm sure that she was looking for you. When she didn't see you, she just said *Hey, Jacqueline* and went back into the house."

Mallory furrowed her brow. "You know, that's what I don't understand. She and I were never friends. Our daughters are friends, so we've talked during plenty of parties, play dates, and jamborees. We've been on field trips together. I've kept Abbie as often as she kept Zoe. But, she acts like she's mad at me."

"No, she acts like she wants to talk to you about me," Jacqueline pointed to herself.

"She better not."

"I can take it. I just don't want it to get weird for Zoe."

With a heavy sigh, Mallory blew the words, "Me either." She rested her head against her cream leather headrest and reached out to hold Jacqueline's hand.

~~~~~~~~~

As they pulled into the Pelican Cove subdivision, Jacqueline rolled her window down again. Driving past houses that were all versions of one another, she glanced around at the near symmetry of this life. Weaving along bird named streets, she quickly recognized that the house at the entrance of the subdivision had been duplicated in a pink lemonade, cream, pale blue, and gray stucco throughout the neighborhood. Some had the garage on the left side rather than the right side, but they were all the same. After several turns, she encountered a looming two-story brick version. It was the only one of its kind. Staring at it, she wondered why it had not been selected more often. With glass windows in the garage door and four paned windows in the rooms overhead, the house glared at her as she passed by. Even as she passed it, she looked back at its disapproving scowl. Anxious to be past it, she continued on.

She turned left onto Hawks Den Road, then she maneuvered right onto Egrets Way. It came to a dead end and she was forced to turn onto Coven Court. Passing house after house and making turn after turn, she felt as though she had left the world she knew and wandered into to some new territory. Jacqueline thought how Paige was as crafted for subdivision life as subdivisions are crafted to be their own sphere of living. With homemade treats and a husband who coached their children's co-ed soccer team, they were perfect for this new universe. This place where no one offended anyone, because all of their opinions, likes, dislikes, hobbies, and interests were the joint thoughts of middle America.

She made the right onto Crow's Nest Lane and caught the whiff of charcoal. She knew she had arrived. She edged the Mercedes around the shoulder of Paige's corner lot and parked the car. Exiting the car, she sought to take a closer look at the world she had entered. She wondered if this was the life of families and she was the outsider from the foreign land who just did not understand. She stood outside in the night air staring at the basketball goals at the end of the drives. She imagined how children pushed them to the end of the driveway in order to share. She saw bikes lying casually in the grass awaiting their riders. She could see over fences into backyards with swing sets and pools. She could hear the sounds of children playing and the hum of parents talking. Her eyes gravitated to the similarities of their cars. Every yard had a mid-sized sedan and a SUV. She thought *maybe this is perfection, maybe this is the goal*. This was the American Dream in which a couple joins other couples and together they achieve the dream of homogeneity. It is what Paige had done and seemed happy doing it. Gathering the bags, she walked behind Mallory to the door and wondered if this is what she wanted. As she stood at the front door, next to her girlfriend, she inhaled a big whiff of it all and awaited her invitation inside.

"Hey, you two. I was starting to wonder if you were gonna stand us up," Paige teased as she leaned in to hug Jacqueline whose hands were full.

"Are we late?" Jacqueline asked as she entered the house.

"Well, I thought Mallory was only going back to the house for a few minutes. I didn't realize that you two..."

"Were gonna have to do it before you could leave," Alex chimed in.

Jacqueline rushed to Alex. With bags in her hands, she hugged her close. "Well, you know how I do."

"Yeah, I know how you do," Alex smirked.

"So, how's the big time magazine business?"

"I miss you guys. *Upbeat* is so different than the Sun. I mean, the people are different. There isn't the...friendliness. I don't know I guess it doesn't feel like family."

As she took bags from Jacqueline, Paige said, "You could always come back."

"Don't say that. I just might," Alex responded as she drank the watery ginger ale that she swirled in her glass.

Jacqueline glanced around Paige and Brett's home. It was an intermingling of personalities. His sixty-inch television was mounted to the turquoise painted zinnia-stenciled accent wall. The mantle was decorated with candles and family pictures. The tan leather couch was draped in a red throw decorated with vintage cars.

It was as much of an eclectic mix as was the company. On the loveseat sat Olive, in a tie dyed shirt that was twisted up above her navel. Her jeans may or may not have been denim. Without feeling for spandex, Jacqueline couldn't be certain. Next to her sat Drew, her new boyfriend, who was clean shaven with neatly moussed hair. His chinos and red polo were the perfect uniform for box store retail. Leering from the couch was Pam, Elet's middle brother, Reese's girlfriend. While Pam sat dressed in a designer jumpsuit that would have received a compliment from Alex if it were worn by anyone else, she would never be cordial to Pam. Despite still being married to one man yet living with another man, Pam saw herself as far better than Alex and was certain to express it. Hoping to bypass some of the usual tension, Jacqueline waved to all and exited the Pandora's box that was the living room. She followed Paige to the breakfast nook.

Having left the scarcity of authenticity in that room, Jacqueline felt more at ease. As she gazed around the kitchen, she admired the hand-sewn curtains that dressed the bay window. The material was white with tiny little yellow flowers. The nook table was new but was made to look antique. She smiled as she thought of what do-it-yourself artistic technique Paige had perfected just for that table. To add to the shabby chic decoration, there were vintage white and yellow vinyl chairs. This space felt genuine, like classic Americana. Jacqueline thought how the room could only be made better by Paige appearing in a matching ruffled apron while hand-churning milkshakes.

Upon closer inspection, Jacqueline noticed the placemats were in the same fabric as the curtains. There were two clean ones and two that appeared to be stained with spaghetti and juice. Staring down at the evidence, Jacqueline asked, "Where are the kids?" Paige had her back turned. She was arranging the sodas and cake that Jacqueline had brought inside, but she nodded in the direction of the back of the house. Jacqueline walked near her, so that she could peer into the backyard. Outside, she saw the big smiles of small people as they ran about.

Bryce and Kelsey were twin five year olds who spoke and moved in unison. Neither child looked like Brett or Paige. The two aliens favored themselves. Like most parents, they drew conclusions about their children's looks from long since deceased relatives. Brett determined that the children's long appendages reminded him of his paternal grandfather who stood well over six feet tall. Paige said her grandmother had curly hair similar to her children's locks. Instead, the kids look as some kids often do, as though they didn't belong to these people at all. Bryce and Kelsey were long, thin children with curly blonde hair and big, bright eyes. Yet, Paige and Brett were both short, full-figured people whose eyes disappeared when they smiled.

Jacqueline was surveying the backyard when Alex walked up behind her. "Daydreaming?" Alex asked.

"No, not really. I was just enjoying the view of Bryce and Kelsey running around while Brett starts up the grill. The rest of the guys are talking to him, but he's looking after the kids and, barely, listening to the guys. It's cute."

"It's something," Alex said as she turned around and rested against the sink.

Assuming that Alex was as moved as she was, Jacqueline agreed, "Yeah, it is."

Alex hit her arm. "Have you gone soft? They're probably out there talking about us."

"No," Jacqueline denied.

"Definitely," Paige chimed in.

"I'm gonna go find out," Jacqueline responded. She could care less if they were or they weren't talking about them. She just wanted to run away from the conversations that suspected the worst.

"You can't do that. They'll stop talking when you come outside." Paige warned.

As she walked out of the kitchen towards the sliding glass doors in the dining room, Jacqueline responded, "Nope, you guys forget I get to live in both worlds."

~~~~~~~~

Florida weather can be stifling. The summer humidity can leave newcomers panting for air, or worse, suffering from heat related illnesses. But, an evening in September is better in Florida than in any other state. Jacqueline exited a climate-controlled seventy-eight-degree house to enter a warm breezy evening cookout. The crackle of charcoal mixed with the sounds of children's laughter and men's voices. It wasn't just the sixty-eight-degree weather. It wasn't just the sound of children gleefully playing tag around the yard. It wasn't just the voices of old friends recollecting stories with revelry; nor was it the clamor made about her presence that made her feel wonderful. All of these moments were running simultaneously. All of them were speaking to her heart and, rather than answer or reply, she stood still and allowed a space in herself for them all.

After moments of standing in front of a closed glass door with a smile etched on her face, she spoke, "So, these are the men of my life." And, they answered with a roar. Their words jumbled together in unison with the clanking of beers and the sizzling of meat. She approached Brett and patted him on the back as flames tried to escape from the grill.

Beating back the gift of Prometheus, he responded, "Well, how are ya, Jacqueline?"

"Things're great, Brett. How 'bout you?"

"Can't complain. Can't complain." He wouldn't complain even if there had been a complaint. She patted him on the shoulder once more and turned to the guys who had scattered resin chairs around the fire show.

"Gentleman, how are we tonight?"

Elet arose from his plastic throne and gave her a hug. "We're all great. I'm glad you came."

"Where else would I be?"

Teasing, Reese responded, "Never can tell with you. Mexico? Italy? France?" As he chuckled, his shoulders heaved up and down. She thought of how odd it was that he was the second born Walden child but he had received a much larger physique than his older brother, Elet. Reese was thickset with a strong neck and wide chest. He sat in his teal colored resin chair in a plaid button up and khaki shorts.

Before she could mount a witty reply to Reese's jab, Brett chimed, "Those days are long over. She has a family, now." Tapping the top of the grill with this spatula, he went on, "This is where she's gonna be from now on."

As Elet passed her a red plastic cup of some dark liquor that smelled of shoe polish, she said, "Seems like this is where I am supposed to be."

~~~~~~~~

From the sliding glass doors, Mallory watched the animals in their natural habitat. "Do you hear them? They're giving her a hard time about not being somewhere better."

Sitting at the whitewashed farmhouse dining room table overlooking the living room where Olive, Drew, and Alex were interrogating Pam, Paige said, "Sounds to me like she's fine being in my backyard."

"You think your backyard is better than some tropical vacation spot? Come on, get real."

"Heck yeah, it is. Elet and Reese helped Brett with all the pavers and the raised flower beds. They made an outdoor kitchen with that grill he wanted. Oh, it's nicer than wasabi flavored almonds."

Mallory was stunned by the last part of Paige's statement. Rethinking what had been said, she stuttered, "Paige, you know what I mean. I wish they'd all shut up before she realized that she might be happier somewhere other than taking my kid to a sleepover."

Drew overheard the conversation. He was sitting in the living room attempting to be a good boyfriend, but wished that he could go out and play with the other beasts. "You know, Mallory, I don't know you guys too well, but I've really enjoyed being with Olive and the kids."

Olive hadn't expected that admission. She squeezed his hand and looked into his eyes.

Quick to respond, Mallory said, "That's because you aren't always around. You're easing into dating a woman with kids."

"Ouch," Drew said. "I'm there as much as she'll let me." Olive looked at him with confusion.

"I get what Mallory is saying," Pam stood up and pulled her ponytail tight. She entered the dining room with her wine glass in her hand. "When Reese and I started dating I wondered how he would react to a woman with a child. At first, he backed off a little bit. But, little by little, I think he got swept up in how good I was for him."

Alex rolled her eyes. Looking at Pam, she extended her hand and rotated her wrist in a skeptical circle as she said, "Yeah, I don't know about all of that. But, I have known Jacqueline for years and if she was unhappy, we'd all know." Alex and Olive joined the rest of the party in the dining room. "Look at her. She's sitting in those horrible cheap chairs drinking Elet's disgusting homemade beer laughing and joking."

"Homemade beer?" Drew perked up.

"Yeah, one of Elet Walden's great many talents." Alex reiterated.

"Actually, all the Walden boys," Pam corrected.

"What the fuck ever."

Drew saw this as his perfect opportunity to exit the ice shelf that had formed inside the house. He kissed Olive on the top of her head and proceeded in the direction of alcohol and smiles.

~~~~~~~~~

After hours of food and revelry, the night began to draw to its natural end. Olive and Drew were the first to exit. Cheerfully, Olive kissed everyone good night as Drew stood at the open door admiring her. When it appeared that she was coming to the end of her farewell wishes, he extended his hand. As she neared him, she slid her thin fingers into his open hand and squeezed. He said good night on their behalf and closed the door behind them.

Peering outside, Alex said, "I didn't think he was gonna stick around." Paige swatted her with a dish towel. "I'm just saying. She met a man at a club while we were on vacation."

Looking out the other side of the blinds, Mallory agreed. "Yeah, it's great. I think things are getting serious. She says she's supposed to meet the rest of his family."

"Our little Olive Juice," Alex sighed.

Outside, Drew walked her to the passenger's side of his car. He opened the door and closed it after she was inside. As he walked around the back of the car to the driver's door, he smiled and nodded to himself. He grasped the door with confidence and folded his long torso into the car. Before he cranked it, he turned and looked into her brown eyes and said words he had never told a soul. "I love you," he said slowly, making certain that she heard him.

A smile grew wider and wider across her face. Rather than immediately replying, she bounced up and down in the seat. While he took this reaction as a confirmation of her love, he waited hoping to hear an actual affirmation. With her arms reaching for him, she said, "I love you, too." As she kissed him, her elbow beeped the horn.

To which, Alex replied, "Well, I guess that's my sign." She left the living room only to locate Elet in the kitchen. She walked behind him and tugged at his t-shirt. He knew what it meant. In mid-sentence, he stopped speaking and followed her out the front door. Unlike Olive, she didn't say good night or farewell to anyone. Without conversation, the two walked to the driver's side of her yellow Mustang. She opened her door and flung her purse into the passenger seat. He waited for her to turn to face him. Once she did, he kissed her.

"I can't wait until we're heading home together," he said.

"You're the one who doesn't want to move into the apartment with me," she said.

"You're the one who doesn't want to live in the house yet."

She groaned. The night had been far too wonderful to rekindle that battle. "Elet," she said, defeated.

"I know. I know." He would live to fight another day.

She leaned towards him and placed her head on his chest. She knew that it would calm him. "Don't stay at Reese's tonight. Drop them off at his place and come and stay with me."

"Will you be awake?" he asked as she turned to get into her car.

As she turned the key, the Mustang roared and she looked up at him and said, "Wake me." Then, she winked and backed away.

He stood outside and followed her every turn. He would stand there until he could no longer see her tail lights. He thought of how she was his fiancé and yet, she wasn't quite his. He shared her with everyone and everything else, but he never knew exactly who or what. He slid his paint-stained fingernails into his pockets and walked back to the house.

When he re-entered, Pam was standing at the door. He overheard her say, "It doesn't make any sense to me."

To which, he asked, "What? What doesn't make any sense to you?"

Quickly, his brother, Reese, interjected, "Nothing, Elet."

"No, let's hear it. Pam, what doesn't make any sense to you?" Elet asked again.

She didn't dare look at Reese. She knew his face would be disproving, but she felt that someone had to tell Elet the truth. She straightened her blond hair back into its tight ponytail and said, "It just doesn't make sense to me why you two aren't living in that house yet. Why you are living with me and your brother? And, why is she still living in her apartment? My God, you're getting married in a few months."

For a second, Elet didn't respond. He heaved his chest out and folded his arms, then he rocked his trim frame on the balls of his feet and said,

"Well, I guess you don't have to understand, Pam." Before Reese could apologize or defend his girlfriend, Elet held his hand into the air. His calloused fingers brought an end to the conversation. He walked over to Paige and hugged her. In her ear, he said, "Thanks for having us." He shook Brett's hand and patted him on the back. He hugged Mallory. When he approached Jacqueline, he didn't move. He stared into her face.

She lowered her head and looked up at him over the rim of her eyeglasses, then she drew him into an embrace. Before he could speak, she said to him, "Haters gonna hate." She could feel his chuckle. Without any further discussion, he, Reese, and Pam were gone.

~~~~~~~~~

The house grew calm. Only Jacqueline, Mallory, Paige, Brett, and the kids remained. Mallory began helping Paige clean the kitchen. Brett carried his sleeping children to their beds. With no assignment, Jacqueline stood at the sliding door and stared into the backyard. Mallory walked up behind her and ran her hand over her shoulder, "Whatcha thinkin' about over here?"

"Nothing. Just wondering where everyone goes from here."

Mallory withdrew within herself. "I guess we'll have to wait and see."

"It'll be fine," Paige said. "It'll all come together. Just wait for it."

Jacqueline sighed and said, "I'm glad you think so." As she waved farewell to Brett who had toys and books in his hands, she headed out into the warm night. Leaning on the Mercedes, she stared up at the moon. When Malory joined her at the car, she didn't notice her.

"Are you still thinking about them?" Mallory questioned.

Startled, Jacqueline jumped, "Oh, sorry." Then, she opened Mallory's door. Before she walked to the driver's side, she leaned into the car and kissed Mallory a sweet and simple kiss that always felt like the perfect end to an evening out. As she got inside the car and pressed the button to start it, she said, "I'm glad that we're going wherever we're going together." As they pulled away, she turned to her and said, "Wait, where are we going?"

Chapter 5

Mallory emerged from the bathroom engulfed by a cloud of steam. Her hair was twirled inside of a towel that rested precariously atop her head. Her skin was luminous from her fresh steam bath as she glided towards the bed. Jacqueline failed to look up from the screen of her tablet. Instead, she felt the sudden heat from the bathroom and began to speak. "I had a great idea for a wedding gift."

Sensing her excitement, Mallory did not deter the conversation, "Oh yeah. What?"

"An arch."

"An arch?"

Still, typing away on the tablet that rested on her lap, Jacqueline explained, "Yes, an arch. I was lying here in bed thinking that as best person that we should really get them something great. Then, I thought about all the things that I loved the most and I couldn't decide between the doors and the bed. Buying them a bed is too personal and the doors on that house are the originals, so Elet would replace them. But, I thought that I could probably have an arch made. That'd be cool."

"This seems like a lot of trouble for a little thing that they are only gonna stand in for a few minutes," Mallory replied.

"That's what I thought at first. Then, I checked out some arches that other people had. There's ones out there that are big enough to keep. I mean they are so big that after the wedding they could put it in the backyard." She continued to type. "They could go out there and sit under it."

Mallory lowered her head and let the towel unravel itself from her hair. As it unwound and slid into her waiting hands, her waves of red were abound. It was a routine that Jacqueline had enjoyed watching. The secret highlight of every evening. Sitting in the room bright with the fluorescent lighting, Jacqueline admired the contrast of her crimson red locks resting on her ivory shoulders. As usual, she was rendered speechless. Her face beamed. Mallory hadn't noticed that she had stopped typing. Feeling amorous, Jacqueline said, "Come here."

Having heard Jacqueline's whispered plea, Mallory responded, "No, honey. I'm tired."

"You're too tired to come over here?" Jacqueline placed the tablet on her nightstand and swung upright on the edge of the bed.

Mallory's arms and head went limp as she trudged to Jacqueline's side of the bed. "It was a really, long day. I took a nice long shower and was looking forward to curling up beside you in bed and dozing off to sleep."

With her hands on Mallory's waist, Jacqueline looked up into Mallory's pleading eyes and coyly responded, "Who said that's not what I wanted, too?"

As Jacqueline began to kiss her stomach, Mallory wiggled free, "All right!"

Defeated, Jacqueline moaned and returned her blown legs back under the covers. Smirking, she recovered her tablet from the nightstand.

Mallory eased into bed and nuzzled against her arm until Jacqueline lifted it and held her close. Lifting her head to look at the screen, she said, "That's not an arch. It's a damn gazebo."

"Well, I guess. Kinda."

"How much is that gonna cost?"

"I'm not sure. I bet it would be less than the bed. I sent an email to Noah, the guy who helped me with the doors and the bed, to get the all the info, but I need him to hurry. It's only a few weeks until the wedding."

Mallory sat up. "You made this entire decision in the last twenty minutes? Price unknown?"

Realizing that she was traveling down uncertain waters, Jacqueline responded cautiously, "Well, I've been thinking a lot about what to get."

"No, I understand that. But, it sounds to me like you've decided."

"Don't you think that it would be really nice?" Jacqueline faced her. "Do you have a better idea?"

"No, I think it's an awesome gift. I'm sure they'd love it, but don't you think that we should've talked about it?"

"That's why I mentioned it when you got out of the shower," Jacqueline retorted. Then, she feared that she should not have spoken with such haste. She could tell that something about this had upset Mallory. And, while she was not completely sure what she had said wrong, she knew that she should clarify this misunderstanding. "If you thought it was a bad idea or a bad gift, then that would've been the end of it."

"I don't think you understand." Mallory retracted to her side of the bed. "You were alone for twenty minutes. And, in that time, you decided to spend a few thousand dollars on a wedding arch for our friends and all you wanted to ask me was, is this a nice gift?"

Jacqueline stared as Mallory said that. She had no response. Mallory had explained what had occurred. She didn't disagree, so she sat still waiting on Mallory to continue. But, Mallory didn't continue. Instead, she looked into Jacqueline's dark brown eyes and blinked away her tears. As Mallory turned her head and began to roll onto her side, Jacqueline said, "Please don't cry. I didn't mean to make you upset. I was just thinking about a gift. I just wanted it to be something special."

"You don't have to spend thousands for them to feel special."

Jacqueline leaned against Mallory's back. "I didn't think I had to. I just wanted them to have something nice. Something that I thought would be nice."

"But, don't you see? Don't you see why I'm upset?" Mallory began to cry. The tears that rolled down her cheeks were filled with a concoction of emotions.

Jacqueline no longer cared about the arch. She had forgotten about the nature of the argument. Instead, she wanted the tears to stop. She wanted to end whatever was so deeply troubling Mallory. She placed the tablet on the floor hoping that if it was out of sight that it couldn't cause any more harm. Then, she rolled onto her side and curled her body closer to Mallory. Stroking her arm, she pleaded, "Tell me what's wrong. Please."

Mallory shook her head against the pillow as Jacqueline continued begging to be told what had caused this outpouring. After a few moments, Mallory rolled towards Jacqueline and turned her head into Jacqueline's chest. Fearing that she might smother, Jacqueline rolled onto her back. Through her sniffles, Jacqueline understood little of what Mallory was mumbling, but she did understand, "I don't know what we're doing. I don't understand what's happening. Just when I think I know what's going on, something new happens."

"What does that mean? What we are doing is being together. We're just living."

The crying stopped. Mallory lifted her head. Her eyes were blank. Her emotions had been stilled. Jacqueline thought she'd made things better until Mallory spoke. "Just living? Just living? What does that, even, mean? Is that what you want from your life?" Then, the crying returned. This time, the tears seemed heavier, stronger. Somehow, they contained more anguish than they had before. As the emotions raged like a brush fire, Jacqueline was not searching for the source. She was putting out the fire. She rubbed Mallory's back and made quiet sounds that she hoped would soothe her. As it started to work, Mallory returned to talking. "I love you," Mallory continued. "I love you more than I've ever loved anyone else. It's almost instinctive, but at the same time, I'm so scared. I never know what you're thinking or feeling or planning. You won't let me in." Then, there was no more. Those were the final words she spoke for a long while. Her head rested gently upon Jacqueline's chest, but her eyes continued to unleash a flood.

For what felt like hours, Mallory sobbed and Jacqueline held her tight. She kissed the top of her clean hair. She rubbed her cool skin. Softly, she tried to reassure her. "I love you, too. It's all fine. There's nothing to be upset about. There's nothing to worry about. Everything's working out great. Don't cry, baby. Try to relax."

After Mallory had emptied her tear ducts, she took quick breaths. She was almost panting. Jacqueline pulled the cover from her hoping it would help. In time, she began to calm. She caught her breath and wiped her eyes with her hands. She said, "I'm sorry."

"For what?" Jacqueline asked as she drew the hairs from her face. Her eyes were swollen. The end of her nose was red. Her usual pale skin was flushed with color. Jacqueline cocked her head and marveled at how Mallory's pain had been painted on her face.

"Freaking out," with bloated lips, Mallory breathed.

"Don't worry about it," Jacqueline said as she kissed her forehead. "I'm sorry I don't think about how tough things are for you. I should've thought about how tough things are on you just being with me. I'll try to do better."

"Jacqueline," Mallory cleared her voice. With Jacqueline's full attention, she continued, "I don't want you to think that you've done anything wrong."

Holding her close, Jacqueline replied, "Clearly, I have."

"Not really. I mean, I know this is all new to you. And, you're doing great. You really are. It's just that.... it's just that..."

"Just what?"

"I don't know. There are too many things," and the tears flowed again.

"Well, tell me the first thing that comes to your mind."

Sniffling, she said, "Okay...okay...where are we going?"

Jacqueline started to snicker, but stopped. She knew that that was the wrong response. Running her hands through her flattened hair, she said, "I don't know. I mean, I guess we're going as far as we want to go."

"What does that mean?" Mallory looked confused. She'd asked the question that plagued her. She'd asked Jacqueline what everyone was asking her. She said, "The future. You know, a year from now. Do we have a future a year from now? What does a year from right now look like?"

Jacqueline was scared to say all of the things that she had thought in the past five months. She didn't want to mention her long range plans. As frightened and as anxious as Mallory was, Jacqueline was as well. "A year from now things are still good. I don't know. I mean, things are good right now. And, I think we should just go with it. Let's go wherever we want to go. As far as we want to go. There's no reason not to." It was a good evasive answer. It was meaningless upon close inspection, but, in a moment filled with tears, Jacqueline knew it would work.

"Yeah, I guess so." Mallory wiped her damp face on the sheets. Jacqueline stared at the wet spot her tears had left. "But, what about money?"

That was unexpected. Jacqueline had never considered having this conversation, "Money?"

"Yes, money. You know exactly what I make."

"Yeah, I do, but that's only because I'm your boss. A fact that I'd rather not discuss at the moment."

"But, I don't know what you make. I mean, I have an idea. And, I have an idea of what you made for all the years that you've been at the Sun, but it doesn't make sense. I mean, all of this," she swept her hand up into the air and around the room. "I can't figure this out."

Defensive, Jacqueline recoiled, "Whaddaya think? I'm selling drugs."

"No, honey. I just don't know. I've got questions you never address."

"Actually, it sounds more like accusations." Jacqueline felt unnerved. She didn't want to talk about finances.

Aware that this conversation was heading in the incorrect direction, Mallory said, "That's not at all what I mean. I love you. I want to be a part of your life, but you keep me out of so many things. I don't know your family or your friends. What do you tell all the people that you used to hang out with? What do you tell those girls who still text your phone? Why is it all such a secret?" And, her sobs returned.

Letting down her guard, Jacqueline began to stroke her back, "Honey, you worry too much. I love you. You know all of the friends that matter to me. Those girls who text my phone are from my past and I block them as they text me. You know that. You know that none of them matter. As for my family, we aren't very close. That's got nothing to do with you. I'm here with you. I don't have any secrets from you. You've got a key to all the things that mean anything to me. You have access to everything." She stroked her back. "I think you're just exhausted. You need to try to rest. This'll make more sense in the morning. I promise." Jacqueline stopped rubbing her back and slid down in the bed, so that they could face one another. She gently kissed her lips and said, "I'm going to change my shirt and get your washcloth."

Jacqueline removed her shirt and exchanged it for a dry one as she headed to the bathroom. After heating the water to a comfortable temperature, she dunked Mallory's washcloth and wrung it dry. She returned to Mallory's side of the bed and sat down. Gently, she wiped Mallory's face. For a moment, she sat there staring into her sea green eyes that were now marred by strands of red. She felt responsible for her unhappiness that Mallory was feeling. And, then, she became overcome with her own sadness. Fearful that she would become emotional as well, she smiled down at Mallory and lifted up from the bed to return the washcloth to the bathroom.

As she slipped back into bed, the tablet vibrated. She knew that Noah had responded, but she thought against checking. Instead, she drew Mallory close and said, "Come here and let me hold you, so you can doze off." Having kissed once more, Mallory rested her head on Jacqueline's chest and tried to relax. Hoping to muffle any further sounds that may come from the tablet, Jacqueline turned the television on and surfed through the channels searching for any possible distraction.

It was to no avail. Mallory heard the repeated buzz of the tablet, but she was too tired to fight again. There would be another day.

Chapter 6

"Mom, when are we meetin' Jax?" asked Zoe.

"How many times have I told you that she isn't coming over?" Mallory had grown tired of answering the onslaught of questions. She left Jacqueline's penthouse after lunch and picked up Zoe from Abbie's house. Since then, she had listened to a barrage of questions and pleas about Jacqueline, the penthouse, dinner, and tomorrow. "I thought it might be nice if we went to our house and spent a night alone. Just me and you. You know, like old times." As she said these words, she was half-convincing Zoe and half-convincing herself. She looked up into her rearview mirror and saw her daughter's displeasure.

Zoe's long, thin legs had reached the length necessary for them to comfortably fold over the back seat. She looked as if she had grown inches overnight. In a sunshine colored t-shirt and jean shorts, she sat in the backseat with her head rested on the palm of her hand. Her elbow was firmly planted on the arm rest and she stared outside. While Mallory was sure that she wasn't looking at anything, she was unaware that Zoe was mounting her offense.

As Mallory drove towards their house, she continued to try to talk to her daughter. "How were things at Abbie's this time?"

"Fine." The one word responses had begun.

"No fights this time?"

"No."

"Who's birthday was it? One of her cousins?" Mallory looked into the rearview mirror again. She had hoped to make eye contact.

"Yes." The car started to feel chilly.

"Macy, right? It was Macy's birthday. How old is she now?"

"Nine."

Mallory was starting to seethe. She had done her best to be honest with her daughter. She had picked her up from her birthday sleepover. She had come inside and talked to her best friend's mother. She had taken her daughter for a much needed trim of her dirty blond hair. Against her better judgment, Mallory had agreed to frozen yogurt before dinner. But, now, it was time to head home. It was not time to head to Jacqueline's penthouse overlooking the Bay with a private elevator and a wraparound balcony. It was time for Mallory and Zoe to be at the place that Mallory paid rent for them to reside. And, it was her decision to make without an interrogation from her daughter. "Zoe Rhiannon Russell! I have had enough of your sulking. I've tried to let you be upset, but this has gone on long enough. We are going home. It is not a punishment. This is our home."

Zoe only responded with the folding of her arms. As Mallory's mother had wished when Mallory was pregnant, Zoe was, in fact, just like her. She was tough, but smart. She questioned everything and emerged with her own opinions. As the car inched into the driveway, Zoe collected the overnight bag that Jacqueline had bought her and opened the car door. While her mother was inside the cabin of the car removing her sunglasses and gathering her purse, Zoe slammed the car door in disgust. As she sprang to the front door of their house, she faintly heard the screams of a woman who had just had the car door slammed on her.

Mallory exited the car and stalked to the front door. "I have had enough of you. When I open this door, I want you to go to your room."

Zoe didn't respond. She had been sent exactly where she most wanted to be.

When the doors opened, Zoe stomped away and Mallory collapsed into her loveseat. Enveloped by its pillows, she sighed and rubbed the ever-protruding vein that throbbed in her forehead. She looked around the small house that she had once loved. The place she had enjoyed decorating without the help or opinion of any other person. The place that she had loved felt wrong today. All of the contents were as she had left them on Friday morning when she headed off to work. Yet, something wasn't quite right. The light colored furniture mixed with the printed, overstuffed couch and loveseat made the room feel airy and inviting. It was the exact definition of a home that she had dreamed of living in. But, none of this mattered at that moment. At that moment, all of the decorations and furniture did not help how Mallory felt.

Rather than moving to the couch that had a better view of the television, Mallory reached for the remote on the coffee table and brought the room to life. However, the first words uttered from the instrument that was supposed to bring her solace were: "Bases are loaded and Nelson doesn't look like he has got anything left. It'll be a miracle if he gets to finish this inning." Mallory leaned her head back against the couch and a tear rolled down her cheek. That was the moment that she knew that nothing was out of place. Rather, someone was missing.

~~~~~~~~~

Dinner was subdued. Zoe swirled the mini-raviolis on her plate without admonishment. Mallory finished all of her salad, but she had not left the table. She sat back against her chair as if she were physically exhausted.

Finally, Zoe spoke, "Mom, you can tell me if you broke up with Jax. I'm old enough to understand."

"What? No. I didn't break up with Jax."

Zoe heaved her shoulders forward and thrust her hands in the air. "Then, what are we doing here all alone? What happened?"

Mallory leaned forward placing her elbows around her salad plate. She spoke with her head rested in her hands. "Zoe, NOTHING happened. I just thought it would be nice to be like it was. I thought it would be nice for Jax to have some space."

"Space?"

"Time alone."

"To do what?"

"Whatever she wants to do without having to worry about you and I being there."

"What'd she say that she wanted to do?"

"Well, nothing. I didn't ask."

Zoe stared at her mother. She moved her head from side to side hoping that someone else would appear who could better explain this. When she saw no one was there to help, she returned to her mother, "Will she be finished doing it tomorrow?"

"What?"

"Whatever it is that she needed to do will she be finished doing it tomorrow? Will we see her tomorrow?"

"I don't know, honey. We'll see."

Frustrated by her mother's lack of answers, she asked, "May I be excused?"

For a moment, Mallory did not respond. She thought of how Jacqueline had changed their lives. They were eating in the dining room. Her daughter had asked if she could leave the table. These were things that they hadn't done before Jacqueline became a part of their life, but now, they felt very normal, very right. Realizing that her daughter's blue eyes were peering in her direction awaiting an answer, she said, "Yes, go take a bath." Without responding, Zoe placed the chair under the table, rinsed her bowl and glass, and placed them in the empty dishwasher. Mallory watched her from the table. She hoped that Zoe would take a bath and settle down for the night. She didn't have the energy to have any more discussions about her romantic life with her seven-year-old daughter.

After Zoe had finished in the kitchen, Mallory cleaned up the little mess that they had made. Then, she headed off to her bedroom on the other side of the house. When she opened the door to her bedroom, she smiled at the sight of her wrought iron bed. She had been so pleased the day it was delivered that she rushed out to purchase a flowery duvet cover and down-filled pillows. She glanced around the room and admired the glider rocking chair that sat in the corner under a curved lamp. It was her reading spot. She fondly remembered all the evenings that Zoe had sat on the ottoman rocking in tandem with her begging to stay up just one more hour. This place was her design. It had been crafted by her. It was her place, but tonight it failed to give her the comfort she sought.

As she went about searching for her remote, her phone sounded. Waiting on the television to turn on, she retrieved the phone only to see that she had missed two calls. One call was from Jacqueline and one call was from Paige. Also, there was a text from Jacqueline. It read:

```
I hope you and Zoe are having a blast. I love and
miss you both.
```

Mallory felt worse. Jacqueline hadn't asked for time alone. On the contrary, she had planned to go with her to pick up Zoe. She thought that they were all going to get the haircut and go back to the house for a few nights. It was Mallory who decided to go home without her. Jacqueline had asked repeatedly if she had done something wrong, if she had said something wrong, but Mallory couldn't explain. Rather than try, she told Jacqueline that she thought that she should spend some time with her daughter to make certain that she was okay. She knew that Jacqueline would not refute her needing to do it. She knew that Jacqueline would do whatever Mallory thought was best for Zoe. But, Zoe was fine. She was better than fine. She had adapted to her mother having a black girlfriend. She enjoyed the time that she and Jacqueline spent together and the time the three shared.

Feeling the rise of emotions in her chest, she placed her phone beside her on the bed and turned to face the television. And, there was baseball. Nelson had lost the lead. The runs had scored and he was no longer in the game. Instantly, she wanted to call Jacqueline; and, in forcing herself to not call, the emotions she fought capsized her. She began to cry. Feeling the tears fall down her face, she felt flush. She felt warm, almost feverish. She had not come here to cry. She had come home to get control of herself. So, she sprang from the bed and headed to the bathroom.

~~~~~~~~

When Jacqueline first began watching Zoe in the evenings to allow Mallory to work late, she had noticed the inquisitive nature of the child. Rather than stifle it, she had allowed her to ask any question she had. In most cases, the questions were things that she had overheard adults discuss, but she did not quite understand. Jacqueline made great effort to explain both sides of the topic and give Zoe the range needed to discover her own opinion. These were the moments that Jacqueline enjoyed most. Zoe never hesitated to ask anything of her, and tonight would be no different.

Zoe went to her desk and unplugged her tablet. She took it back to her bed. Sitting cross-legged and unbathed, she sent a text to Jacqueline's cellphone:

Zoe: What are you doing? She thought that it might take a few minutes for Jacqueline to respond, but, there was no delay.

Jacqueline responded: Watching the game

Zoe: did you go with friends

Jacqueline: No. I am at home. I am watching the game on the couch.

Zoe: alone?

Jacqueline: Yes. Just me. Then, Jacqueline sent a picture of herself sitting on the couch.

Zoe: what're you doing with your space

Jacqueline: My space? What do you mean?

Zoe: mom said you needed space to do stuff alone.

Jacqueline: Nope.

Zoe: will I see you tomoro

Jacqueline: It is spelled t-o-m-o-r-r-o-w. And, if you and your Mom don't have plans, I would love to see you tomorrow. I am lonely without you two.

Zoe: I dont get it.

Jacqueline: Get what?

Zoe: if you are lonely, why did you need to be alone?

Jacqueline: I don't need to be alone. Your mom wanted to spend time just the two of you. Did you have fun with her tonight?

Zoe: no

Jacqueline: No? Why not?

Zoe: we used to be alone all the time.

Jacqueline: Moms like to be alone with their kids sometimes. It's nice.

Zoe stopped typing. With her tablet in her hands, she walked across the dark house to her mother's room. She knocked on the door and waited for her mother to welcome her inside. Before Mallory could ask what Zoe wanted, Zoe said, "If Jax didn't want alone time, then why did you make us leave?"

Drying her hair, Mallory said, "I can't do this with you all night."

Zoe noticed her mother's eyes. "Were you crying?"

"No, Zoe."

"Mom, look." She handed her the tablet. Zoe hadn't noticed that Jacqueline had sent another message telling her that she loved her and to behave. As Mallory read through the conversation, Zoe continued to talk. "Mom, she doesn't want space or whatever. She isn't doing anything. I bet she would come over here and be with us."

Mallory sat down on her bed and patted a spot next to her. "Zoe, come and sit next to me. I'm going to try to explain this to you. Try to understand. Jax has to go out of town in a week."

"Where's she going?"

"Baltimore."

"Is she gonna come back," Zoe started to look worried.

"Yes, she will. She's going to drive with Mr. Elet to pick up his wedding gift."

"How long'll that take?"

"A few days, I guess."

Zoe's spirits lifted. "Mom, can we go?"

"You have school, remember?" Zoe collapsed dramatically onto the bed. "Besides, when Jax is out there driving, she may start to feel different about me. She might remember what it was like to be without a girlfriend and a little girl in her life. What if she doesn't want us when she gets back?"

Confidently, she said, "That won't happen."

"Oh, really, how do you know?" Mallory asked.

"We're a family," Zoe said with ease. She slid from the top of the bed and started to leave. At the doorway, she stopped, turned back at her mother, and asked, "Can we see her tomorrow?"

Mallory sat in disbelief. She only half-heard what Zoe had asked, but she responded as all mothers do. "We'll see."

As she closed the door, Zoe said, "Okay, I'll ask her."

Mallory fell back against her bed and lost the battle against her tears.

<div align="center">~~~~~~~~~</div>

After a few hours of lying atop her flowered bed linens, she heard the vibration of her phone. Rustling amongst the covers, it beckoned her. Her face felt stiff. Her cheeks hurt. Forgetting that her voice might sound as she felt, she answered the phone. "Hello."

"Hi, honey. How's it going?" It was Jacqueline.

Mallory sat up in her bed. "Hi, there. How are you? What'd you do tonight?"

"Nothing." Jacqueline was distant. "Nothing. I just hung out here at home. I watched the game and took a shower. Now, I'm just sitting in bed." Jacqueline chuckled, "I keep waiting on you to join me, but you aren't going to."

"No, I'm not," Mallory rubbed her forehead.

"I miss you." Jacqueline admitted.

"I miss you, too." And, Mallory did. She had returned to her house hoping to run from her fears, but when she arrived, the fears were there, too.

"How'd things go when you went to pick of Zoe? Was Lauren weird?" Jacqueline asked, trying to lighten the mood.

"Uh," Mallory rolled onto her stomach and swung her feet in the air. "She's so weird. I rang the doorbell and Abbie answered. I told Abbie to go get Zoe, so we could go. So, I was standing outside just waiting, right?"

"Right."

"So, Lauren comes to the door and invites me in. I didn't really want to be bothered, but I went inside. She showed me the nursery and all the clothes she had for Mason. She took me to look at the bottles and the breast pump. It's not like we're twenty and this is her first baby. I've seen all this stuff before. So, there we are standing in her kitchen. She's putting the bottles she took off the shelf back up and there's silence. I'm not saying anything and she's not saying anything. She's still got her back to me when she says 'how are things with you.' I said fine. She said 'no really, how are things with you.' She said it like I was lying. So, I'm getting mad, you know."

"Uh oh," Jacqueline added.

"Right. So, I asked her what does she want to know. And, she says she wants me to know that she's here for me. I said thanks."

"Is that how it ends?" Jacqueline become interested.

"Yes, Zoe came in the room. I told her to say her good-byes and we left. But, isn't that so weird?"

"What does she want you to tell her?"

"Maybe, you're keeping me captive and I have to pass her secret messages to help free me."

"I think that she thinks you have some secret you need to get off your shoulders."

"What secret?"

"Well, I don't know, but she wants to be the confidant."

"Even if I had a secret, I don't know I'd tell her."

"Who would you tell?"

"You," Mallory said quickly.

"I think she thinks the secret is about me, so you can't tell me."

"It doesn't matter. We aren't that close."

"She thinks you are."

"Ya think?"

"Duh." Mallory was silent for a while. The jovial nature had given Jacqueline the confidence to admit why she'd called, "I was wondering if...maybe...since the day's over. And you spent time with Zoe alone. Maybe, I could come over and stay the night. We can rent a rom-com and watch it in bed. And, I'll even bring you ice cream," Jacqueline sounded nervous.

"That would be nice," Mallory began to smile. She didn't want to be without Jacqueline. She wanted nothing more than for Jacqueline to want to be with them. And, in this moment, talking to her, Mallory's fears were quelled. She thought back to the text conversation between Zoe and Jacqueline and her heart warmed. She wanted Jacqueline there and she knew that Jacqueline wanted to be there.

"Okay. I'm on my way." Mallory was about to hang up when she heard the best words she had heard all day, "I love you."

"I love you, too," Mallory responded with exasperation.

Chapter 7

As Jacqueline inched out of bed, she was careful not to wake Mallory. In prior months of their relationships, she had made a mental outline of the layout of the room. Carefully, she crept around the wrought iron bed hoping not to stumble into it. Perceiving the placement of the glider and its ottoman, she danced towards the bathroom door. She had almost achieved perfection; but, her super sleuth talents failed to remind her that the bathroom door was closed and she walked into it. Resisting the temptation to swear, she grunted and entered the small room. Turning the light on, she stared at herself in the medicine cabinet mirror that was suspended above the pink pedestal sink. The day before had been exhausting, but it had ended well. She hadn't let Mallory go to asleep alone. She hadn't let her go to sleep angry with her. She had sought her out and made peace. She had watched the rom-com movie of Mallory's choice without complaining about how they were all the same. She had eaten ice cream in bed as Mallory always wanted to do. She had held her close and tried to make amends for the rift the arch was going to cause. The arch. The arch was too large to be shipped to her. It was being shipped to Baltimore and she would have to find a way for it to be delivered here unless she was prepared to cause more damage by going to retrieve it.

Releasing her tight grip on the sink, she thought of how she had changed. Six months ago, she would have given no second thoughts to traveling to Baltimore, but not anymore. Now, she was concerned about how her travel would impact Mallory. Proud of herself, she thought of how Mallory must know the depth of her feelings, because of that change alone. Smiling and nodding at herself in the mirror, she was quite pleased of this indication of her commitment.

Having brushed her teeth and washed her face, Jacqueline proceeded into the kitchen. She started a pot of coffee for Mallory to enjoy when she awoke. She retrieved bacon and sausage from the refrigerator and placed two pans on the stove. While they heated, she began to mix a box of muffins. As she cooked a quick breakfast, she thought of how comfortable Mallory's house felt. It was smaller than the penthouse. Yet, it contained all the amenities of a home without seeming sterile, as Mallory complained that the penthouse did. She looked around the tiny kitchen as the bacon sizzled and thought that the back wall should be moved to expand the room. She ran her brown hands along the textured walls looking for the one that was weight-bearing. She peered into the tiny dining room and thought that her table would never fit in there. She was prepared to discard it and buy something new. She thought how she'd like to add a third room onto the house as well as a patio. Then, the smell of the muffins reawakened her. Mallory had not asked her to move in. In fact, she had come to her house yesterday to get away from her. Jacqueline was deflated. Her confidence was shattered and her appetite lost. She emptied the muffins from the muffin tin onto a plate and placed them with the breakfast meats in the microwave. She murmured as she cleaned all the pans and utensils and placed them into the dishwasher.

Quietly, she returned back to the bedroom. In the far back of Mallory's tiny closet was a place for Jacqueline's clothes. She selected a pair of khaki ants and a blue, pink, and white striped long sleeve shirt. Sitting in the rocking chair, she put on her socks and glanced at a peaceful Mallory who looked very much at home in her bed in her house. Now, she wondered what Mallory thought of a future for them. Jacqueline did not mind sharing time between the penthouse and Mallory's house. She was fine in either place as long as they were together, but what had Mallory wanted? More time in her own home? It would make sense. This little bungalow in Clearwater was closer to Zoe's school and friends. It was closer to their life. But, Mallory didn't own that home. She rented it in haste when she relocated from Daytona. She had talked about Zoe changing to a better school. She had mentioned on a few occasions looking into the schools around the penthouse. Jacqueline had and discovered the schools in her area were not the best. Then, she sought out the best schools in the area. She contemplated relocating to give Zoe the best, to give Mallory the best, and to find a place that felt like home for them all. It would need to be a place with a pool and space for entertaining and room for Zoe's friends to visit. In recent days, she had thought about checking out the market. She thought maybe it was time. But, she wasn't sure. She looked back over at a sleeping Mallory and wondered, *what does she really want?* Before her thoughts intruded on her day any further, she removed her pants from behind her and slide them onto her long, brown legs. Once on, her feet found her brown boat shoes resting under the window. With her pants still undone, she removed her t-shirt and replaced it with her button up. Buttoning it up and tucking it into her pants, she gazed outside at the rising sun. It was nearly six in the morning and the day beckoned. While carefully folding her sleeves to the elbow, she returned to the heated curling iron in the bathroom to place a few curls in her closely cropped hair, then tussled them about with her fingertips. Once the look was complete, she leaned down and kissed a sleeping Mallory, before she exited the room.

Crossing through the tiny house, she entered Zoe's room to kiss her good-bye as well. She found her asleep in a tiny ball with her quilt on the floor. When Jacqueline leaned to kiss her good-bye, she smelled the scent of an unbathed child and shook her head. As she was leaving the room, Zoe spoke, "Jax?"

"Yes, it's me. Go back to sleep."

"When did you get home?"

Home, she thought. "You were asleep when I got here."

"Did you get all your space?"

"Yes, now go back to sleep."

"Will I see you tonight?"

"Yes, but I've gotta go to work, so I can pick you up from school."

"Okay."

That appeared to be the end of the conversation and Jacqueline closed the door softly. Before she could make it out of the front door, Zoe had come out of her room. She was approaching Jacqueline who had stopped and placed her hands on her hips. "Zoe, it's not time for you to be up yet. Go back to bed." Zoe continued to walk to her as though she hadn't heard her. Jacqueline placed her messenger bag on the floor and waited for Zoe's arrival.

Still rubbing her eyes, she walked to Jacqueline and hugged her. With her head in Jacqueline's stomach, she said, "I love you."

Jacqueline closed her eyes and melted. With her hands against Zoe's back, she said, "I love you, too. Now, go back to bed. I left you a treat in the microwave, but I want you to shower before you eat it. Okay?"

Zoe gave a faint agreement and returned to her bedroom. Jacqueline thought that she had better leave before the child returned. As she locked the front door, Mallory closed her bedroom door.

~~~~~~~~

While Mallory and Jacqueline had dated for only five months, it had been nearly a year that Jacqueline had been picking up Zoe from school. It started as one friend with no children offered to help a friend who had to work late. But, now, it was a ritual. In truth, Jacqueline and Mallory could have dropped Zoe off at school together, traveled to work together, and left together to retrieve her from school. To Jacqueline, it seemed like too much togetherness; to Mallory, it seemed like too much time in the Laredo. As the engine started, the new twin exhausts garbled. Jacqueline loved the sound of it. She turned down the radio to listen. As she backed out of the driveway and headed down the tiny neighborhood street, she turned her phone on. She had turned it off when she arrived at Mallory's house the prior evening. She had not wanted any unexpected texts or phone calls to ruin the already delicate visit. The phone vibrated and alerted her to two voicemails. The chime of emails rang and text messages filled her inbox. As she waited to turn onto the US19, she checked her text messages knowing that this would be a good time to block any former women who had tried to make contact in the night. The times that she hated the most were the moments when all was going well and then, there was an unexpected ding of an unwanted text message. Whenever it occurred, she worried that it was from some woman from her past that was saying hello, asking how she was, inviting her to do something, or, worse, sending a picture. In truth, this had happened for years. She had had the same cellphone number since college; so, often, she received unwelcome conversations. Rarely did she respond, but now, five months into a relationship the contact had become burdensome. This morning, she sorted through only a few hellos and G-rated pictures. She blocked the senders whose phone numbers were no longer listed with names in her phone.

Finally, she saw a name, Clementine, and a text notification. Happy that it was a text from someone she knew and someone who knew that she was in a relationship, she opened it. Much to Jacqueline's surprise, Clementine had sent a picture. As Jacqueline waited for it to download, she cruised along I-275 east into Tampa. She had read Clementine's comment:

```
Time to get up and get back on the grid.
```

Eager to see the picture, Jacqueline continued to check. She expected some picture of the telecommunication wires or an Internet reference. She thought it might be a picture of where she had gone over the weekend. Much to her surprise, it was a picture of a naked woman lying face down in a disheveled bed. Jacqueline could not look away. She had seen plenty of naked women in life, but she was stunned. She wasn't quite certain why she had received the text. She raised her hand up to her mouth with the phone still in her grasp. The picture of the naked woman lying across the bed flashed in her mind. She knew from the woman's size that it was not Clementine, but she had not understood why her employee would send her such an image. She was baffled. She had been working long hours with Clementine to configure the paper's online presence. Their conversations had been friendly, but they were never explicit. Jacqueline thought of past interactions and conversations making certain that she had never acted or been inappropriate. By the time, she whipped into her space in the parking garage, she had decided that the text was probably sent to her in error. She thought that she would not mention it to Clementine; she did not want to embarrass her. She would just delete it and no one would ever be the wiser. Especially not, Mallory.

~~~~~~~~~~

She was sitting behind her desk working hard at work when the staff began to pour onto the news floor. From her vantage point, she could oversee much of their activities from her desk. While she had not been looking, the sounds of voices and the presence of lights brought to her attention that it must be close to eight. She stood from the behind the desk, reached for her cup of tea, and walked to her observation area. From her glass wall, she could see Mia, the Business and Finance editor, removing her tailored black suit jacket and hanging it on a coat rack she had added into her cubicle office. She glanced past Mia to Nelson, the Metro Editor, who occupied the cubicle parallel to Mia. He was surrounded by his staff members. Jacqueline assumed that they were already discussing the stories to be featured as well as drafts of ones being worked. Pleased, Jacqueline smiled. As Managing Editor of the second largest paper in southwest Florida, the Tampa Sun Tribune, she was orchestrating a monumental change. She was perched at her surveillance post delighted with her success when Mallory came into her office.

"Good morning."

Startled, Jacqueline whirled around, "Hey, there. I didn't see you come in."

"I noticed," and she smiled. Jacqueline thought how nice it was to see her smile, to see her face light up. "I brought you something." Mallory had had her hands behind her back since entering the room, but Jacqueline had not noticed. As Jacqueline approached her, Mallory revealed a small white cake box, which had been hidden behind her back.

With a rush of emotions, she said, "You stopped at the bakery?"

"Yes, I did and," she opened the box, "I got you the honey drizzled croissants you like." Her smile was so wide that her eyes smiled, too.

"Aw, hon.." Jacqueline stopped herself. "I know. No display of affection in the office." While the office was aware that they were dating, the two had decided to keep their personal life as private as they could. They restrained from pet names, personal business, hugs, and other displays of affection. Their efforts were futile. The office knew of the relationship. They could tell by the quick glances, smiles, the pauses in their speech, and the words that were not being said. "However, I'd like for you to know that I really appreciate this surprise and I'm very grateful to have you in my life," Jacqueline said.

As Mallory turned to leave the office, she whispered, "I love you, too."

Yelling behind a closed door, Jacqueline replied, "Hey, that's not fair." She smiled to herself. She knew what had evolved between she and Mallory was love. Rocking in her office chair, she was swooning. When she heard her office door start to reopen moments later, she started to speak before she looked up, "I didn't get to say I love you."

"Yeah, and you probably shouldn't say it now."

Jacqueline looked up immediately. The voice that responded was not Mallory's voice; it was Clementine. Embarrassed that she had been caught having the kind of personal moment that she and Mallory had sought to prevent at work, she replied, "I'm sorry, Clementine. I thought you were..."

Interrupting, she said, "Mallory. Yeah, I know." Standing at the far corner of Jacqueline's desk in black slacks, a black pinstriped jacket, a white collared shirt with a black tie decorated with gold pineapples, she twirled Jacqueline's globe about its stand. But, she did not look at Jacqueline. Instead, she glanced through the side of her black horn-rimmed glasses and continued, "Hey, did you get my pic?"

Stunned that it was sent to her on purpose, Jacqueline frowned. "Yes, I noticed it this morning."

Shocked, she walked to the front of the desk and placed her hands firmly down and leaned forward. "You noticed it? You noticed it? Man, what has happened to you? Have you lost it?"

Irritated, "Lost what?" Jacqueline questioned.

She fell back into one of the black leather chairs that sat on the other side of the desk. "Saturday night, I went out to Livewire. Out in the Grand Central District."

At first, Jacqueline was upset that Clementine would presume that she did not know or had not been to Livewire. Just more than a year ago, Jacqueline had been there three to four times a week. She was prepared to explain that to Clementine when a cooler head prevailed. Instead of sharing her prior experiences at the bar, she feared where this might be leading. Rather than engage her prior to the staff meeting, Jacqueline collected her folio, laptop, and a pen, then said, "Before you get too far into this, we have a nine o'clock."

"Oh yeah. Okay, I'll tell you the story after the meeting."

"Actually, I have another meeting after the team meeting."

"Oh, yeah. Well, you are the Managing Editor." Clementine stood from the chair and headed towards the door. "I'll catch this afternoon."

"Okay." After Clementine had left the office, Jacqueline stood up and let out a long breath. She was starting to replay the odd conversation with Clementine when Grant entered. He was wearing his short sleeved saffron shirt with black boxes. The shirt was usually the cause of great conversation in the office. She had thought on many occasions to intervene on his behalf, but she had never been certain what her responsibility was. She assumed that Grant was aware that his penchant for fashionable dress, vast knowledge of men's grooming products, and healthy lifestyle had been reason for office chatter. Despite all the years of knowing each other, she was unaware of his sexual orientation and, truthfully, she had no need or desire to know. She had only fended off conversations about Grant when they impacted the work environment, but, on many occasions, she wanted to protect him from the cruel world that surrounded him.

"Are we ready, boss?"

"Morning, Grant. How are you today?" She grabbed her tea and headed towards him.

"I'm marvelous. I contacted Victoria Prescott like you asked. I haven't heard back from her, but I'll let you know when I do. And, here is this morning's agenda. I would've stuck my head in earlier, but you've had a line."

Taking the agenda, Jacqueline said, "Thank you, Grant. I appreciate your help. Forward me Vicki's responses when you hear from her."

"Of course," biting his lip, he said, "Are you really gonna do this? I mean, are you really gonna..."

She stopped him before he could finish. "Grant, you're my assistant. Some things I need held in the strictest of confidence."

"I know. I was only asking since you and I were alone."

While reviewing the agenda, she continued to look at it, but answered him, "Grant, no final decisions have been made, but it is on the table. At this point in my life, there are no bad options." Surprised by her candor, he did not ask any further questions. Instead, he waited for her next move. She finished her review of the agenda and said, "Looks good. Let's get this party started." Then, the two exited Jacqueline's office and crossed into the Conference room.

Previously, the room was used only for Board meetings and the delivery of bad tidings, a truth Jacqueline had regretted. Since the restructure, she had begun holding meetings of varying importance in the Conference room to reassure the staff. As Grant distributed the agenda and straightened the high back leather chairs, Jacqueline took her place at the head of the mammoth mahogany table. At the far back of the room, she was the first face that latecomers would see. However, today, she turned her chair and stared out at the boats that filled Tampa Bay. She imagined herself pulling her boat out from the dock in her backyard. She could see herself relaxing on its bow. Wearing sunglasses and a Rays hat, her hands were firmly holding the wheel as she felt the breeze brush her face. She was at peace until Mia spoke.

"Oh, Jacqueline. Oh, Jacqueline. It would be better if you could wait to daydream until Nelson begins speaking." The shrill undertone of bitterness filled the air.

"Such spice so early in the morning, Mia," Grant responded as he brought in a cart of breakfast refreshments.

"My God, Grant," Mia said as she rolled her eyes.

Jacqueline had her head resting on the back of the chair. She had returned to her boat when she heard the only voice that made her reality more desirable than her daydream. "Good morning, Mia," Mallory said. She was wearing dark gray slacks and a light pink short sleeved shirt. Jacqueline did not speak, but she sat upright in her chair and smiled in Mallory's direction. Mallory met her eyes and smiled, then quickly, she turned away. She sat at the far end of the table as she always did. The Tampa Sun Tribune was a well-respected paper with regional recognition. In recent months, the paper had gained national attention, but, at heart, it operated as a small company. The Boyd family had controlling interest in the paper. Relatives had worked together. People celebrated on another's successes and mourned each other's losses. Jacqueline was the Managing Editor. She had promoted a team of editors, which included her girlfriend, that represented the various departments of the paper with the blessing of the Editor-in-Chief, Jack.

The office had been aware of the burgeoning relationship prior to the two of them becoming aware of it. When the two returned from vacation in the summer, the editor promotions were announced by Jack. As the early retirement program reduced the staff, the Sun became both leaner and more focused. In the weeks after the announcement, staff was reallocated to specific departments. Lines of supervision were announced and employees settled into their new expectations. In the midst of the changes, Jacqueline was seen about the news floor more often. She was engaging staff and being more accessible. She had decided that her presence might reassure them. Instead, the staff became aware of that the rumor of a relationship was truth. There were no missteps, no inappropriate acts, but the stares and smiles had become apparent.

~~~~~~~~~

Wanting to reassure herself that she was not being unethical or irresponsible, in the summer, Jacqueline scheduled a meeting with Jill Hanover, the Human Resources manager. When Jill entered her office, she fumbled to explain, "Jill. Thanks for coming. I know that you're probably busy."

Unsure of the formality, Jill responded cautiously, "Uh, sure, no problem."

"Listen, I know that things are changing around here." Jacqueline stood from behind her desk and began to pace her office. "And, I want to make sure that I'm a good...partner?" she seemed to question the choice of her word aloud. "Yes, partner with you."

Unsure where this was headed, Jill simply said, "Of course."

Placing her hands in her pockets, she went on, "I now have a group of editors who report directly to me and each of them has a staff of people reporting to them."

"Yes, I know. We wrote the job descriptions and created all of the teams together."

"Yes. Yes, we did." Feeling more confident, she removed her hands from her pockets and folded her arms across her chest. "I want to be fair to everyone and be transparent. I want them to know that I'm accessible to them and act as a good steward for them."

"I agree."

"Good, but I need your help to make sure that happens."

Still in the dark, Jill asked, "My help?"

"Yes, you see, I'm as complicated as the rest of the staff is. I have a personal life that sometimes intersects with my professional life, but it doesn't drive my decisions." Standing at the window overlooking the writing floor, she whispered, "But, they won't know that. I mean, they won't believe it if you don't help me."

Then, the light came on. Jill knew that Jacqueline and Mallory had been dating. The entire office knew and HR was no different. And, while Jacqueline appeared unaware that the world was watching, it was always watching. "Don't worry about Mallory."

Jacqueline's eyes grew big. She swung her body around and faced Jill. "What? I never said anything about Mallory. I mean, I want to be fair to everyone."

Nonchalantly, Jill asked, "Aren't you dating?"

Jacqueline had not planned this to be her coming out moment. She had worked at the Sun for years without discussion of her sexual orientation. There had been co-workers who had assumed she was a lesbian, but she had never shared the details of her life or discussed relationships at work. So, she stood stunned when Jill asked so earnestly. Fearing that she could not lie to the Human Resources Executive and request her help, she responded, "Well, yes, but no one knows that."

"I think everyone knows it."

"We haven't told anyone. I mean, Paige knows, but no one else knows," Jacqueline stammered.

"Jacqueline, you don't have to tell people for them to know, but don't worry about it. I have not had any concerns brought to my attention. The structure that you created prevents you from having any direct involvement in her annual review process, compensation, bonus, or employment status. If anyone asks me, we are well prepared to prove that you didn't give her the job and you have limited control over her financial package. You make requests. I make the determinations. Jack approves or disapproves us both. We have a check and balance." Rising, she said, "Are we done?"

Deflated, Jacqueline nodded, "Yes, I guess so."

"Good." And, Jill exited the office.

Silent and alone, she returned to her desk and went back to work. There would be no fanfare. No PowerPoint presentation, no email or cake to congratulate her having just come out of the closet at work.

~~~~~~~~

Leaning back in her seat, she remembered how she'd felt that day. For a second, she had forgotten that that was in the past, and that the present needed her attention. The room had filled with the department editors bustling about enjoying pastries and beverages selected by Grant. They clamored about the room until Clementine entered. The sudden silence as they turned to face the opening door awoke Jacqueline from her thoughts.

She boomed, "Ah, Clementine, I'm glad you were able to join us." Clementine nodded and flashed her broad smile as she proceeded to the chair to Jacqueline's right. She continued, "I think that we have everyone here, so let's get started. As you can all see, I have asked Clementine to join our Monday morning staff meetings."

Immediately, Mia spoke, "Well, we can see that, but why is she here?"

Tapping her silver pen upon the table, Clementine nodded in Mia's direction. She preferred the open hostility that oozed from Mia to the sarcastic pleasantries she received from other members of the staff.

Now, energized, Jacqueline stood up and walked to the dry erase board Grant brought to every meeting. "Thanks, Mia, for asking that question. As you all know, our creating a sound and effective online presence was one of the chief goals of our mission. The goal was not to, merely, place the paper online in a very static form, but to enliven the Tampa Sun Tribune as an active forum within and beyond the community. Clementine was hired to help achieve that goal. I have had each of you meet with her and her team to discuss layout and format of your departments' online presence. It's my understanding that those conversations have been beneficial to all of you." She paused. Glancing around the room, she waited for signs of confirmation. Paige was nodding in unison with Jacqueline; but, as Production Editor, Paige had had very little contact with Clementine. Guy Flynt, the Sports Editor, sat in a too tight shirt comparing the sizes of his fists. He had them both squeezed and stared from one to the other. Next to him sat Nelson, the Metro Editor who had been the most resistive to the notion of engaging the public. Through Clementine's report, Jacqueline had given Nelson's concerns great thought, but, siting in the meeting next to Clementine, he nodded as though he agreed. Across the table, Grant was dutifully recording Jacqueline's every word while Mia stared cross-armed as though she may spring into a brawl with Guy. To her left, Bob, the Politics and International News Editor, had various stacks of papers placed in front of him anxiously awaiting a presentation of some kind. To Mia's right was Mallory who sat in her chair assuredly smiling at Jacqueline as a supportive girlfriend might. As Jacqueline caught Mallory's eye, she felt the right corner of her mouth rise. Knowing that looking at her for longer than a glance could cause her to lose all focus, Jacqueline returned to her chair and her thought. She continued, "So, I thought it would be better for her to just join these meetings. If this proves to be more of a distraction or not beneficial, then we can certainly rethink it. Agreed?" No one agreed.

For the next hour and a half, each department provided updates on larger stories being investigated, researched, or written. There was talk of scandals from the prevalence of performance enhancing drug use in Florida to changing Environmental Protection Agency guidelines and how it affected the Bay Area. There was talk of the Chamber of Commerce's involvement in major league sports which caused a fiery debate between Mia and Guy. Mallory presented the near completion of a project being worked between Lifestyles and Production that would yield a smaller, weekend paper that discussed local events. In all of these conversations, suggestions were given by other department editors as well as Jacqueline, Paige, and Clementine. As the conversations came to their natural close, Jacqueline said, "I want you to know that Jack and I are very proud of all of the hard work each of you have been doing. Your efforts are very appreciated. If there is anything that any of you need, please do not hesitate to let me know." This was how she closed each of her meetings. It had become her sign off message. Typically, when she said it, people began collecting their belongings. Rarely did anyone ever speak after the statement and when they did, it was done after most, if not all, of the room's occupants had left in hushed tones.

But, today was different. Today, Clementine pointed to Mallory with her silver pen and added, "Was that for all of us or just Mallory?"

There was silence. Mallory, who had been gathering her belongings, lifted her head and stared into Clementine's direction. She wasn't used to be taken off guard. People rarely surprised her, but she had not expected this quip. Clementine sat facing Mallory with her back to Jacqueline.

Jacqueline arose, squinted her eyes behind her glasses, and batted her eyelids repeated. As she spoke, she sighed audibly, "No, that was meant for you all. Is there something that you need, Clementine?"

"No, nothing at all," she smirked as she winked at Mallory.

Seething, Mallory stood up and left the room. The other editors followed her. Paige dallied about the room hoping to have a word with Jacqueline. When it was obvious that Jacqueline was waiting for the room to clear before she reprimanded Clementine, she nodded in Jacqueline's direction and left.

With the room empty of everyone except Grant, Jacqueline said, "Do you wanna tell me what that was about?"

"What?"

"Let's not play games. What's on your mind?"

"I was just having a little bit of fun."

"Fun?"

"Yeah, fun. Come on, it was funny."

"No. It wasn't. Not at all."

"Relax. No one took it seriously. Everyone knows that you two are fu..."

Before Clementine could finish, Jacqueline interrupted, "Don't say it. Don't you dare say it. What I am doing in my personal life is personal. While everyone may know, we do our best to keep our personal life out of here and I will not let you make light of that. But, when it is time for business, it is time for business. Do you understand me?"

"Yeah, yeah. Sorry. I was just having some fun. Lighten up. I know things about you that you don't even know that I know. I've heard things about you, so don't pretend like you're all business."

"I don't know what you think you know, but I am all business here." She pressed her fists into the table. "You got that?"

"Okay. Okay," with her head bent, she slipped out of the Conference room.

Jacqueline turned and hit her fists against the window frame. She was staring outside. Her eyes had found a houseboat when Grant said, "She's just jealous."

She snickered, "What?"

"J-E-A-L-O-U-S. She's jealous of you."

With her head against the glass, she yearned to be on the houseboat drifting around the Bay. "I'm pretty sure that's not her problem."

"Nope. I know people. She's just jealous. Mark my words," he said as he wiped off the table. "She's got an angle."

"Grant, I don't have time for angles. I have my hands full with the straight edges," and she walked out of the Conference room with her hands in her pockets.

Chapter 8

When Alex left the Tampa Sun Tribune, she knew that it would be hard to make a fresh start with a new company. But, she never imagined that it would be hard to meet new people. At the Sun, she felt special and unique; she was the pinnacle of fashion. She had a youthful presence that was contrary to the serious notions of the newspaper business. At *Upbeat,* she was not the only woman wearing expensive, new clothes that were designed to look vintage. She was not the only African-American woman proudly displaying her natural hair. She was not the only woman with youthful exuberance. In fact, youthful exuberance was a job requirement.

UpBeat Magazine was a regional magazine that was a subsidiary of a national entertainment conglomerate that owned other magazines as well as radio, television, and online channels. It was the door that led her into the mansion where she knew she belonged. One of the perks of being part of the *UpBeat* family was that she had invitations to fashion shows, gala events, concerts, and festivals all around the state. At Miami Fashion Week, she had smiled and cajoled her way into the front row of center stage. She had met world famous designers and runway models. Then, after a week of partying in posh South Beach destinations, she returned home to write. As she pranced through the *UpBeat* doors, with sunglasses wedged in her waves made from her loosened locks, no one asked about the Art Deco district. No one made mention that she had worn an authentic Cesar to work. She did not have the opportunity to tell people that the Latin American designer had lent her the piece. Or that it was not worn in the show, because of poor planning; or, that she had thought of keeping it outright. Instead, she passed through the brightly colored open space, searching for a place to write. Without assigned offices or spaces, employees had freedom to create in vacuum or community. *UpBeat* welcomed friends, not employees, to explore the creative style that worked best for them. They had not known that a chair, a desk, and a space to share with a co-worker is what Alex needed most.

Balancing her weight atop a large rubber ball while wearing Cesar's thin, silk pink and white dress that was created to wear from the office to a cocktail party proved difficult. She slid about the ball in the most unfeminine way. Scooting about, she wrestled to maintain balance. While her mother always told her that a woman should keep her ankles always crossed, Alex was having a difficult time keeping her thighs together. After some time, she mastered some balance. Sitting upright with her legs slightly apart, she bore her weight through her torso to her pink shoes. Made to be elegant with thin gold-tipped heels, she had pressed firmly on the soles of the shoes. The heel tips anchored into the tile. Confident that she had mastered the ball, she nodded at her accomplishment and reached down to remove her laptop from its bag. Once on her lap, she powered it on and began to type. After a few words, her mind had focused upon the art of writing. Her body went lax as her faculties concentrated on who she saw and what was worn. She was clicking her teeth and trying to determine if the Madeline Amaro piece with the small golden bow in the center of the bust was more flamingo or taffy colored when things fell apart. The laptop started to slide off her charmeuse dress. Tilting to reach for it, her feet released their lock on the tile and she skidded off the ball. The laptop thudded on the tile. Her body splayed across the floor. Quietly and quickly, she propelled herself upright. Her arm was pounding, but she didn't dare rub it. Immediately, she glanced from side to side. She thought no one had seen her fall, but they had. Of course, they had. The sound resonated over their Bluetooth headphones. They just didn't come to her aid.

Standing, she looked for a chair. A real chair. A chair with a seat and legs. To her far left, she saw one - it was wooden with sturdy metal legs. But, there was no table. No desk space upon which she could write, but she decided that she would forgo a rough draft of the article in pencil for a seat. Gathering what few belongings that had toppled out of her purse after her spill, she kicked the ball and headed for the chair. Walking amongst other co-friends who sat cross-legged on the floor or who laid upon their stomachs with laptops in their faces, she tiptoed careful not to step on anyone. As she exited the open space, her stride became more confident as she heard the click of her heels on the tile floor. Careful not to be turned away, she asked the man who sat next to the open chair, "Excuse me, is this seat taken?"

He did not answer immediately. He typed frantically.

After a few seconds, she thought that he may not have heard her. So, she repeated, "I'm sorry. Is anyone sitting here?"

This time, he moved his gaze away from his machine. His hands stopped typing and squinted at the sight of her as if he had looked into the sun. She saw his look of confusion, but her own anger built as he failed to answer. The man to his right answered on his behalf, "Please sit down. You don't have to ask. If the seat is empty, just sit."

"Thank you. I just didn't want to sit down if he was saving it for someone."

The stranger laughed. "No. He's definitely not saving it for anyone." Alex cocked her head to the side and wondered if she had missed something. The man had seemed normal enough. He was wearing vintage high-top basketball shoes, torn jeans, and a sweatshirt. His head was covered in large brown ringlets that Alex thought could be nicely maintained by the use of some hair product. Noticing how long Alex stared at the silent man, the stranger spoke to her again. "His name is Langston. He's in charge of the Gaming division. He's playing the BETA version of a persistent multi-player universe. Don't be offended, but he's not gonna pay you any attention."

"Oh." She said and bent forward. Looking into Langston's face and smiled to see if he would make eye contact. He glanced over the top of his laptop at her, but quickly he returned to his game. "Well, it was worth a try."

The stranger laughed, "If it makes you feel any better, that's more than most people get. By the way, I'm Clark."

"Hi, Clark. I'm Alex."

"Hi, Alex. New 'round here?"

"Kinda, it's been a coupla months now, but it still feels.... a little foreign."

He looked around the non-conventional room and said, "Yeah, I bet it could. It's definitely not for everyone. If people come to *UpBeat* too late in their career, I think it's hard for them to transition into such an alternative work environment." Alex didn't respond. She was too busy sizing him up. Even seated, she noticed how tall he was. Her mind gauged that he was at least six foot four. He sunk into the black vinyl chair and crossed his corduroy covered legs to make a desk for his laptop. Shaking his size twelve plain toe oxford, she saw a glimpse of his brightly colored socks. He noticed, "The socks?"

"I've gotta see these for myself." She placed her bag in the chair next to Langston and walked in front of him. "May I?" she said. Clark nodded. Careful, not to expose herself, she slid her hand along the backside of her dress as she sat on the edge of the glass table next to him. Alex ran her hand under his pants leg to expose his socks. She felt him shudder. "Relax. I don't think you have anything unexpected down here, do you?"

"You never know."

"Well, if you did, it would be an even better surprise than these multi-colored paisley socks." And, as abruptly as she walked over, she stood and returned to her chair.

"You're a very interesting woman, Alex. Very....interesting."

"I was. I once was more than you could have ever imagined."

"I'm certain this is very true, but this new version is interesting as well." He ran his hand over the sock where her hand had been, then he stood up. Adjusting his pants and retucking his shirt, he looked down at Alex. "I hope to be further intrigued by you, Alex." Alex looked up at him and smiled. As she did, he turned and walked away.

Alex was replaying the interaction in her head, so she only faintly heard Langston say, "Clark Matthus, Vice President of Media Operations."

Alex smiled and sat back in her chair. "Thanks, Langston." She thought, *UpBeat isn't gonna be so bad after all.* With new energy and new focus, Alex removed her laptop from its bag. As it was powering up, she retrieved her phone that had been sitting in her bag violently vibrating. The text messages and pictures began to appear. Smiling, she placed the phone on the arm of the chair and checked her face.

In another whisper, Langston confirmed, "Project meetings last about an hour."

"Good to know, bestie." and closed the compact.

Langston smiled as he typed voraciously.

Before she could begin typing her article, the texts and pictures were available. There was an avalanche of compliments and pictures. The messages included the usual teasers like, *Hello Gorgeous* and *I can't wait to be near you, again* and *Is it almost time.* The pictures were unlike the things that Elet sent. There was a picture of the chest of a man she hadn't seen in years. His rippled muscles and dark skin made her feel flush. The next photo was of his arms. Hairless and glistening in the Florida sun, she remembered how it felt to be wrapped within them. The final picture was his face. By the time she saw it, she was brimming with excitement. Despite the years that had passed, his dark skin and a strong jawline reminded her that he was a very attractive man. His teeth gleamed in the cellphone picture as she thought of his name, Cooper. The two hadn't seen or spoken to each other in years. In fact, she had blocked him from her mind. But, now, he was back in town.

~~~~~~~~~

When her cellphone rang last week, she thought it was Elet. It was midday on a Tuesday. In her mind, only one person would call her, so she answered without hesitation. "Hello, baby."

"Well, hello, baby."

Instantly, she knew that the baritone who had answered was not her fiancé. Since summer, she had pledged herself to complete fidelity. She hadn't entertained the flirtations of the opposite sex. She hadn't had any inappropriate conversations or rendezvous. To guarantee that she would not be swayed, she had changed her phone number. So, the confidence of this stranger to react in such a way unnerved her. Finally, she responded as any upstanding semi-outraged woman would, "Excuse me?"

"Well, you said it to me first. I thought it would be wrong to leave you hangin'."

"Um hmm. Who is this?"

"That hurts. After all the years, we've known each other I can't..."

"You have just a few seconds to tell me who you are before I hang up and block your number."

"Okay. Okay. Alex, it's me. It's Cooper." She relaxed her guard. She was shocked, but she didn't say anything in response. "Oh, baby, have you missed me?" She thought about the question. She wasn't sure if she had or she hadn't, but she had forgotten how much she enjoyed the sound of his voice. The certainty of his speech. The correct choice of words that danced along the lines of decency. "Well, I guess the cat's got your tongue. You know, I've been dreamin' of you for a while now. I wondered if the past was far enough behind us that we could talk like the fine adults we've become. How long has it been?"

"Six years."

"Ah, you do speak. Six years. Hmm, so much has happened in my life in the last six years. I'd love to get together with you and catch up."

"Aren't you in Atlanta?"

He howled, "Look who is keeping up with who. Have ya checked me out online? You stalkin' me?"

"No, no, I'm not. I believe those are some of the last words you said to me. I think it went something like 'Baby, I need to go to ATL and get my head right. I need ya to understand.'"

"And, that's one of the biggest regrets of my life. I shoulda stayed and gotten things right with the only woman that I've eva really loved." Her guard collapsed. Her shoulders went limp. Suddenly, she felt a chill. He continued, "We've been through so much togetha. I can't believe I just let you slip away as many times as I have. But, I want ya to know I'm back for ya."

Dizzy with emotions, she uttered, "Where are you?"

"Thought you'd never ask. Heading to my mama's house."

"In Brandon?"

"Yes. You remember the house, don't you? Big ole white house on the corner. The one with the waist-high hedges that you used to hide behind until I'd come outside."

Her mind went back to that corner. It was down the street from her parents' house. Three blocks south to be exact. It was a huge white house with white metal awnings. She stared at it as a kid and wondered why there were no other colors. She never approached it from head on. She walked all the way around the neighborhood to approach it from the side. She would crouch day or night beside the hedges near the stop sign and wait for him. Sometimes, he would come quickly; but, other times, she would wait for hours for him. "Yea, I remember," embarrassed that she did.

"Of course, you do. When I got there yesterday, I checked to make sure that you were sitting by that hedge." He snickered. "Of course, you weren't. I was planning to go to your parent's house today and ask how to get in touch with you..."

"Don't do that!"

"Lemme finish. I didn't have to. I went to Byron's place to get a tape up. While I sat there waitin' my turn and talkin' to my boys, I thumbed through a magazine. *UpBeat.* I think it's called. Have you heard of it?"

She smiled. "I've seen a few copies."

"Yeah, well, it seems they have a columnist that I used to.... know," he amused himself with his own wittiness. "So, I gave them a call and they transferred me to this number. And, just like that," he snapped his fingers so loud that she could hear them through the phone. "I'm back."

"You're back? For good?"

"Who knows? I'm back on business, but I'm open to the idea of stayin' around. Sky's the limit for us."

Her heart beat his name. Coo-per. Coo-per. Coo-per. "I don't know what to say. It's been such a long time and..."

"All I want you to say is that you'll have dinner with me. Or lunch. Or breakfast. Just something. All I want is to see ya. Smell ya. Be close to ya."

"Cooper, I'm going out of town for business tomorrow. I won't be back until the weekend."

"Baby doll, I'll be here waiting."

And, she melted. She had forgotten how she loved being called baby doll. "Maybe, we can get together on Monday. Will you still be in town? Will Monday work for your schedule?"

"I'll make it work. I haven't waited six years just to not wait five days. Lemme give you my number in case you want to call or text me while you're out of town."

As she wrote down his number, she gave no thought to this being in violation of her commitment to fidelity. In fact, she thought of Elet. She thought of how funny it would be to have them side by side. The man she always thought she wanted and the man she was planning to marry. "Okay. Got it."

"Good. Call or text me anytime. I'll be around." Then, he was gone. She hadn't said goodbye. She never got to say goodbye. As usual, he danced away from her and left her feeling as though she should have said more than she did.

~~~~~~~~

Today was Monday and it was time to go see Cooper. While she was in Miami, she sent a few texts to which he responded immediately. She had been playfully reminiscing and enjoying his attention. She hadn't told anyone that she was speaking with him. She had wanted to, but considering all that happened over the summer, she wasn't sure that anyone would understand. Cooper wasn't some stranger that meant nothing to her. Cooper was her first love. And, as she sat next to Langston, she mumbled, "Maybe, Cooper's the love of my life." She wanted desperately to talk to someone about whether or not that was true. She wanted Langston to turn and let her tell him the condensed version of the thirteen years that she and Cooper had known each other. Instead, Langston turned his head and furrowed his brow at her. She assumed that the look meant that he was annoyed by her sudden comments. In truth, that was his retort.

When her face was ready, she stood up and said, "How do I look?" Langston said nothing, but he flattened his already thin lips and nodded with approval. "Oh, Langston, you say the nicest things. I'm gonna go get some lunch. Do you want me to bring you something?"

He groaned, "Food."

"Anything likes, dislikes, allergies." There was no reply. "Okay, I'll bring back whatever screams Langston." She gathered her things and walked towards the front of the building. With her laptop in the bag on her shoulder and her purse in hand, she flounced past younger women in tighter pants and higher heels. Before she deflated completely, her phone rang.

Thinking it was Cooper confirming that he was outside waiting on her, she said, "Hey, you!"

"This isn't Elet."

"Oh, hey, Olive. What's up?"

"You got a sec?"

"Just a few. I'm heading out for a lunch date."

"Aww, that's sweet. Still having lunch dates with your fiancé."

"No, a work lunch date."

"Oh, okay, then. Listen, I was thinking that now that we've got your dress picked out. We need to move on getting these other dresses picked out. Last night, when I got out of the shower, Drew was asking me if I was wearing the same thing as the bridesmaids. And, I didn't know. We haven't really talked about that kinda thing. He said for his sister's wedding that everyone was wearing a different dress, but, in the same color. I thought that was pretty cool. Hell, I even dreamed of it. Ooh, and I just sat here and thought that we could do the same dress but in different colors. That would cool, too. Whaddaya think?"

"I think that you and Drew shouldn't be in bed together talking about me."

"Trust me. It ain't like that, gurl. We were just talkin' while I dried my hair."

"You sure are over there a lot now."

"Don't change the subject. We need to get this show on the road."

"Yeah, I know. I'll think about it tonight."

"No, you won't. But, that's okay, cuz I'm just gonna keep buggin' you until we get this done."

"Thank you so much."

"No need to thank me. It's what maids of honor are for. I love ya. Call you later."

She said, "love you too" as she stepped out of the building onto the sidewalk. In the darkness cast by the other skyscrapers, she looked to her left and right. She hadn't asked what he'd be driving. He hadn't told her. She thought, surely, he wouldn't still be driving his old Honda CRX. Glancing at cars as they passed by, she tried to peer inside to spot a familiar face. She was staring at a dark-skinned man in a Toyota when a shiny, black convertible Cadillac stopped in front of her and the passenger window opened.

Unaware of the car's presence, she was startled when a familiar voice said, "Baby doll, you look beautiful."

Chapter 9

Mallory arrived home to what appeared to be an empty house. Jacqueline's Jeep was parked in the driveway, but, as she entered the house, she saw and heard no one. Perplexed, she said, "Hello," but no one answered. She placed her purse and folio on the coffee table. As she looked around her empty house, she intended to drop her keys on the coffee table, but she missed and her keys hit the floor. Stepping over them, she went in search of Jax and Zoe. The kitchen was dark. The main bathroom was empty. Thinking this may be a weird repeat of Saturday morning, she headed to Zoe's bedroom. The door was cracked. Gently, she pushed it open.

Mallory walked into her room. She leaned down over her daughter and kissed the top of her head. "Hey, Mom."

"Hey, there you. What are you doing?"

"Homework. Jax says that I've gotta get it all done and eat dinner before we can go to the carnival."

"Are you almost finished?"

"Yeah, almost. I've only gotta do my math."

"Saved the best for last?"

Zoe groaned, "No way. Math's the worst."

"Okay. You better get it done."

"I know. I know."

Mallory left her room. She peered into the kitchen once more, but there was still no sign of Jacqueline. Wondering if she was lying down, Mallory headed to her bedroom. Jacqueline wasn't in there, either. As she stood in her room, holding onto the frame of her bed, she could see a shadow in the backyard. She crossed back through the house to the kitchen. This time, she exited through the kitchen to the laundry room and outside into the backyard. Her nose caught wind of dinner.

"Well, there you are."

"Here I are," Jacqueline said from behind the open grill.

"Seems like you've got things under control."

"Do I?"

"Well, yeah, you have dinner and homework going."

"It was easy tonight. She wants something. No homework. No dinner. No carnival."

"Nice move."

"Thanks. Chicken should be ready in a few minutes. There's a salad in there and some rolls. I figure we'll keep tonight's meal light since you've gotta work and she's gonna jump around like crazy."

"Ugh. How'd I get roped into manning a booth? I don't even want to go. You know, we used to not even go to these carnivals."

"Really?"

"Really. That's why Zoe asked you. She knew I'd say no."

"We've been bamboozled."

"Nope. Just you. I knew what was up."

"Damn it. No one told me."

"I have to go get changed, so we can eat and leave."

"Okay, baby. I'll call you when I get the plates ready." Mallory walked over to Jacqueline. She threw her arms around her neck and kissed her slowly. "What was that for?"

"You're the best."

"I can cook more chicken if it'll get me another one of those." Mallory giggled and went inside.

~~~~~~~~

As Jacqueline pulled into the parking lot of Palmetto Elementary, she glanced around at the transformation that the school grounds had undergone in the few hours since she had picked Zoe up from school. The parking lot was full of bounce houses. There was an arcade trailer in the bus lane. Local food trucks had filled the kindergarten parking lot. The rows of the other parking spaces were filled with a series of games to interest the children and snacks to spoil their appetites. As she stepped out of the Jeep, the air was cool, but comfortable. She had forced Zoe into a pair of jeans, but she was wearing shorts. When she pulled her seat forward to allow Zoe to get out, she saw the look of a caged animal in her eyes. "Simmer down, tiger. Don't run too far away from me. I know it's your school, but we won't know everyone who will be out here tonight. Okay?"

Mallory was standing on the passenger's side with her door open. She was adjusting her makeup one last time before leaving them to head to her booth. "Zoe, stay with Jax. Do not make me spank you in front of all of these people." Mallory pointed to the slowly forming crowd with her mascara wand.

"I know, Mom. I'm not going anywhere." Zoe stood in the door frame staring at the slide. "I can't wait to go on that." Jacqueline reached up and placed her hands under Zoe's armpits. Zoe jumped up into the air as Jacqueline whirled her around and down to the ground.

Watching from the other side, Mallory said, "I can't believe that you let all of your friends see you do that."

"What?" Zoe asked innocently.

Now, pointing at Jacqueline and Zoe with her compact, Mallory said, "That airplane whirl. You won't hold my hand when I drop you off to school, but she can whirl you around and down to the ground like a five-year-old."

Jacqueline had walked to the passenger's side and leaned against the Jeep next to Mallory, "Airplane rides are cooler than handholding."

"I don't know. I'd prefer to just hold your hand."

"Well, let me know when you're ready. My hand will be over here waiting."

Mallory put her makeup back into her purse and placed her purse under the passenger's seat. She locked the door and turned to face Jacqueline. "Are you sure?"

"Sure. I think the school is onto us anyhow."

"You think?"

Laughing, Jacqueline stretched out her large brown hand and Mallory wove her thin ivory fingers with hers. They walked hand in hand with Zoe run-dancing beside them. When Zoe spotted the ticket booth, she began to run ahead. Jacqueline called out, "Zoe!"

Zoe turned and screamed, "I'm just going to the ticket booth to see how much the tickets are. I won't go anywhere else. Promise."

Mallory released Jacqueline's hand, "It's gonna be a long night."

"Yeah, I think it is."

"Do not spend more than twenty dollars tonight."

"How much are the tickets?"

"Jacqueline, no matter what she says. Do not spend a million dollars at a fake carnival in her elementary school parking lot."

"Okay. Okay." Jacqueline watched as Mallory headed across to the parking lot towards her booth. She would never grow tired of watching her walk.

~~~~~~~~~

Zoe had been on the slide four times before Abbie arrived. Standing on top of the slide, Zoe could see Abbie inside the jump house parallel to where she was. Hastily, Zoe slid down the slide and ran to Jacqueline who had been standing at the exit. Out of breath, Zoe ran to Jacqueline and said, "Abbie's here! Abbie's here! Can I go where she is?"

"Where is she?"

"Over there in the bounce house. Can I go? Can I?"

"Okay. Okay. Calm down. You can go over there. Here's the tickets. I'll be standing by the exit."

As she darted towards the bounce house, she yelled, "Okay."

They had been at the carnival for almost an hour. Jacqueline had not spoken to any of the parents. She had not congregated in any of the groups that had formed. She hadn't given any thought to the idea that she should attempt to talk to them. When they spoke, she politely responded, but with brevity. She shook hands and returned hugs, but she never lost sight of Zoe. She had stood alone watching her, but, as she headed to stand at the opening for the bounce house, she heard a familiar voice.

"Hey, Jacqueline. When'd you get here?"

It was Josh, Abbie's father. "Hey, Josh. How's it going?"

"It's good. We've been here about ten minutes and I think I've spent about ten bucks."

"That's nothing. We've been here about an hour and I've probably spent about twenty bucks."

"No way am I spending that much."

"Should I write that down and remind you later that you said it?" she teased.

"Please don't. So, how'd you get duped into this?" Jacqueline shrugged her shoulders. She had not been duped or tricked. In fact, she just assumed it was what was to be done. "I've got duty early tomorrow morning, so we're definitely not staying long."

"Did you all ride together?"

"Yeah, Abbie and I brought Lauren up here earlier, so she could man the booth with Mallory. Then, Abbie and I went home and ate, so she didn't fill up on crap. Then, we came back up here. I figure it won't be a long night. Lauren can't stand on her feet for too long."

"How much longer does she have?"

"Just a couple of weeks. The doctor said that he wouldn't stop her from going into labor anymore, so when he's ready, it's go time."

"It's so great that you got back here before Mason's born."

"Yeah, Lauren woulda really been a basket case if I hadn't been here. I know she asked Mallory to be in there with her, but I don't think she can handle her all on her own."

This was news to Jacqueline. She hadn't been told that Lauren had asked Mallory to be present at the baby's birth. As Josh recalled the story of how anxious Lauren was at Abbie's birth, Jacqueline tried to think about past conversations. Perhaps, Mallory had told her and she had just forgotten. Maybe, it was not a secret. Maybe, it was just an oversight. Having ignored the entire conversation, Jacqueline decided that she was indifferent to Mallory's presence in the hospital and had better return her thoughts to the conversation that she had been having with Josh.

"So, how are things going with you guys?" Josh asked.

"Oh, things are good."

"Really?" He questioned as if things would be otherwise. Jacqueline furrowed her brow. "No, I guess that I thought it would be tough on you to adapt to life with a family and hard for them to adjust to life with you. Lauren said that Mallory has barely spoken to her since you two got together. She said she was gonna try to talk to her and find out how things were going. I said to leave it alone, but Lauren never leaves anything alone."

"Nope, no problems. Things're fine." She said. Before he could respond, Zoe and Abbie ran towards them. Both girls were speaking at the same time. With sweaty matted hair, Zoe ran straight to Jacqueline and wrapped her arms around Jacqueline's legs. "Are you having fun?"

"Yes," escaped her panting breaths.

"Hi, Miss Jacqueline," Abbie said. "Daddy, can we go to the next row? They have games and a petting zoo over there."

"Can we, Jax? Can we?" Zoe begged.

"Okay, Abbie. Let's go," Josh said.

As they walked to the next row, passers-by spoke to Josh. They welcomed him back, saluted him, and asked about this tours overseas. Leaving him to talk, Jacqueline motioned that she would look after the girls while he spoke to his well-wishers. The girls stopped at the balloon rainbow. Giving each girl five tickets, they took turns popping random balloons in search of prizes. Groans of disappointment were heard when some balloons were only filled with confetti. After a few tries, Zoe returned to Jacqueline and announced that this game was a trick and they were stealing her tickets. Then, she told Abbie, "I'm leaving. This is dumb. Come on."

Protesting, Abbie replied, "It's the best. You just don't know what you're doing."

"Do, too."

"Nuh-uh."

"Uh-huh."

Hoping to prevent a skirmish, Jacqueline interceded, "Enough, you two. Zoe, go try the baseball toss. It's right there on the other side." She moved between Abbie at the balloon rainbow game and Zoe at the baseball toss. She wasn't really paying a lot of attention to the people who were hovering around her. Instead, she was collecting the various trinkets each were winning.

"You must be, Jacqueline, Zoe's mother's girlfriend."

Jacqueline was silent. Not because she hadn't wanted to be recognized or because she did not know the man who was speaking to her. She wasn't certain how she felt about being called a girlfriend at this point in her life. Partner felt professional. Lover felt too personal, but girlfriend felt very casual. With her hand outstretched, she said, "I'm sorry. You are?"

"Oh, I get so used to everyone knowing me. I'm Ben, one of Dalton's fathers."

"It's very nice to meet you. Zoe speaks of Dalton, all the time." In truth, Zoe mentioned Dalton as much as she mentioned any of the other kids in her class. At almost eight years old, kids were either her friends or only characters in a story. Jacqueline remembered Dalton, because Mallory had told her. Dalton was the son of Ben and Danny. They had been in a relationship for a number of years when they decided that they wanted to be

124

parents. They tried to adopt a child and the state forbade both men's names being placed on the birth certificate. After many pleas and phone calls, the couple joined three other couples and filed a lawsuit against the state denying their right to adopt. The case drug on for years. There were local trials. Then, the case went to the Appellate Courts and finally, there was a Supreme Court decision. In the meantime, they chose to have a surrogate birth a child for them. Ben and Danny had the doctor mix their sperm prior to fertilizing the egg; so, in essence, neither knew whether or not he was the biological father of Dalton. But, the boy's features led Jacqueline to think it was Danny's son. His dark hair and brooding eyes were in keeping with Danny's features. He was a tall, brawny man. He had served in the military and still worked on base as a civilian. Maintaining the closely cropped military crew cut, it was obvious that he was dark haired. In contrast, Ben was coltish. He was more angler. His pace and temperament was swifter than Danny's, but each adored their son.

As the girls returned to request more tickets, Jacqueline said, "Girls, say hello to Mr. Ben and Dalton."

"Hey, there, Dalton. Do you want to hang with us?" Zoe asked.

"Dad, can I?" Dalton said in a voice deeper than a boy should have at eight.

"May I?" Ben corrected.

"May I?" Dalton replied. Zoe rolled her eyes at this exchange. Noticing her attitude, Jacqueline tapped her shoulder.

"Yes, you may, but keep a look out for me." Ben approved.

"Thanks, Mr. Ben. Come on, Dalton! Come on, Abbie," Zoe screamed over her shoulder as she headed back to play.

"Those girls are so cute together. Sometimes, I wish we had another one. A boy and a girl would be perfect."

"Well, why don't you?"

"It was a fortune just having Dalton. Besides, Danny says that another kid would take away our ability to give Dalton the world. I guess he's right. What about you?"

"Me?" Jacqueline wasn't sure what he meant.

"Are you two going to have a child together?" She didn't answer. She had never thought of it. Mallory had never mentioned it. Noticing her hesitation, Ben continued, "Well, you've only been together a little while. There's plenty of time to figure that out. But, it might be nice for Zoe to have a little playmate."

"She'll be eight next month, so, even if we had a baby, it couldn't be her playmate. Besides, Abbie's Zoe's best friend. They run as a pack. I don't know that a sibling could get a word in with those two." With that, the girls returned to Jacqueline to deliver her their winnings. As she talked, they filled her pockets with rubber balls, candy, erasers, and friendship bracelets; then, Dalton appeared with his own handful of trinkets. The children compared the games they had played and the ones that they hadn't as the adults tried to organize the children's loot in more comfortable ways.

"Danny!" Ben called. When Danny did not respond, he pointed in his direction. "That's my husband. He was hoping you'd make an appearance at the carnival. I was going to volunteer for a booth, but it was full. Then, I saw that Mallory was going to be working the Feeding the Animals booth with Lauren, we had really hoped that you would come. So, we could finally meet you."

Embarrassed, Jacqueline said, "Well, I hope that I am not disappointing you."

"Oh. I'm so sorry. Silly me. I guess I shouldn't make it seem like such a conspiracy, but there has been a lot of talk about you. You had to know."

"Actually, I had no idea."

"Girl, yes." He grabbed her wrist. "It hasn't been bad. I mean, after the controversy of Danny and I, I think the worst is over. Most people have only said that you're quiet and keep to yourself. That Zoe adores you and that you have been a great asset to the class. Dalton said that you send food and snacks. You had paper, markers, pens, and pencils donated from the newspaper."

"Oh, yeah. There was a list of needs for the classroom. I thought we were supposed to make donations."

"Yes, people give what they can, but, typically, just a few things. I think you gave so much that other classes had their wish list met by you."

Jacqueline was not sure how to respond. She wanted to walk away. She wanted him to stop talking. As she glanced from side to side looking for an escape path, she saw Josh approaching her. She noticed that with him there were two other parents and Zoe's teacher. She hoped new blood might draw some of the attention off of her.

Right on cue, Josh said, "Sorry that took so long, Jacqueline. Thanks for looking after Abbie." Jacqueline handed him Abbie's pocket full of tiny toys. As he wrangled them into his pockets, he spoke to Ben. "Hey, man. How's it going?"

"Good. You're Abbie's dad, aren't you? Yoshi?"

"Actually, it's Yoshiya, but I go by Josh. It's easier."

"When they had their geography lesson and Abbie did her presentation on Japan, Dalton came home and told us all about it. He wanted a Japanese name. We had to eat Japanese food. He was enthralled for months."

"That's cool. I didn't even know she had done a presentation on Japan. My parents are Japanese. They moved to California in the late seventies. I was born in San Diego. I've been to Japan a ton of times visiting family and their friends, but I'm a SoCal boy."

"That must've been so cool."

"You know, I never thought anything of it. I mean, I can speak Japanese, but my parents speak English primarily."

"Oh, really," Ben asked, "Did you teach Abbie?"

"My mom did. She talks to her every day in Japanese to keep her skills up."

"That's awesome. Does it ever come in handy when you're on missions?" Ben pressed.

"It definitely didn't in Afghanistan." As Josh regurgitated his war stories, Jacqueline was happy to take a backseat. But, she noticed one of the other mothers staring at her. Jacqueline moved to the other side of Josh to break her gaze.

Then, Danny appeared. "Welcome home, Airman. How's it been?" Carrying Dalton on his neck, he stuck his thick hand out to shake Josh's.

As Josh restarted his story for Danny's sake, Mrs. Yates, Zoe's teacher introduced the two silent women who had walked over with Josh. Speaking as though we were all eight year olds, Mrs. Yates said, "Jacqueline," firmly. "Jacqueline. I wanted to introduce you to Celeste Bevie, Emma's mother, and Angela Sanchez, Isla's mother. Their daughters share a table with Zoe. Ladies, this is Jacqueline Emerson, Zoe Russell's..."

Before she could search for the right word to explain their relationship, Zoe appeared. "Hi, Mrs. Yates."

"Hi, Zoe. Aren't you going to say hello to Emma and Isla's mothers?"

Zoe gave them a wave. Then, she tugged at Jacqueline's shirt as she often did when she wanted a private moment. Jacqueline bent down and Zoe said, "Can Abbie stay the night? She says they're gonna have to go soon, because Mr. Josh has to go back to the base in the morning. We're having so much fun. I don't want her to leave. Please. Please."

"Zoe, did she ask to stay the night or are you asking on her behalf?"

"We both want to know. See, she's over there asking Mr. Josh." Jacqueline glanced over to Abbie in Josh's arms trying to talk to him. "Mom can drop us both off at school. It's not out of the way. I'll even share my lunch with her. We've both eaten dinner. And, I promise we'll be good."

"First of all, we can make two lunches, but, let's wait and see what Mr. Josh says."

"Does that mean it's okay with you if it's okay with him? Does it?" Zoe asked anxiously.

"Yes, Zoe. It's okay with me if it's okay with her parents, but you two cannot stay up all night or fight or argue or act crazy. This is still a school night."

"I know," Zoe said as she ran off to collaborate with Abbie.

"You're so good with her," Celeste said. "Emma tells me you live in a penthouse. Must be nice."

Angela said, "Isla says you've got a huge boat."

"And, superpowers," Jacqueline teased. Neither of them smiled. She wondered if they had gotten the joke or if they suspected that she might really have superpowers.

Before she could apologize for her sarcasm, Josh reappeared with the girls. Since he was no longer telling the story from overseas, Danny, Ben, and Dalton began to chat with Celeste, Angela, and Mrs. Yates. "So, I hear something's up. Abbie wants to stay the night with you guys, so she can stay at the carnival longer."

"That's what I hear, too. They're surely getting craftier."

"Well, it would definitely help me out if she stayed the night, but I don't want you to think I put her up to it."

Jacqueline chuckled, "Never thought it. These two are masters. We're just their puppets." As Jacqueline and Josh laughed, the other adults rejoined the conversation and shared stories of their children's antics. With the heat off of her, Jacqueline felt more at ease. The group moved to the next row as the children moved from station to station. When Jacqueline noticed that the kids were heading to Mallory and Lauren's station, she excused herself and joined them. Mallory was helping a first grader aim for the shark's mouth when Lauren noticed Jacqueline, Abbie, Dalton, and Zoe approaching.

"Here comes Zoe and Jacqueline." As the child successfully tossed a fish into the shark's mouth, Lauren let her select a prize. Then to the kids, she asked, "Are you having fun?"

Abbie nodded, but Zoe answered as if Mallory had asked, "Mom, a ton of people are here. I saw, like, my whole class. Jax was walking around with the other parents. She and Mr. Josh were talking to Dalton's dads and Emma's mom and Isla's mom. Even Mrs. Yates came over to talk."

Mallory eyed Jacqueline. "Everything okay?"

"Yep."

"We can talk about it later. Let me know if I need to say something."

"No, honey, it's fine. They're just more forward than I had expected."

"Mom, look at all the stuff I won," Zoe reached her hands into Jacqueline's pocket to retrieve her winnings.

"Okay, Zoe. I got it." Jacqueline pulled out the handful of trinkets to show Mallory.

"That's great. You better go play with Abbie. They're gonna go soon. Miss Lauren needs to get home and rest."

"Abbie's coming home with us," Zoe announced.

"What?" Lauren said.

"Dad said it was okay. I didn't want to leave, so Zoe and I asked if I could spend the night with them. Okay, Mom." Abbie begged.

"Please, Miss Lauren. Mr. Josh and Jax said it was okay. We swear," Zoe added.

"Stop saying you swear," Mallory mumbled under her breath as she rubbed her forehead.

"It's fine with me, girls. I just wish someone would have come over and mentioned it to me."

"Us," Mallory added.

"The girls have promised to behave, to stay settled, and be ready for school bright and early tomorrow morning," Jacqueline tried to soothe both mothers.

"Are you sure about this?" Lauren asked Mallory.

"No, it's fine. Abbie's never any trouble. And, after all the running they've done tonight, I'm sure they'll pass out before we ever get home."

"Jacqueline, do you know where my husband is?" Lauren asked.

"He was talking to the others at the end of the row when we last saw him. Everyone wants to talk to him and Abbie was so excited to go and play that I told him that I'd look after her."

"Has she been good?"

"Absolutely," Happy that the conversation was going well, Jacqueline pressed for more, "How are you feeling? Josh said that it'll be anytime now."

"Yeah, I can't wait until he punches out."

"I guess I'll start preparing myself for the middle of the night call. You know, if you need me to, since Mallory is going to go with you to the hospital, I can keep an eye on Abbie. I mean, unless you want her there with you."

Confused, Mallory asked, "I'm going to be where?"

"At the hospital. Since you're gonna be at the hospital, Zoe and I can go to their house and wait for news. Or, we can drop you off at the hospital and pick up Abbie and bring her home with us to wait for news. Then, when Mason is born, I can bring her up to the hospital. She can stay with us for the couple days you'll spend in the hospital if you want."

Looking at Mallory, but speaking to Jacqueline, Lauren quietly said, "That's very nice of you. You know, Josh and I hadn't talked about what to do with Abbie. We may have to take you up on it. His parents are going to come from San Diego after Mason's born, but for those first few days, I may need your help." Before Jacqueline could respond, the girls pulled her off towards the next row.

In the distance, Lauren heard Jacqueline say, "It's no problem at all."

Now, with her arms folded, Mallory sucked on her tongue. Rolling it around inside her mouth, she tried to phrase her thoughts as gently as she could, "So, do you want to tell me what this is all about?"

Removing the fish, the last child threw into the shark's mouth, Lauren said, "I've been trying to talk to you. I wanted to ask you if you would go with me when it's time."

"Why?"

"To help me."

"Help you do what?"

"Have Mason."

"What? Josh's here."

"He's no help. You know how he is."

"Actually, I don't."

"Exactly. He's doing his own thing. He's either at work or busy with that damn motorcycle. He has no idea what I'm going through."

"Why me?"

"Because you're my closest friend."

"I am?"

"Yes, you are. That's why I've been so upset with you."

"What? You're upset with me?"

"Nevermind. You haven't even paid me any attention. You're just like Josh. You think everything is pregnancy related emotional outbursts, but I have feelings whether or not I'm pregnant."

"I don't even know that the hell you're talking about."

Chapter 10

Jacqueline was sitting behind her desk feeling the heaviness of her eyelids when Mallory entered her office door. Despite their newfound relationship, Mallory knocked on Jacqueline's office door before she entered. "Are you going to come in?"

"I was waiting on you to invite me in," Mallory held the door and stuck her head around it.

"Good morning. Again."

"Good morning," Mallory drug into Jacqueline's office and slouched into the chair. "You snuck out of the house this morning."

Laughing, she said, "I did not. I kissed you goodbye."

"Well, you sure as hell didn't dillydally around. You were in a hurry to get away."

Jacqueline laughed as she rested her head on her desk. "I'm so tired. Two little girls are exhausting. Even when I tell them to calm down, they don't. I just don't understand how they have so much energy."

"It was your bright idea to have a mid-week sleepover."

"What could I do? Zoe was begging. Abbie was begging. Josh looked like it would really help them out. I was trying to do the right thing. The good thing, you know?"

Mallory laughed, "Oh, I know."

Realizing she should apologize, Jacqueline atoned, "Sorry, I didn't check with you first. I tried to clear all bases. I knew we didn't have any plans that would exclude Abbie. I tried to make them promise to be good and take baths and not fight. I really did think this over."

"I'm okay with it. I know you had Zoe's best interest at heart. And, I, also, know," she leaned forward towards her face and said, "you needed to learn the lesson."

"What lesson?"

"Sometimes, you're too tired for your own kid. When you are, you definitely don't have energy for an extra kid."

"No joke," She smirked. "Did Lauren call you this morning?"

"How'd you know?"

"She always calls the next morning after Abbie has spent the night."

"Oh my God, she does. That's weird."

"Nah, it gives her a good excuse to talk to you. Think about it. She says you're her closest friend. That means she wants to talk."

"She's so weird. This morning, she was going on and on about how we used to talk. She told me that she misses the conversations and wonders what happened."

"Yeah, Josh mentioned something to me about that. He said she told him that you stopped talking to her when we got together."

"Oh my God, is everyone talking about me?" Mallory sat back in the chair. "She says that we used to talk about what was going in my life. She said I used to share who I had dated and what had happened, but, now, we don't talk at all."

"Is that true?"

"I'll tell you what I told her. When I was dating, it wasn't going well, so when we would have events and she'd ask how things were going, I would just tell the latest story. Some of them were funny. But, then I started having feelings for you and I wasn't sure what they meant. Then, you and I were together more, so I didn't see her all that often. But, when I did, I was distracted by thoughts of you. I just couldn't figure it out myself. I couldn't talk to anyone. It wasn't personal. Anyhow, she said that she wished I knew that I could talk to her. I said I'm sorry. I guess I haven't talked to a lot of people. There weren't a lot of nice reactions from the few people I did tell, so I've just stopped sharing. She said that I didn't have to be that way. She said that she was still there to listen if I wanted to talk."

Jacqueline lifted her head, "That's nice."

"Or crazy."

"I think I get it. You thought that you were just rambling to Zoe's friend's mom. You thought nothing of it. But, to her, you were sharing. You, two, were bonding. She was telling you what was going on in her life and you were telling her what was going on in your life, then you just stopped. She thought she did something, but she didn't. So, she's been pissed off that you stopped being her friend, but you never knew you were her friend. Are you friends, now?"

"I guess so. She told me that she likes you and that Josh has a gay cousin."

Jacqueline teased, "People always think that it helps the awkward hurdle to say 'Hey, I know a gay person.'"

"I think she felt that way, too. She told me all about his cousin like it was going to make me feel some kinda way."

"See, it's classic. Well, now, that that's all hashed out, are you going to the hospital?"

"Yeah, I guess so."

"Then, the gay cousin story has worked," Jacqueline teased. "What'd she say about me?"

"Oh, that you're really nice and are good with Zoe and love me."

"Well, it's good to know I've got her approval." As she saw the lights fill the news floor, Jacqueline said, "I wonder what the people 'round here think when they see the two of us together."

"Probably not much. I think they've gotten used to it."

Jacqueline stood up and walked to her window. "They're thinking something. They don't come over when we're talking. They assume it's personal. If you're in my office, Grant blocks my schedule. He sends them away." She turned back to Mallory, "I've told him not to. I've told him that it's okay."

Mallory was indifferent to what they thought, but she entertained Jacqueline's curiosity. "I bet they wonder what things are like at home. What you are really like when you aren't here? What am I like? Are we talking about business? Are you telling me corporate secrets?" She moved her hands about the air like a ghost.

"No. I mean, on mornings like today. We both look exhausted. I want to put my head against my desk and nap. You're in here slouched down in the chair. We look like we had some late night. I wonder if they think it's late nights of drinking and partying and sex.

"They probably do think it's late nights full of sex. Great sex, I might add."

"If only they knew that two little girls having a sleepover on a weeknight after a school carnival is the cause of our exhaustion," They laughed.

Mallory stood up from the chair, "Well, we've gotta suck it up. My boss has called an all-employee meeting this morning and the subject of the meeting is top secret. Do you know how many people asked me what the meeting was about? They really do assume that we sit around and talk about business all day and all night long. Even, Paige asked and she knows us both. They ask me if we're all fired, if the paper is bought out, if Jack has resigned. I get all the questions."

"Sounds like it's tough being the boss' girl..." Jacqueline stopped. She was going to say girlfriend, but she remembered how she didn't like that when Ben said it. She flashed through all of the euphemisms and decided to make light of the situation. "Ole lady," she chirped and gathered her belongings for the meeting. She noticed the look on Mallory's face.

"Well, your ole' lady thinks that if it was something really bad, then she would know ahead of time. She has a daughter to raise, after all."

"Of course, she would. Now, let's go. Apparently, they're stewing out there." Jacqueline watched Mallory move towards the door. She was wearing dark pants with a cream colored silk top that was decorated in small yellow polka dots. Jacqueline liked polka dots and Mallory knew it. She wondered if Mallory wore the shirt on purpose. She wondered if she thought of her while getting dressed this morning. Whether she did or she didn't, Jacqueline had convinced herself that it was, at the very least, a possibility. And, that was just the jolt she needed to overcome the hours they had spent yelling at two second graders in the middle of the night.

Quickly, she caught up to Mallory, so that they could exit her office together. As they did, Jack was exiting his door.

"Good morning, you two," he spoke through his yawn.

"Good morning, Jack. How are you?" Jacqueline replied. Mallory walked into the conference room ahead of them as though he had not spoken to them.

"Tired. I came in for a morning meeting. Do you know what time I have to leave my house to get here by seven-thirty?"

"No, but I can only imagine the horror of getting up early, getting dressed, and waiting on the driver to bring you into the office." Jacqueline teased.

"Well, I do have to stand outside and wait on him, you know?"

"Outside of what? The house? How long are you out there? Minutes?"

"That's not the point."

"Oh, the problems of the rich."

"Hardy har har. You're so funny." He said. Jacqueline jeered. "Let's get this show on the road. I need a nap."

As the two entered the room, with smiles on their faces, the faces of the in-office staff relaxed. At that moment, Jacqueline realized that Mallory was not being dramatic. She was not just curious about the nature of the meeting. People really were concerned about what was going to be announced. Grant had had the oversized mahogany table removed from the Conference room. But, in its place, there was an odd collection of other chairs that had filled its void. She hadn't like the look of it. It was as if the once charming Conference room had been transformed into a supply closet. This debacle was an insult. Her eyes drifted all around. There were chairs from other conference rooms, some from the lobby, some looked like they might be desk chairs. It was a horrible sight. Thinking of how different things felt in the absence of the correct furniture, she jumped, when Jack spoke to her. "Am I up or are you doing this?"

She didn't respond. Jack nudged her. She didn't respond. As she glanced across the room, she met Mallory's eyes. Jacqueline lifted her eyebrows and smiled at her, but Mallory did not smile back. Instead, she nudged her head forward. Without speaking, she knew that Mallory wanted her to snapback from her thoughts to this moment. "It's all yours, Jack," she said. She had not known what Jack had meant by his question, but that felt like an appropriate answer. As Jack proceeded to the front of the room, she stood beside him but a step back.

"Ladies and gentlemen. Thanks to those of you, like myself, who got up and came in early for this quick meeting. I'm sorry that you were given such short notice, but we have an announcement to make." The room felt silent. Jacqueline scanned the crowd and noticed all eyes on Jack. All eyes except for Mallory. Mallory was not looking at Jacqueline nor was she looking at Jack. Mallory was staring at Grant who was behind Jacqueline. Jacqueline turned to look at him. In gray linen pants and a long sleeve cobalt blue shirt, he was slouched against the conference doors playing on his phone. She cleared her throat and glared at him. After he placed his phone in his pocket and stood upright, she turned back around to find Mallory smiling at her. Jack continued, "We're a family here at the Sun. We have gone through ups and downs together. We have had to say goodbye to many of the people who were legends in these halls, in this town, in this industry, but we forget that the ones of us that are left are legends in the making. Ladies and gentlemen, that's why we're here today." He pounded on the podium. "One of our own has been recognized and we're so proud that an email just wouldn't do. We needed to get as many of us together as we could to show our pride and offer our congratulations. Later this morning, the whole world will know what we are about to share with you. Clementine Porter, the most recent addition to our family, has been awarded a Wetty for the web design and management of our Tampa Sun Tribune's new web presence." The room filled with applause.

While quietly clapping, Jacqueline leaned into Jack's right side and said, "It's a Netty, not a Wetty."

While clapping and smiling, Jack retorted, "What the fuck ever. I was on a roll."

"It was a really nice campaign speech. I almost thought of voting for you."

"Hmm, I might try that next."

Jacqueline teased, "I think you'd be great over at Waste Management." He elbowed her.

As the clapping started to subside, Grant opened the doors to the conference room to reveal a cake. "Come on up here, Clementine. We got a cake for you. Thanks for all you do." With that, Jack patted her on the back and left the conference room.

Jacqueline smiled as he passed her. "I've got the rest."

"Thanks. I'm gonna go lie down in my office until it's time for our meeting."

"Okay." As Jacqueline stood there, speaking to the staff members as they poured out of the conference room doors, Mallory approached her. She stood to Jacqueline's side waiting for most of the room to empty. Recognizing that she was there, Jacqueline said, "What are you doing staring at Grant in meetings?"

"What are you doing staring at me staring at Grant in meetings?"

"I was just scanning the room."

"Uh huh," and she snickered and left the conference room.

Grant was in the atrium between Jack's office and Jacqueline's office when the room cleared. She walked to him. "Grant, I'm fairly certain that what happened in the conference room today should never ever happen again." She leaned into her office door and pushed it open.

Behind her, Grant sulked in, "Sorry. I was just making sure all the preparations were made. I wasn't playing a game or watching a movie or whatever."

"Grant! I mean all of those damn mismatch chairs that look like they came from your back porch. That's the room we use for Board meetings." Anger was filling her body. "I know that we have to move the table out for full staff meetings, but there has to be a better setup than a hundred chairs you found at a thrift store."

"That's all I could find."

"Buy some. We are a multi-million-dollar company. You got a cake the size of pickup truck. Can we get some new fucking chairs?" She was pounding her right hand into her left hand. It was not often that she lost her temper at work anymore, but there were still occasions for the temper she had sought to wrangle. "Is that too much to ask? Let's do a chair inventory. Research chairs, desks, and tables in other conference rooms. Make that your project. Get with the building people and make that happen. Will you do that for me?"

Unfazed by Jacqueline's outburst, Grant saluted. "Sure. I can't wait. I'd love to do a whole redesign. I can absolutely get on top of that."

"All right." Shooing him out of her office, "Go get the fuck on top of it." She watched as Grant spring back to his desk.

For a moment, she thought that she might have been rude to him. Before she could decide if she should apologize or not, the door opened. "What is Grant getting on top of during company hours?" Clementine entered. Wearing a pair of dark jeans, a black button up, and velvet ivory blazer, Jacqueline wondered if she should have human resources send a reminder about business casual attire. "Thanks for the big hurray. I know it was all you."

"All me? You did all the work. You got the award. We just wanted to congratulate you." Jacqueline was still semi-seething. She wanted to tell Clementine it wasn't a good time, but the new Open Door policy ensured that the employees could have access to her at almost any time. With a hard swallow, she sat up in her chair hoping this interaction would be brief.

"I do love a good Wetty," she said slyly.

Jacqueline shook her head and apologized, "I'm sorry about Jack's mistake."

"It's cool. It was funny."

Jacqueline began to clean her glasses. "So, any big plans tonight to celebrate?"

Clementine removed her non-prescription black horn-rimmed glasses and began wiping them against her jacket sleeve. "Oh, I was thinking of going down to a bar we both know and picking up a girl we both..."

"What is wrong with you? I mean, honestly. Why can't we ever just have a regular conversation? This is a big day for you. I was trying to be happy and supportive, but you're in here with jokes."

"I'm sorry. I'm just fuckin' with you. I'm on cloud nine. After all of this time, I've been given the chance to really do what I do best. You have given me a great opportunity. I'm not part of some bullshit team. I lead the damn team. I didn't do a redesign. That site is my design. And, now, I got my Netty for it. I'm so stoked. I couldn't be happier." Clementine was up from the chair. She was walking about Jacqueline's office.

Happy to see Clementine excited by her success and not trying to talk about her personal life, Jacqueline stood up as well. She walked from behind her desk and sat on the desk's edge, "Hey, I'm really proud of you.

When we were doing the interviews, after only a few minutes of talking to you, I knew that you were exactly what we needed. You have the energy and the vision to do great things. Now, I would love to see you have a long career here at the Sun, but I know you. I know that we're just a springboard onto to bigger and better things. And, I want that for you. I don't want it anytime soon, but I want that for you."

While Jacqueline sat poised on the corner of her desk, Clementine stopped pacing about her office and barreled towards her. Before Jacqueline knew what was happening, her face was met with velvet. Clementine had hugged her. Wrapped in her cocoon, Jacqueline wanted to shake loose, but she chose to ride out the embrace. "Thanks, man. I really do love you and love working for you. We should go out sometime."

Jacqueline inched back behind her desk, "Sure, maybe we can catch a game or have dinner or something."

Clementine laughed. "No, Grandma. I mean, we should go out. You remember what it was like to go out, don't you? Lights? Dancing? Women? You've only been dating for a few months, right? How have you already forgotten what it was like to go out?"

"Okay. That's where this ends. You have a cake to eat and I have a meeting with Jack. Keep your eyes open for an email that Grant will be sending. I think there's another surprise." Jacqueline picked up her folio and headed out of her office. When she reached the door, she turned and waited for Clementine to follow.

Passing by her, Clementine said, "I'm gonna get you to go out with me. Just you wait."

"With baited breath," she replied as she placed her folio against her chest and batted her own black eyelashes.

~~~~~~~~~~

Paige was motionless. She leaned against the corner of Mallory's desk thinking of the right words. She was aware that word choice would be paramount. She needed to help Mallory overcome what she'd just witnessed. "Mallory, I'm sure it was nothing. Come on. She did just get a big award."

"But, did you see that hug? Who am I kidding? Everyone saw that hug. The wall is made of glass."

"Mallory, it looked like a congratulatory hug."

"Yeah, the kind that Jacqueline doesn't give."

"She was probably caught off guard. You know, Clementine."

"And, that's what worries me," Mallory was rubbing the makeup from her forehead.

"I wouldn't worry about it."

"How can I not? Tell me that."

"Because Jacqueline isn't like that."

"Like what?"

"Secretive or untrustworthy."

"That's easy for you to say. You aren't there when her phone goes off and she hides it. I know it's pictures that are sent to her. I don't know who sends them or if it's more than one person."

Paige was stunned. She was not sure what to say. "Honey, have you asked her about them?"

"Of course, I have. She doesn't lie. She tells me that she has had the number for years. She has given it to people for business and pleasure. That she isn't in contact with those women anymore, but that they still contact her. She says as soon as the pictures or texts appear that she deletes the conversation and blocks the number. I have seen her do it, but it makes me sick to my stomach every time the damn thing goes off."

"Why doesn't she change her number?"

"Too many business contacts have that number. She has had it for years. And, really, would it matter if one of the people sending pictures or invitations was an employee?"

Paige sighed. "Try to relax. I am sure that it's nothing. I don't know why I want to say this, but, honestly, I don't think that Clementine is her type."

Mallory hit her with the stack of papers on her desk. "Gee, that makes me feel better."

Paige placed her hand on her shoulder. "You guys are coming tomorrow night, right?"

"Of course, we'll be there. Do you want us to bring anything?"

"Good spirits and open hearts."

"Okay. That's enough, Glenda the Good Witch. I've got work to do. Skedaddle."

Chapter 11

Jacqueline was outside loading Mallory's overnight bag into the trunk of the car when she exited her house. They had had dinner with Jack and Misty on a few occasions. In all the prior dinner dates, Mallory had worn her work clothes to their house. Dressed in her business professional outfits, she said that she felt underdressed and out of place. Misty was a model. She had started her as a child model doing commercials and print ads. The exposure spring-boarded her to pageants. After winning Miss Georgia and participating in the Miss America pageant, she did fashion modeling for years. Now, in her early thirties, she had returned to her roots in commercials and print advertisements in national magazines and websites. She was stunning. Her long, thin frame and straight blond hair made Mallory reevaluate her look and body. She wondered what Jacqueline thought of Misty and feared that she might be comparing her to a former Miss Georgia. Anytime she addressed her concerns with Jacqueline, she said not to worry; but, Mallory was distressed. She wanted Misty to know that under the striped blouses and dress pants that she was attractive. Therefore, she had planned that this dinner would be the occasion to prove that. Tonight, Mallory had Jacqueline drop Zoe off to Lauren and Josh's while she rushed home, jumped in the shower, reapplied make-up, and curled her hair. Her long, red locks that had sat inside a pencil-made bun, for most the afternoon, would cascade down her back tonight. And, it was going to be a very visible back.

When Jacqueline stood up from leaning into the trunk, Mallory was approaching her with a maroon glittery clutch that caught the sun's last lights. She was wearing a flowy, cranberry top that exposed her well-defined collarbone and dipped down her back to that space above her bra line that always begged to be touched. The bow that decorated the back of the shirt appeared to be the only seam that might be holding it together. Mallory had paired the top with slim fitting black skinny jeans and a pair of black ankle boots. Jacqueline closed the trunk and stared for a moment. After some thought, she said, "Maybe, I should have done more than change my shirt."

"You like?"

"Of course, I like, but I'm wondering why I haven't seen this outfit before."

"You stopped taking me out."

Walking to open her door, Jacqueline said, "Well, this is a good way to remind me to do that more often." As Mallory sat down, Jacqueline leaned in for a quick kiss. Her attempt was thwarted as Mallory had begun to apply red lip stain. "Okay, do you need to tell me something? Do you want to be with Misty?"

"Of course not. But, this bitch isn't going to keep showing me up."

Jacqueline trotted to her side of the car. "You know, she's not showing you up. Jack only has eyes for her and I only have eyes for you. There's no battle for attention. There's no competition."

"She doesn't think that I'm hot."

Jacqueline giggled. "Baby, she will tonight."

~~~~~~~~~

As they left Clearwater, Jacqueline groaned and yawned.

"Are you okay?"

"Oh, yeah. I'm just tired. It has been a long day."

"Yeah, who knew that you'd planned a whole party."

Wiping her eyes, she said, "I didn't plan any of it. Mia told me that she heard that Clementine was going to get the award. Grant was in my office. Before I could make any plans, he said that he would take care of it. I hadn't thought of it anymore until late that afternoon. He had the damn giant cake ordered, the table was being moved, and that damn lunch was planned. It was like the President was coming. All I did was text Jack and ask him to come in. It seemed like a good show."

"Yeah, the whole day was about her. How could she not enjoy it? She got a meeting, a cake, an email, lunch on the company, and a hug from the Managing Editor." There was silence. Mallory did not turn to look at Jacqueline. She sat in her seat checking her mascara, but she could feel Jacqueline looking at her. "Did you think that I didn't know?"

"There wasn't anything to know."

"You hugged her."

"I didn't and I wouldn't. She hugged me. You know me well enough to know that I didn't hug her." Make-up was still being applied. There was no eye contact, but Jacqueline continued to look in her direction. Nervously, she said, "Mallory, I'm serious. I absolutely have zero interest in her. I think she is amazing at what she does, but, very often, I want to strangle her."

"I don't think that's what she's hoping for with you."

"I hope you're just joking."

"I don't think you want her, but I do think you need to watch yourself with her."

"She doesn't want me. I can promise you that."

"Then, what does she want?"

"I don't know. I think she just likes to start the fire for the sake of feeling the heat." Jacqueline reached over and placed her hand on Mallory's thigh. "I love you. And only you."

"I know that and you know that I love you," Mallory stopped checking her face and returned the car visor to its upright position. She looked at Jacqueline and said, "But, does Clementine know that I'll fuck her up?"

"If she doesn't yet, I get a feeling she may find out."

~~~~~~~~~

In salmon colored shorts and powder blue button up, Jack opened the door for Jacqueline and Mallory. He was a holding a half-full highball in his hand. "Greetings and salutations! How the hell are you two doing tonight?"

"Well, I don't think that we're doing as well as you are Jack," Jacqueline teased.

"Mallory, you look amazing. I had no idea all that was under there. What are you doing swimming in the deep end with this one?" and he pointed to Jacqueline with his cocktail hand. He never noticed the alcohol that sloshed from the glass onto the floor.

A shadow fell upon the foyer as a long silhouette approached. Before Misty arrived, Mallory could hear the clank of her stilettos against the tile floors. Click. Clack. Click. Clack. Click. Clack. Then, there she was.

Approaching Mallory with a confidence, there was the five foot ten former Miss Georgia turned swimsuit model angling for her. She had on jeweled, white stilettos and a skintight black romper jumpsuit with gold buttons. Of the seven buttons, only the bottom four were buttoned. The top ones were open, giving sight to her well-designed and very expensive bosom. With her arms outstretched, Misty approached Mallory, "Oh my God, I love your outfit! We're gonna have to get togetha and raid each other's closets someday." Then, she pretended to kiss Mallory on the cheek.

"I love that jumpsuit. You're gonna have to let me borrow it," Mallory lied.

"I've made some punch. Jacqueline, help me get some glasses of it for the ladies." Jack and Jacqueline left the foyer and headed to the wet bar in the den. Mallory closed the front door and followed Misty to the kitchen, the place where they normally sat and talked while they waited on dinner.

~~~~~~~~~~

Mallory followed Misty through the foyer, down the hall, and into the kitchen. She had been to the house a few times. Jack enjoyed having dinner and a meeting with Jacqueline at the house every other week. In the beginning, Mallory had not come to these occasions. She had stayed home with Zoe, enjoyed a quick bite from a drive-thru, and watched television or painted her nails as she waited on Jacqueline's return. But, one late summer day, Jack was in the office. His door had been open and he saw Mallory leave Jacqueline's office. From across the hall, out his open door, he screamed her name, "Mallory!"

She was slightly stunned. The office was always buzzing with activity. It was the hum of work to be done, but rarely was there a direct yell of a single name. From Mrs. Pennington's desk, she peeked her head into his office. "Yes, Jack?"

"Come in." Confused, she walked into his office. "Close the door." He had been lying on his leather couch. It appeared as though he might have been asleep only moments prior to her arrival. His white shirt was rustled in the back. He stood from the couch and she noticed that his hair was disheveled and the creases in his suit pants no longer existed in the back. In his black dress socks, he walked about his office. Stretching his back and combing through his hair with his fingertips, he said, "So, you were the one?"

Unsure what that meant, "The one?"

"Yes, my wife, Misty? Do you know her?"

"We have made acquaintance a few times. When she has come to the office," Mallory was stumbling with her words.

"My wife said that Jacqueline was interested in someone at the office. And, it was you, eh?" Mallory didn't speak. She blinked repeatedly. "Relax, Mallory, it's not a criticism. It's just odd. That's all."

"Odd? What about it is odd?" Mallory did not like where she thought this might be heading.

"Surely, you know that Jacqueline and I have our dinner and a meeting at the house every once in a while."

"Yes, I know."

"Well, why don't you come with her? I tell her all the time that she can bring someone. But, she doesn't. Then, I have to hear from Mrs. Pennington's gossip circle that you two are dating." Mallory must have looked stunned. "I thought Jacqueline and I were close. Is the relationship a secret?" He sat back down on the couch and tilted towards her as if to offer himself as a confidant. "Let me tell you this, if Pennington knows, I can guarantee that the whole damn office and her bridge team knows," he scoffed.

Half-smiling, "I think we are well aware that the office knows that we are dating, but I want to assure you that we are always professional in the office and at offsite business functions."

Starting to lie back down, "I don't give a damn. I trust Jacqueline. We're a great team. I just don't know why you won't come out to the house. Misty says that I need to make Jacqueline feel at home. I keep offering. I keep hinting. I keep trying to tell her that I know. And, nothing. You never come."

"I guess I assumed that they were business meetings between you and her and I should stay away."

"Hell no. We have drinks. We eat whatever horrible meal that cook and Misty have concocted. We sit by the pool. We laugh and joke. We talk about business. I tell her what I want to do and she tells me why we can't. Then, she comes to work the next day and texts me how we are going to make my dream come true. I love her." Then, his eyes rolled around in his head. He had an idea. He sprang from the couch and went to his desk. Mallory sat quietly in the chair across from the couch and awaited his return. She didn't look to see what he was doing or where he had gone. However, before he returned, there was a light knock on the door and she heard it open.

"Yes, Jack," Mallory heard Jacqueline say.

"Jacqueline, get in here. Mallory and I were just talking."

Jacqueline looked at Mallory confused. "About?"

"About us," he said.

"Who us?"

K L FINALLEY

Swirling his hand as he returned to his couch, "All of us." The room remained silent. "Us. Me. You. Misty. Mallory."

Jacqueline said, "Okay?"

"Why is there no us? Why don't you invite Mallory to our dinner meetings at the house? She is the one, right?"

"Right?"

"Dammit, Jacqueline, don't make me look like an ass. I keep telling you if there is someone that you want to bring that you are welcome to do it. I have rolled out the fuckin' welcome banner. So, why won't you bring her?"

"I don't know. I guess I thought she wouldn't like to come. I don't know." Jacqueline turned to Mallory, "I'm sorry."

Jack exclaimed, "Wonderful. We'll see you both at the house next week. Misty will be so happy that I finally fixed this." That sounded as though it was a dismissal, so Mallory rose to her feet and stepped in front of Jacqueline.

"Thanks, Jack," Jacqueline said as she walked behind Mallory out of Jack's office. Without talking, the pair crossed the hall back into Jacqueline's office. Once inside with the doors closed, she asked, "What was that about?"

"I have no idea. He caught me as I left your office and I was being grilled on why I never came with you to their house."

"I really am sorry if you wanted to go and I had made you feel left out. It's not that great of a time."

"Well, it looks like it's going to become a bad time for us both."

"Looks like it," agreed Jacqueline.

~~~~~~~

After that day, Mallory had joined Jacqueline at all of the dinner dates at the Boyd's Mediterranean-style home on Harbour Island. This night, she followed the clickety clack sounds of Misty's shoes to the kitchen. She reclined against the cream colored cabinets with their gold knobs and handles and stared as Misty slung her tresses from one side to the other as she wrangled platters from the refrigerator. She didn't offer to help. Instead, she wondered when Jacqueline might return with some kind of alcoholic beverage. Alcohol would be needed tonight.

With her head in the refrigerator, Misty was speaking, "You know, I was tellin' Jackie that we've got to stop just having you two over to the house. We outta go out and do somethin'."

Half-listening, half-staring at the black slate tiles and wondering if Misty had designed the kitchen this way or if it was this way when they moved in. Then, her mind flashed to the kitchen in the penthouse. She imagined a different color countertop and made a mental note to tell Jacqueline that they should redecorate the entire penthouse. Remembering what Misty had asked, she responded with, "That'd be fun," but thought, *I never want to do that.*

As she lifted the platters onto the black marble island, "We've had a hard time making real friends. You know what I mean?" Misty's forehead should've wrinkled. The sentiment required a facial expression, but it appeared the muscles in her face could not or would not allow one. "I mean, Jackie and the money and me and the modeling. You know? You just don't find people who like you for you."

"Oh, yeah. That must be tough."

"Jacqueline has always been so sweet to me. She's just incredible. I completely understand how you could fall for her." Mallory had not really been listening before that comment, but, now, Misty's babbling had her full attention. "She's a real catch. Successful. A doll. She has a great place."

"You've been to the penthouse?"

"Once. Jack had some papers she needed. We were out on his horrible boat. He got an old sailboat from Big Jack when he was fifteen or so. The thing is tiny. It has none of the new upgrades. My God, we could get a yacht, but, instead, Jack makes us cruise around in his tiny childhood sailboat. I hate that damn thing. Every time I lay on the bow, I'm scared the damn sail may fall on me." She even appeared disturbed by the thought of it. "Anyhow, we met her at the marina at her place. She came down and we had a few drinks at that little bar thingee."

"Oh. We've sat down there a few times," Mallory relaxed some.

"We didn't get to go upstairs or anything. I was so bummed, but Jackie said we could some other time. He wanted to get out of the Bay before all the traffic. But, man, I bet it's nice. Is it?"

"Yes, it's very nice, but come on, you've traveled the world modeling, you live on Harbour Island, and you're married to a Boyd. Who could want more?"

"Jackie is wonderful. I love him, but I bet Jacqueline's a load of fun. I mean, she's got more....so much more fire than Jackie could ever even dream of." It was official. Mallory hated her. "You're really lucky to have her all to yourself."

As she came into the kitchen, with two drinks in her hand, Jacqueline was speaking, "Babe, I tasted Jack's concoction." Noticing that she might have halted an existing conversation, she said, "Oh, I'm sorry if I interrupted."

"No, honey, go on," Mallory said with a huge smile on her face.

"That punch of his is okay for me, but there's no way that you were going to drink that. So, I opened a bottle of Pinot for you. Here you are."

"Thanks, honey."

"See, that's so sweet," Misty said. As Jack entered the room., Misty asked, "Jackie, did you bring me some wine, too?"

"No, I got you some of the punch."

"But, Jacqueline says it's not great."

"No, she said that Mallory won't drink it. That it's too strong for her. I told her that you'd be fine. I told her my woman may look delicate, but she can hold her liquor like a sailor," Jack boasted as he slapped her backside. Mallory quietly giggled as Misty sipped Jack's homemade gasoline. She coughed as she swallowed her first sip. Encouraged, Jack clucked, "See, that's some good stuff." She would have disagreed if she could have spoken, but her throat was ablaze. Reaching for the platters on the table, he said, "Let's eat. Jacqueline, give me a hand with this." Jacqueline collected the bowls of salad and Mallory removed the noodles and rolls from the countertop. Misty followed.

As they entered the dining room, Misty slid her arm up and down the red and ivory damask wallpaper. With her highball and the platter of chicken in her hands, she was not able to locate the light switch. Jacqueline noticed that she was struggling and returned to help her. "I got it, Misty."

Misty praised, "You're such a doll. Jackie, isn't she a doll?"

"More of a Cabbage Patch kid, if you ask me."

"Thanks, Jack," Jacqueline retorted. "You know, you should have the motion sensing lights put in here." She pointed up at the ceilings. "Then, you never have these problems."

Standing beside her stirring the chicken piccata, Misty asked, "What's that?"

Jacqueline did not answer. She stared at Misty's movement. She had seen women stir meals all of her life. Her mother, grandmother, waitresses, friends' parents, and Paige had all stirred dishes as she watched. None of them had ever moved their hips. None of them had ever sashayed the way she did. Waiting for her response, Misty stood staring down at Jacqueline. Her big blue eyes and bright bleached smile mesmerized Jacqueline. Looking half at her face and half at the rhythmic movement of her hips, Jacqueline stuttered, "Motion lights."

"But, what are they?" Misty questioned again. Aware that she had hypnotized Jacqueline, her smile widened. "Are they those kinda lights that flash on when someone comes in the room?" Her Georgia accent drew the question out. Jacqueline hung on every word.

Observing the spell that Misty had cast upon Jacqueline, Mallory answered, "Yeah, it's something like that. Tell her about it, honey."

And, the spell was broken, "Oh, yeah. So, the penthouse has sensors. When it senses someone's presence, it triggers a number of automated features. The lights, the water in the sink, the flush of the toilet. You know, some of the features in stores or airports."

"Well, I didn't know you could do those things at home. Mallory, do you have those things at your house?" Misty drawled out her jab.

"No, I don't have them at my house, but we have them at the penthouse," she snarled and placed her hand on Jacqueline's leg.

Hungry, Jack interrupted. "Baby, you've stirred the shit out of that chicken. It's dead already. Come sit down, so we can eat." Laying down the serving spoon, Misty brushed past Jacqueline and headed for her seat next to Jack. "Thank God. Let's eat." To the clang of spoons and serving forks, plates were made. Wine goblets were refilled and gasoline was poured.

"This is very good, Misty," Mallory remarked.

"Shit, she didn't cook it. You know, we pay a chef to teach her to cook, but he does all the cooking and she does all the watching."

"Jackie, I do cook. We discuss the menu. We go over the recipe. He cooks a little, then I cook a little. Then, we have a meal," She sat back against her chair and folded her arms.

"Oh, I'm sorry, baby." Jack bent over to kiss her. "This one is wonderful." She stroked his face as he kissed her cheek.

"It sure is. I love chicken piccata," Jacqueline agreed.

"Well, I'm glad I could make one of your favorites. Maybe, one night while you and Jack are working, I can teach Mallory to make it for you." Mallory smiled as she thought of horrible ways to hurt her.

"That's okay. I do most of the cooking," Jacqueline replied.

"You do?" Jack asked with shock.

"Yeah. I cook. Why's that surprising?"

"I never thought of you as domesticated."

"I can cook. I'm the oldest in my family. I had to help my mom with dinner. I don't know. I guess I just picked up on it."

"You don't bring snacks or cookies or anything you make into work like other women," he remarked.

Chuckling, she said, "Well, no, I'm not doing that. I guess before I didn't have any reason to cook, but, now, I do." She glanced in Mallory's direction, made eye contact, and smiled. Mallory would have kissed her, but, in the presence of Misty and Jack, she lifted her hand to behind Jacqueline's head and stroked her neck.

"That's so sweet," Misty remarked.

She reached for Mallory's hand. "I don't know. You know, making a meal and eating it together is what you're supposed to do. It's the kinda things that kids need. Structure. Family. Happiness. And, it breaks up her dreaded homework time."

"You've really gotten into this?" Jack remained amazed.

"Sure, it's good stuff. The three of us sitting at the table eating and talking. No TV. No iPad. No cellphones. Just us and dinner."

Placing her hand on Jack's leg, she admitted, "I decided to learn to cook, so I could be more of a wife to Jackie. You know, give him a home."

With half of a roll in his mouth, he muffled in disbelief, "You did?"

"Yes, Jackie, why'd you think I was doin' all of this?"

"Hell if I knew," Jack retorted. Mallory laughed. Then, he laughed harder, because she laughed.

"Really, Jack, I don't think you listen to me."

"Of course, I do. Why don't you tell them your good news?"

Misty sat up tall in her chair. She cleared her throat and announced, "Since you two are our closest friends, I want you to know my big news first." She cleared her throat again. "On January first, I'm gonna have my own afternoon talk show." Jack put his napkin in his lap, clapped, and beamed with a mouth full of bread.

Jacqueline rested her fork on the side of her plate. "What? This is great. You're getting your own show?"

"Yes, ma'am. It's gonna be on from noon to one on Channel Four."

Holding her wine glass, Mallory's eyes scrunched and she asked, "A talk show?"

"Yeah, a little local show. I thought I'd interview people and events from around the area."

"Weekends or weekdays," Mallory's questioning continued.

"Just Monday through Friday to start, but we might expand to a Saturday morning episode as well."

"Jack, is this under the Boyd umbrella?" Jacqueline inquired as she thought of the possible impact to the newspaper.

"Nope, this is all my beautiful wife. No Boyd money. No Boyd affiliation." He waved off her concerns. "You know, she's been doing little local commercials for Channel Four. Then, the station started getting requests from other networks to hire Misty for their commercials. I'm sure Channel Four figured they'd better contract her to something big before she got better offers with another network."

Interjecting Mallory asked, "Do you still have a contract with Miris perfume and that clothing line? What's the name?"

"Cipele."

"Yes, Cipele. Can you do all of this?"

"Sure, there's no affiliation between the perfume, the clothing line, and the network."

"No, I don't mean are you capable. I'm saying you're going to be incredibly busy." Mallory started to outline her responsibilities. "The show, interviewing the guests, preparing for the segments, photo shoots for the two companies. Don't you have commercials for Miris?"

"Yes, they only show in large markets, though."

"But you have to film them."

"Nat, my agent, says I'll get to hire staff for the show, so that'll help some."

Having finished his plate, Jack interjected, "Of course, it will. It'll be great. Besides, those shoots only take about a week or so." Rinsing his palate with gasoline, he reassured her, "It's gonna be great."

Jacqueline said, "Well, this deserves a toast." She raised her glass and praised, "Here's to beauty, wit, and friendship. May you experience all the success you are due."

"Thank you, Jacqueline, you are the best. Isn't she such a doll, Mallory?" Misty asked.

"Um hmm," Mallory grumbled as she finished her drink.

~~~~~~~~~

After dinner, Mallory slipped off to the restroom to enjoy a moment of solitude while Jack and Jacqueline headed to the pool, their usual post-dinner station. Unlike most nights, Jack rushed Jacqueline outdoors and closed the French doors behind them.

Noticing his anxiety, Jacqueline asked, "Do you want to talk shop before the girls come outside?"

"No, I want to tell you something."

Jacqueline had gotten used to Jack and his directness. She was no longer offended. She had discovered that the true drawback of Jack's wealthy life was reality. He had failed to have people in his life who were not sycophants or parasites. "Shoot."

"Misty and I have a pre-nup."

"Okay."

"There's an infidelity clause. There are a bunch of financial clauses to protect her past earnings, my family money, the family name, the paper, all kinds of shit. She has a clause that limits the amount of weight I can gain and the kind of lifestyle she is to maintain regardless of her future earning potential. I prohibited drug use, eating disorders, and excessive plastic surgery."

"Wow. I didn't realize that you could do all of that."

"Oh yeah. You can do anything. You can add anything. I called my guy and made an appointment for you. Lemme give you his card."

"Wait, what? Why?"

Sloshing his drink as he walked to her, "Because you're getting all gaga in there. I may not know exactly how much you have now, but remember Dad had me put you in touch with our financial adviser years ago. And, I know how much you make, now. So, between inheritance, earnings, stock options, 401K, and the investments that I'm sure Evan set up for you. It's gotta be a ton. It's at least six digits. And that's more than whatever she has, so we need to talk about you protecting yourself. Gay marriage wanted to be like every other marriage. Well, join us with a goddamn pre-nup."

"Hang on. We aren't getting married. We're just dating."

"Uh, no, my friend. You aren't. Is she with you all the time?"

"Yes, we're usually together."

"Are invitations required or assumed?"

"Assumed, I guess."

"Vacationing?"

"Well, we have. We're planning a little birthday trip for Zoe next month and a family trip out of the country next year."

Jack said, "Family trip? Uh huh. Let me ask you this - do you want her to move in?"

Without thinking, she said, "Well, sure."

"You answered that pretty quick."

"She and I haven't talked about it," Jacqueline was whispering, "But, I would like for them to move in with me or me with them."

"She got all hot for you tonight. Did you see that outfit?"

"That's not about me. She's showing up Misty."

"Yeah, so you don't look. I know how this works. I'm married to the model. Other women start off being themselves, then, eventually, they start overdressing at little events. They don't care about Misty. They worry what the guy...well, I guess, girl, in your case, thinks when they see those legs walking around." He went to the summer kitchen and made himself a fresh drink. She followed him. Continuing his speech, he said, "And, you can't tell me that you've never thought of closing the deal. It wouldn't be you if you didn't."

"Whether I have or I haven't, she and I haven't talked about it."

He knocked his knuckle against her forehead. "There's nothing to talk about. You ask. She says yes. That's the whole thing. Then, you wait on her to tell you the terms of the deal."

"What are you two doin'," Misty asked as she came outside. She had changed from the bodysuit and stilettos into a black and white plaid one-piece swimsuit with a sheer black cover. The cover-up was either too big or was not being worn correctly. It hung loosely about her frame, revealing her bronze shoulders. "I asked this one," she said pointing at Mallory who was behind her. "If she wanted to take a swim with me, she refused. I guess I'll have to swim alone. Unless one of you wants to join me." The accent had returned. It lingered in the air. Her sentences swayed about their ears and gracefully landed in their thoughts like a song.

Jacqueline tried to resist the siren's song. She reached out for Mallory, hoping that her resolve would keep her steady. "Unfortunately, we can't tonight. We need to head out soon. We still have to pick up Zoe and get her off to bed." That was another lie. Zoe was spending the night with Abbie.

"That's too bad. Jackie heated the pool up just for us." Misty let the wrap that never quite covered her fall to the ground. She stepped over the fabric heap it left. Jack was at the bar. Focused on his drink, he was oblivious to all of this. Mallory was busy watching Jacqueline watch Misty dive into the pool. She glided deeper and deeper into the lit, parakeet-colored pool. Just when it appeared she may reach the bottom, she ascended to the top, folded her arms and rested on the pool's edge. Batting her full eyelashes while water streamed down her back, Misty remarked, "The water's magnificent. Y'all don't know what you're missin'."

Jacqueline was mesmerized by the dive, the beads of water, and the night air. She could not respond. However, Mallory said, "And, she won't tonight," and led Jacqueline to the car.

Chapter 12

Having a conversation with Elet dressed in a red and white striped long sleeve shirt and the matching knit beanie was difficult for Jacqueline. She was unaware that it was equally difficult for Elet to talk to her as she wore a jagged orange and black shirt that was designed to look like animal skin. "Fred didn't wear khaki shorts," he teased.

"I'm sure he had something on under the tiger skin."

"It was prehistoric times."

"Yes, it was, but they had technology. I think he probably had short shorts or something on under there. And, that's what I'm representing. It's the spirit of the show," she replied

"Uh huh. Well, I call bullshit. I need you to pull off those shorts and be pure prehistoric," he tugged on her shorts.

"Not gonna happen, but I will slip outta my shoes and be barefoot." The two laughed. As they stood in the backyard drinking ciders, they were surrounded by a collection of costume covered children playing on the swing set. Raggedy Ann, Kelsey, was swinging without her wig on. It had come off in the windstorm the swinging had caused. Snow White, Destiny, had recovered the wig and held onto to it for Ann. Raggedy Andy, Bryce, no longer had rosy cheeks. The sweat and the grubby hands of a five-year-old had caused them to smudge about his face. Brett, Frankenstein, had tried to clean Raggedy Andy's face on a number of occasions, but he had only made matters worse. His green make-up had mixed with Raggedy Andy's red make-up. Now, Andy looked like he had been in a bar room fight. Andy was climbing up the end of the slide towards Thing 3, Jess, who was waiting to slide down. Thing 3 was arguing with Thing 2, Jeremy, who was eager to slide and thought that the others were being unfair.

"This is a nice turn out. I can't believe that we never came to these before." Jacqueline said as she checked on Wonder Woman, Abbie. Wonder Woman had convinced Frankenstein that she was old enough and capable of making s'mores over the firepit. Frankenstein had been overseeing the gooey debacle but had stepped away to check on Raggedy Andy. When Jacqueline realized that an adult should probably be present, she and Waldo edged towards the children. Standing near the open fire, Wonder Woman roasted the s'mores as the assembly line, made up of Zoe as Pebbles and Levi as Batman made the tiny sandwiches. In the absence of Frankenstein, no one noticed that Thing 4, Jarret, Olive's youngest son, had eaten most of the supply. Upon arrival, Jacqueline lifted Thing 4 into the air. Recognizing that he had been caught, he squirmed in her arms and yelled as he tried to bury his face in her shoulder. His oldest sibling, Thing 1, Jason, never looked up from the iPad, the Angel, Drew, had bought him for his birthday. He was too involved in the game he was playing against the leader of the SWAT team, Isiah. The Things had learned to ignore the squeals of three-year-old, Thing 4, but Zoe looked up.

"What's wrong, baby?" Zoe asked.

"Get me a wet washcloth," Jacqueline directed her.

In her green and black tank top and blue shorts, she ran to the sliding glass door. She pounded her chocolate covered hands against it rather than opening it.

As Elet yelled for her to open the door, Paige, her Fairy Godmother, pulled the door back, "What's wrong, honey?"

"Jax needs wet napkins for the baby," Zoe announced.

Leaving the door open, Paige went to the kitchen and wet a dishcloth. The noise from the inside of the house flooded outside. The ears of adults perked up as they tried to guess the name of the song playing indoors. Before they could decipher the tune, Paige reappeared to the door and handed Zoe the wet rag. As Zoe ran back to Jacqueline who was certain chocolate had been smeared on her neck and shirt, Paige closed the door.

"Here you go, Jax."

"Thanks, little one."

Jacqueline began cleaning up Jarret. He had stopped wiggling in her arms and was allowing the adult that he barely knew to clean him. "Jarrett, I think you've ruined your shirt."

Having watched all of this, Elet said, "I never would have thought."

Not looking at him, she said, "Thought what?"

Brett had returned to his post. "Thought you would be cleaning someone's face."

"Oh, I'm sure that there have been plenty of nights that I've wiped your face," she teased Elet. Having cleaned as much as she could of Jarrett's face, hands, and shirt, she swatted him on the butt and sent him off in the direction of the swing set. At only three, his run was not very certain. But, they watched as he waddled quickly off towards the corner of the yard.

"I don't think anyone ever sees kids coming," Brett replied.

"She did," Elet pointed to Jacqueline with his index finger as he continued to nurse his beer. "She chose a woman with a kid. She knew what she was getting herself into."

"Trust me, you never know what you're getting into with kids. Even when you think you know, you don't know," Brett said.

"No, I'm not downing it. I support the new and improved Jacqueline. She's less introverted. She's at friendly get-togethers. She's sleeping and eating. This life's good for her," Elet placed his hand on her shoulder.

"You know, I can hear all of this," she said. "Listen, I've picked up a few things. There's no denying it. But, life is good. All is well."

Brett asked, "Well, what's the plan?"

"The plan?" Jacqueline questioned.

"Yeah, next steps. Marriage? Officially moving in together? It's been like six months. It's time for a new phase."

Mumbling, Elet said, "Here comes the bullshit," and took a swig of beer.

"It's not bullshit. We're happy. We're enjoying each other's company. We're having a great time together. We haven't talked about what's next. I guess we'll just wait and see."

"That really is bullshit," Elet muttered.

"No, it's not."

Twisting open his own beer, Brett said, "Look, you may really believe that, but I'm pretty sure that she's inside talking about what she wants to happen," and he pointed inside.

"She hasn't mentioned it to me."

"You really might be a dude," Elet said as he leaned down and got a s'more. She hit him in the stomach as he chewed.

"She's not gonna mention it to you. She thinks you will disappear if she pressures you. She's gonna ride the roller coaster and have mini breakdowns until she knows what the hell you're thinking."

"Nah, she's not like that."

"Really? Really? Um, from what I understand, she's had a breakdown over the arch."

Jacqueline scratched the front of her hair. Sighing, she said, "Yeah, I didn't see that one coming. We have to go in a couple of days and I don't even want to talk to her about it. It was so bad and I have no idea what even caused it."

"Hey, dumbass, you ordered a super expensive gift without even talking to her about it. She was right there. In the bed beside you."

"She was in the shower and she didn't have to pay for it."

"You didn't talk to her about it?" Brett asked. "You just did it?" Brett chuckled. "You are a dude. Girls want to talk about things. Acting like a unit reassures them."

Jacqueline didn't respond. She saw Zoe walking towards her with a s'more in her hand. "I made this one for you, Jax." Jacqueline handed her beer to Elet and bent down. As she lifted Zoe in her arms, she stared into the bold blue sea that surrounded her pupils. Proudly, Zoe smiled and affectionately, Jacqueline beamed.

~~~~~~~~~~

Inside the house, soft classics provided a background for the mixed crowd. Paige and her dress drifted through her living room and dining room checking on guests.

Dressed in a sleeveless, white dress, Mallory was Wilma Flintstone. She had placed a bun at the back of her head and pulled strands forward that she curled and plastered to the best of her Wilma impersonation. She had circulated around the room and talked to work colleagues, Guy and Bob, made quick appearances to the party. Neither were in costume, but having received invitations, they found it important to come. Upon their arrival, Mallory located them in the dining room. Along with Paige, they chatted for a while. The conversation lagged as each discovered that there was little commonality outside of work. After an awkward half hour, during which time, they did not engage any of the other guests, they left and headed to a sports bar.

"Did you get the chance to say hello to Guy and Bob?" Mallory asked Alex after the guys had left.

"Yes, the two pervs caught me on their way out. I swear they were staring at my chest more than talking to me," Alex complained.

"Well, in their defense, this costume doesn't give the mind much to wonder about." Alex was dressed as a genie. She stood in the living room in sheer, turquoise pants and a top. All of her would have been visible had she not worn her two-piece turquoise bathing suit. "I can't believe you aren't cold."

"Hell yeah, I'm cold. That's why I didn't go outside and say hello to Jacqueline. It's cold in here. It has to be freezing out there." As they spoke, she felt a tug to her hair. She turned around to yell at the person. Only to discover, her brother in law, Dominic, and her sister, Josephine. "Hey, Jo," she said as she hugged her sister. "That's cute. Where'd you get that?"

"I had it from a school party, I think. I was gonna go buy one, but everything was either skin tight or all slutty." In a black dress wearing black tights and black shoes, Josephine stood in the living room with one arm at her side and the other on her hip. The arm on her hip had fabric attached from her wrist to her back. With only one arm up, the visual was missed, but when she raised her arms to hug her sister, it was obvious that she was a butterfly.

"Yeah, no joke. I went looking for costumes as well. I couldn't find anything that wasn't over the top, so I decided to make us all something." Mallory said.

"Don't worry, Jo. The costume doesn't make sense until you see them all together."

"It's the Flintstones. I get it. It's cute."

"I didn't," Alex admitted. Dominic had wandered into the kitchen to talk to Drew and Paige. "I see Dom didn't wear a costume. Party pooper." The women stood in a circle in the middle of the room talking and laughing. They were standing there when the doorbell rang.

"Mallory, will you get that please?" Paige yelled from the kitchen.

"Sure," Mallory excused herself and walked to the door. As she was turning the knob to open it, it was being turned. Fearful that the door was going to be opened into her face, Mallory stepped back. Just as she did, the door opened. It was Clementine. She was in a black leather cat suit. In her other hand, she held her Cat Woman mask and the hand of a tall brunette who was also wearing a black pleather outfit except Clementine's guest was not Cat Woman. Her guest's pleather jumpsuit was outlined with the human skeleton. They entered the house in an uproar. The date was falling forward over Clementine as they barreled into the foyer. All the people in Paige's living room stared at the ruckus.

Noticing Mallory in the foyer, Clementine gave her a hug and said, "Hey, Mallory. What's going on? I hope you aren't leaving,"

Already irritated by her presence, Mallory responded, "I had come to open the door for you."

"Oh."

The guest spoke, "I told her not to open the door. I told her that she can't just walk in everywhere she goes."

Mallory had disregarded them already. She mumbled a "Um Hmm" and turned to walk back into the house.

Clementine and her date passed her. Clementine headed into the kitchen. She greeted Paige with a hug and said, "Hey, I'm sorry we're late. I stopped to pick her up and then, we had to pick up something to bring. We went to this gourmet place that Jacqueline always talks about, but I couldn't find anything there. So, we went to the liquor store. And, I think we had such a good time wandering around that we forgot that we needed to grab something and make our way here. I'm so sorry, but I'm so stoked that you invited me." She hugged Paige, again.

"Well, aren't you sweet?" Paige said wrapped tighter than a burrito in Clementine's arms. In the midst of the embrace, she reached out to shake hands to Clementine's date, "It's nice to meet you, too. Make yourself at home."

Abruptly, Clementine released Paige, "Is that Jacqueline outside?" She was pointing out the kitchen window.

"Yes, she, my husband, Brett, Alex's fiancé, Elet, and all the ki....." Before Paige finished speaking, Clementine had snatched her date out of the kitchen and headed into the backyard.

Mallory, Alex, and Jo moved into the dining room for a better look. Olive had left Drew and met them there.

~~~~~~~

Jacqueline had not heard Clementine from outside the house. She had Zoe in her arms and was chewing the special s'more that Zoe had made for her.

In mid-chew, she heard Clementine bellow, "Hey, there."

She turned to face the door. She had wondered about the interaction with her and Clementine outside of work. In fact, she had given it a lot of thought. She was hoping to have time to discuss her concerns with Elet before Clementine arrived, but the night had gotten away from them. Now, Clementine was standing in Paige and Brett's backyard. She was dressed as Cat Woman and she was dragging some woman behind her. As they approached, Jacqueline lowered Zoe on the ground beside her. She placed her hand against the girl's back as if to keep her close, out of harm's way. "Hello, Clementine. I'm glad you could make it. This is Elet and Brett. And, this is Zoe."

"Well, hello everyone. How's it going?" The guys muttered inarticulate responses that Clementine ignored. "For those of you who don't know, this is Tabatha. But, you can call her Tabs."

Jacqueline knew her. And, she had a feeling that Clementine knew that Jacqueline knew her. Pretending as though she didn't, she extended her hand. Through her gritted teeth, she said, "It's nice to meet you."

In a hushed arrogance, Tabatha responded, "It was always a pleasure."

While Jacqueline was greeting Tabatha, Zoe pulled on Clementine's pants and asked, "Are those real?"

Sharply, Clementine replied, "Real what?" and started to laugh.

Jacqueline sharply turned and glared. Gnashing her teeth, she snarled, "Don't!"

"Okay. Okay. Are they real what?" Clementine asked Zoe politely.

"Real leather?" Zoe asked.

"For the shit ton of money, I spent they better be."

Jacqueline leaned down to Zoe thanked her for her s'more and asked her to play with the other children. Once Zoe had scurried away, she took Clementine by the arm and headed to a different part of the yard. When Tabatha attempted to follow, Jacqueline commanded, "Stay there with Elet." When they were at a distance from everyone else, Jacqueline released her arm, "What the hell are you doing? I've had to put up with your shit for a while. But, what the hell is the point of all of this? Did I do something to you in my past that I don't remember? Do you want payback for it? That's fine. But, at least, remind me." Jacqueline was angry. She stood in the back of the yard flailing her arms around and talking to Clementine in very close proximity. She was completely unaware that she was being watched by Elet who was supposed to be talking to Tabatha, but he had left that duty to Brett.

Rubbing her arm, Clementine said, "No. We never crossed paths in the past."

"So, what the fuck is your deal?"

"I don't have a deal. I'm trying to be your friend."

"How? How in the hell are you trying to be my friend?"

"I'm trying to keep you honest. I know what you've done. I know who you really are."

"What? What the hell are you talking about?"

"I moved to Tampa to take the job. I scouted out the scene here. And, as luck would have it, I became a regular at Livewire. You remember the place, don't you?" Jacqueline didn't answer. "So, I went in there. Met some people. Got to talking. Made some friends. What's the first thing people ask the new person?" Again, no answer from Jacqueline. "Where do you work?

So, I told them. People roared. Guess who they all talked about? Oh, I bet you don't wanna guess."

"Okay. So, you're here to remind me of my old life? That's your fucking deal. Do you think that I forgot?"

"No, I think you know. That's why you want to get rid of me. You used to be just like me. Young, brash, full of life. I've heard all the stories."

Jacqueline jeered, "You've heard some stories about me. Now, you think you know me. Interesting."

"I know enough of them to know that what you're doing right now doesn't match up."

"So, you show up with some girl I used to know..."

"Used to know? That's not how she explains it."

"You know, it's fucking weird that you're slumming around in my leftovers." Rage had filled Jacqueline's eyes. She wanted to scream, yell, and fight. She was desperately trying to hold onto herself, but she felt herself drowning. From the corner of her eye, she saw her lifeboat walking toward. She chuckled a bit and said, "Where's Waldo?" and he appeared.

"Hey, Clementine, I think your date has had enough of chit-chatting with Brett. You might want to go save her." Clementine turned to walk away. "We're gonna catch up with you in a second." After she left them, he said, "Drink some of this." He handed her beer to her. "Okay, let's simmer down. She's just a troublemaker."

"You have no idea."

"Yeah, I do," he said and drank some of his own beer. "You forget how great of friends we've been. We've drank all night. We've played pool together. Hell, when we were young and still working together, I used to have to pick you up for events. Sometimes, we met at your place.

Sometimes, I met you at other people's places. Before we got where we were going, you'd tell me more details than I sometimes wanted to know."

Jacqueline's eyes met his. She opened her mouth to speak, but she wasn't sure what to say.

"Yeah, I remember Tabs," he said in a low voice.

She nodded her head. "Clementine seems to think that I've lost my way and it's her job to remind me."

"Well, I figured it was some shit. I saw you over here in the back corner. You were inches from her face. I had a fear that the old Jacqueline might just make an appearance."

"She wanted to," Jacqueline admitted as she finished her beer.

"She shouldn't. The new Elet and the new Jacqueline are gonna stand over here and get it together. Then, we are gonna walk back over there. I don't think Tabs has any part in this plan. She hasn't said anything about knowing you and she stares at me like she kinda remembers me. But, she hasn't said anything outta line."

Jacqueline said, "This has to end."

"Yep, it does."

"How?" She asked.

"I got no idea, but beating her ass at a Halloween party while dressed as Fred Flintstone is a bad idea." Jacqueline snickered. "Now, get over there. Hold your shit together. Let me go inside and get us something stronger." The two walked across the yard. Jacqueline walked up and put her hand on Brett's back.

"Welcome back. I was just telling them about my deck build."

"Oh, I don't think I know the entire story." Jacqueline said as she pulled up a chair.

As Elet entered the house, the women swarmed on him.

"Elet, what the hell is going on out there?" Mallory asked. Her arms were folded.

"Nothing. Clementine came out with her date. Brett is talking about the deck build. Just chit-chatting."

Paige face palmed herself, "Not the deck build."

"Elet, you're such a liar. We saw Jacqueline and Clementine at the back of the yard. You better tell us what's going on," Mallory pressed.

"Why are you guys stalking us? Weirdos." Elet said as he opened the bottle of whiskey.

Olive entered the conversation, "From in here, it looks like something might be going on between Jacqueline and Clementine. Mallory's worried sick. You should tell her what you know."

Elet stopped pouring. He placed the bottle on the table. He said, "Mallory, look outside." He pointed. "She's sitting in the backyard next to Brett with Jarrett in her lap. Zoe and Abbie are running back and forth to her. Does she really look like she has eyes for Clementine? Does she?" With tears filling her eyes, Mallory shook her head. "Look, I know how it might look. But, you've gotta trust me. Clementine's just a troublemaker. Jacqueline took her in the corner to tell her to chill out with the kids around. I promise you. I have known her longer than any of you. She doesn't want Clementine. I swear." After she nodded, he finished making their drinks. Mallory, Olive, and Jo left the kitchen. Standing there cleaning up his mess, he asked Alex, "Is she okay?"

"I think she's just nervous. You know Jacqueline is hard to get to know."

"I dunno. I think she's pretty open with Mallory. I think that Mallory gets caught up in all the shit she sees."

"What do you think is going on?"

"Me? I think Clementine is fucking nuts."

"Does Jacqueline want her?"

"Hell no, but I think she wants to fight her."

"What are you gonna do?"

"Babe, what can I do? All I can do is talk Jacqueline down from getting into it with her in a backyard full of kids on Halloween."

"Hmm, maybe, this needs a little bit of Alex."

Picking up the glasses to leave the room, he said, "Doesn't everything?" He kissed her on the cheek and returned outside.

As Alex returned to the rest of the women, she was carrying a margarita. She tapped the top of Mallory's head. "Here, drink this."

Nodding in Elet's direction, Olive asked, "What'd he say?"

"Nothing new. That this Clementine is just a troublemaker. There's nothing between her and Jacqueline, but Jacqueline is trying to keep her cool for work and the kids and blah blah this and blah blah that."

"Fuck that," Olive bellowed.

Alex, who had been staring into the backyard while speaking to them finally made eye contact, "Don't worry. I've got this." And, she headed out of the house.

As Mallory rose from the couch, Jo interfered, "Let her go. She's the original troublemaker. She can't have two in Jacqueline's life. She'll take care of her."

~~~~~~~~

It was chilly outside when Alex emerged from the house, but she was boiling on the inside. As she approached the adults, Elet saw her, "Hey, baby. Have you come to join the cool kids?"

"Hi, honey," she said with a fake smile in her voice. She walked behind Clementine's chair and tapped her on her shoulder, "Hi, I'm Alex. I don't think we've met."

Clementine whirled around in her chair to look up at Alex who stood over her in a genie costume, "No, we haven't, gorgeous, but we definitely should."

Looking at Tabatha, Alex said, "May I borrow her for a moment? I promise to bring her right back." Tabatha nodded with indifference. Alex tapped Clementine again and said, "Come with me." As Clementine rose from her seat in the backyard, Alex led her through the back gate to the side of the house. Once there, she closed the gate behind her.

"Wanted me all to yourself?" Clementine teased.

"As a matter of fact, I did. I didn't want to talk to you in front of everyone else."

"Oh, don't worry. Tabatha and I aren't serious."

"And, I can see why. You strike as the kinda person who says things to get attention. I wanted you over here to see if I could get some piece of truth out of you."

"Anything," Clementine continued to flirt.

"Drop the act. I wanna know what you want with Jacqueline."

"What?"

"You heard me."

Clementine laughed, "Are you her muscle?"

"No, she is usually her own muscle. But, I wanna know what you're up to." Clementine leaned against the side of the house. She pulled out a cigarette from inside her top. Before she could light it, Alex pulled it form her hand, crumbled it, and threw it into the yard, "Uh, no. We don't do that. Now, answer me. What do you want?"

"I don't want anything."

"Why keep fucking with her, then? Why say dumb things? Why try to cause trouble?"

"I'm not causing trouble. You guys are causing trouble. Do you think this is who she is?" Clementine pointed in a semi-circle. "This shit. Sitting in a backyard making s'mores and shit."

"Howdah hell would you know who she is? You just met."

"I know more about her than you ever could."

"Lemme guess because you're gay."

She leaned into Alex's face, "Baby, you have no idea who she is or who she's done or what's she's told them."

"Do you honestly believe your own bullshit? Do you really think in all the years that we've been friends I've never been to Livewire? Do you think we haven't helped her pick up women, sat at tables when she did, or waited until she got back with them? You're full of shit. You came here with some ho bartender like she was gonna be like oh thanks for reminding of that piece of ass. Let's go party. I mean, really. This was your plan. How was it gonna play out? In your dream, did she push the fucking kids to the ground, cuss out Mallory, leave with you and all your fuckin' pleather? You and her and that ho were gonna high-five in the driveway. Come on. You've gotta have a better plan than that." Alex began to laugh.

Angrily, Clementine said, "You don't know what it's like."

"You're right. I don't know what it's like to not have any friends and to try too hard to get them. The funny thing is Jacqueline doesn't either. She has friends. She wasn't at Livewire alone searching for any. We were all there with her. Me. Silas. Elet. Even Paige. We went to the gay club with our friend when she wanted to go. We're friends. She's not a crazy ass loner that had to go there by herself, because she didn't belong anywhere. She belongs with us. And, we already know everything she's done and everyone's done. I know what she said to them drunk and sober. Most of it was just shit you say and don't mean. But, you don't know that, do you little Clementine? You don't know shit about that."

Angry now, Clementine clamored, "Fuck you, you fucking bitch."

As she howled her wrath, Elet opened the gate. "It's okay, honey," Alex said and held up her hand to stop him from coming further. "She's ain't no troublemaker. She's just what's left of a lonely little girl who never fit in. She came to the city and went to a bar. She name-dropped until a bigger name got dropped. And, now, she just wants to buddy up to that name, so people'll like her." Elet said nothing. He just stared at Alex who was staring at Clementine. He held his hand out for Alex who walked around Clementine to get to him. Once she reached him, he took a hold of her hand and led her back into the backyard.

When they returned without Clementine, Tabatha looked in the direction of the side of the house. Alex said, "You might wanna go get her. I think she's feeling a little under the weather." As Tabatha sprang from her chair to see what had happened, Alex went back inside. While making herself a glass of ginger ale, she heard a car start.

Chapter 13

At lunchtime on Wednesday, Jacqueline tidied her office. She had filed all confidential documents and returned personnel folders that were in her office back to Human Resources. She cleaned her desktop including her keyboard and monitor. She placed the out of office alert on her email and phone. She had done more for these few days of absence than she had done when she had taken weeks off. After all was done, she placed her left hand under her glasses and rubbed her eye. This plan was no longer a good plan. She had decided to order an expensive gift for her friends without her girlfriend's input. She could admit that was a bad idea. The matter was compounded when days later she discovered that it could not be delivered to Tampa, Atlanta, or Miami. That the arch would be delivered to Baltimore and she would need to retrieve it. While she had intended to ensure a wonderful gift for the wedding of her closest friends, she discovered that this had stressed her relationship with Mallory. They had avoided talking about it. They had avoided talking to anyone who talked about it. Last night, as she tucked Zoe into bed, she told her repeatedly that she would be back in a few days. While she wasn't certain why Zoe was so unnerved, she hated to see her so anxious. Jacqueline had tried to mention it to Mallory, but, as she had for weeks, Mallory avoided the conversation. Now, here she was in the office, minutes before she was supposed to leave and she had a feeling of dread. She pushed away from her desk and walked to the glass wall that overlooked the news floor. Panning the room, she looked out over the sea of faces until she found Mallory's face. Mallory was looking back at her. Jacqueline motioned for her to come up. Sensing that there may be an emotional exchange, Jacqueline went to activate the blinds; but, before they could completely shut, she saw Mallory wipe the tears from her eyes. Another pang of pain struck.

"Hi," Mallory said softly as she opened the door.

"Hi," Jacqueline said. Her head was cocked to the side. She stared at Mallory wondering what she might be thinking. Hoping that her words would bring comfort, if that is what Mallory needed. "I know that I should have talked this over with you. I know that. And, I promise that we will discuss any large purchases from here on out. I promise. But, I gotta go, so I can hurry back."

"I know."

Jacqueline crouched in front of Mallory, "I'm sorry."

"I know."

She rested her head in her lap. She was comforted by the feeling of Mallory's nails running through her hair, "Say something else."

"Is there anything you want me to do while you're away?"

"Be here when I get back."

"I'm not the one..."

"Don't make it seem like I'm going to Daytona on Spring Break. I'm driving with Elet in his pick-up to Baltimore. We're gonna sleep in Myrtle Beach, then we're on to Baltimore. We will sleep in Baltimore, then head home. That's it. That's the whole trip."

"I know."

Jacqueline lifted her head. She had tried to be apologetic. She had tried to be reassuring, but she was starting to be irritated, "Stop with the 'I knows.'"

"Tell me what you want me to say."

Jacqueline sat on the floor between the chair Mallory was sitting in and her desk, "Whatever you want to say."

"I don't think you really want that."

Tired of playing the game, Jacqueline replied, "I guess I don't, but I want you to know that I'll see you this weekend. And, I'll make it up to you and Zoe. And, I love you." Jacqueline leaned forward to kiss her, but Mallory pulled away. Dejected, she wiped her hand across the lower portion of her face. "Okay, will you walk me outside?"

"Of course."

Jacqueline placed the messenger bag on her shoulder. She held the door open for Mallory. While waiting on the elevator, she told Grant to have a good weekend and call her if he needed her. Standing in the elevator, she wanted to hold Mallory in her arms. She wanted to let her scream or cry or whatever might lessen the cramps of guilt she felt. Instead, she stared at the back of her head as Mallory stood on the opposite side of the elevator and ran her fingers across the filigree. Upon arrival onto the news floor, Jacqueline directed Mallory to the elevators at the back of the floor. She wanted to forgo all the conversations that were certain to erupt if they transversed the news floor. They were alone inside the elevator, but Mallory was not standing close. Jacqueline walked near her and placed her arm around her. Mallory shook her arm off.

"Honey, we said that we weren't going to do this at work."

"I know, but I'm leaving and you're upset and I just want to hold you."

The doors opened as Mallory replied, "And I want you, too."

Jacqueline sighed as Mallory snaked through the people huddled in the lobby. With her head down, she followed her lead out of the building. Standing outside, Jacqueline thought that Mallory might stop and let her hug her. But, she hadn't. Jacqueline continued walking behind her. Downstairs, past raised flower beds, down the sidewalk, around the corner out of the sun's light, the two walked. Standing at the entrance to the parking garage, Mallory stopped. Jacqueline approached her and noticed her hand was outstretched. She slipped her hand into Mallory's and they walked to the Laredo. Once there, Jacqueline opened the passenger's door and Mallory slipped inside.

"I feel like a high school kid who just took you to the parking lot to score."

"Tell me that you never did that."

Haltingly, Jacqueline lied and said, "I never did that."

"You're so gross."

"Yeah, but you love me."

"I do. Do you love me?"

Jacqueline walked closer to her. She threw her bag into the backseat and lifted Mallory's face to face hers. She kissed her gently tasting her salty dried tears on her lips. "Of course, I do." Then, she held her close. Mallory rested her head on her shoulder and quietly cried. "I'll see you this weekend. We'll talk a bunch."

"I know."

"Here we go, again." Mallory laughed. Pleased that she got a laugh, she went on, "Are you sure that you don't want to go?"

"I can't. You know that."

"Would you if you could?"

Dabbing the corners of her eyes, she teased, "Hell no. I want you to take me somewhere nice on vacation, not Baltimore by way of Elet's truck." They both laughed. Mallory stood up. "I'm gonna go cry to Paige. You get going, so you can get back here. Be safe. I love you." Standing in the parking garage as other employees left for lunch, Jacqueline pulled her close and kissed her for a long time. Then, she stood there with Mallory in her arms. "If I don't go, I'll never let you leave."

"You know, I'm not shipping off to war. It's Baltimore. You could fly there in a few hours."

"Yeah, we don't all have money to just fly to Baltimore whenever we want."

"Maybe, they don't, but you could."

"Oh, okay," Mallory said dismissively. She pecked Jacqueline's lips once more and said, "Go."

And, Jacqueline complied. The Laredo growled to life and she headed out the garage to Elet's house. Her eyes felt misty. Her throat filled with emotion. She wasn't sure why she felt as strongly as she did. In truth, she was overwhelmed. Racing from her feelings as much as through traffic, she placed her foot upon the pedal and dashed to Elet's house. With the music blaring, she was there in minutes. She pulled the Laredo to the far side of his driveway.

He was sitting on the front porch. In a pair of jeans and a t-shirt, he was dressed as though they were headed out on a boat, but he asked, "What are you wearing?"

"I just came from work."

As he headed off the porch, he said, "Well, I know that. Why didn't you change?"

"I don't know. I figured that I'd just wear this since I was just riding. I can change when we check into the hotel."

He threw the keys to her. "You're driving. I'm riding."

Picking the keys up off the ground, she unlocked the doors for him to get into the truck. Barefooted, he climbed into the passenger's seat and reclined the seat back. She laughed to herself as she gathered her bags from the Laredo. She placed two bags in the back seat. As she climbed into the driver's seat, she slid another package into the glove compartment.

"That thing's like a NRA ad."

"Just protection," she said and cranked the Ford Super Duty. Its roar exceeded the Laredo, but she looked over at it tenderly.

"Need a minute?"

"Maybe," she replied. They laughed and she inched the eight-cylinder turbo diesel backward. "Is she gonna be okay?"

"Who? Mallory or that old thing?"

Teasing him, she asked, "Are you giving me shit already? We're still in town."

"Sorry. Just fucking with you. She'll be fine. Besides, Alex said they were going dress shopping. Mallory's gonna pick it up tomorrow, right?"

"That's the plan."

As he turned towards the door, he said, "It'll be fine sitting in the yard overnight. Will it be fine when your girlfriend comes to get it after she spends the night alone? That's the question."

She wanted to reach over and punch in his kidney. She did not. She held her hands tight to the wheel and steered the massive truck onto Interstate 275 North. She had driven it on a few other occasions, so it was not completely foreign to her. But, she was well aware that she was not an expert at it. Within a few miles, she found the ease of navigating it. It was heavy and its weight was obvious. It took a good deal of time to get it moving, but once she did it, the engine sputtered and grunted until the turbo engaged. Elet hadn't been asleep. She had seen him stir and turn his head a few times. He was waiting to make certain that she could comfortably drive it. She knew it, but she pretended that he was asleep. Within twenty minutes, she had transitioned to interstate 75 North and was heading out of town. Then, Elet drifted off to sleep and she sat alone with her thoughts. There was no single thought. Her mind was a mess with scattered fibers of related thoughts.

She shook her head that Clementine was so pompous that she could imagine any good outcome by showing up to the party with Tabs. She didn't know what Alex had said to her on the side of Paige's house, but Clementine and Tabs quickly left after the encounter. She knew Elet knew. She looked over at him. He was asleep in the fetal position. She snickered and thought she would have liked to cover him if they had had a blanket. Then, her mind returned to Clementine. She wondered why she was opposed to her settling down, growing up, growing older. Isn't that all that she had done? Surely, it was time to do that. Jacqueline looked at herself in the mirror. Her big brown eyes stared back at her. They didn't have the answer she was seeking. She had remembered the times she spent before meeting Mallory. They were fun but empty. She had gone where she wanted, when she wanted, and spent as much as she wanted. She had not had to experience the kind of gut-wrenching conversations that she had that morning with Mallory. Then, she thought, *fuck*. She remembered that she was supposed to text her when they got on the road. She decided to voice text.

Jacqueline: Hi, honey. Just wanted to let you know that we've left. I'm on I-75. Elet's already asleep. Trying to adjust to driving this behemoth. Text more later. I love you.

Mallory: Okay, baby. Be safe. I love you too.

Jacqueline was relieved that she had reached out to her, but texting her whereabouts and plans felt foreign to her. She thought back to life before a girlfriend and a child. She had enjoyed not checking in. With no one to remind her of the faculty memory, she had pumped herself up on the merits of the single life. Confident in her driving and alive in the memories of the life she once had, she turned on the radio. Elet's pop music station began to play the newest song on the Top 20. Jacqueline did not know it. She tried hard to enjoy it, but after a few minutes, she turned to another station. It was playing a teen song. She had heard it blaring from Zoe's room when Abbie spent the night. She could hear the two girls singing along. She laughed aloud just remembering it. Then, she changed the channel. It was the classic radio station, the first channel programmed in Mallory's car. She liked the mix so much that she had added it to her station lineup. She left it there. It gave her comfort. It felt like home and that let her settle in for her long, interstate drive.

~~~~~~~~~

Driving from west Florida along the interstate to central Florida was only marked by the height of the hills. No matter what the season, the scenery was awash with green. Green grass. Green trees. It was the same. She had been driving for nearly two hours when she exited in Gainesville. She was a Florida girl. She knew ways around the state. As she steered off interstate 75, she entered the flow of traffic through the business and residential area. She cruised past apartments and strip malls. At stop lights, the roads were shared with pedestrians, motorcycles, bicyclists, families, and mopeds. With the air conditioner off, she lowered her window and enjoyed the sunshine. As highways reduced in size to local roads, she felt the presence of college life. To each side was evidence of sororities and fraternities, of parties and libraries, of restaurants and bars. She smiled to herself as scantily clad young girls passed in front of the truck. She waved when they waved and smiled when they didn't. She wished she was in the Laredo. With its top down, it would have better represented who she was. She was smiling slyly when Elet woke up.

"Uh, why are their girls in short shorts walking on the interstate?"

"Hey there, sleepyhead. Up from your nippy nap?"

"Where are we, pedophile?"

"This is the home for the Florida Gators. Look to your left and you'll see Lake Alice. Up ahead on your side will be the VA hospital."

"Thanks, tour guide, but I think we need to be getting out of the state, not enjoying memory lane."

"We're going. It's quicker to cut through Gainesville and hit 301 than to go all the way up 75 to 10 west."

"What?"

"Just trust me," she said. They weaved through the city and onto US Highway 301. The highway bisected small towns. In the truck, they passed cow farms, flea markets, barbecue stands, and old churches. They traveled through the byways of towns known as speed traps, small towns unknown by non-Floridians. They drove alongside trains racing parallel to them. They cruised at a comfortable speed on the outskirts of major cities until they reached Interstate 10 West, outside of Jacksonville. Fearing being bogged down in travel through town, Jacqueline steered around the largest city in land area in the continental United States. Using the Interstate 295 North exchange, she looped Jacksonville's core. Rather than sitting for hours in traffic, she connected to Interstate 95 North near the Jacksonville airport and headed out of state. As she approached the state line, she sent a text to Mallory.

Jacqueline: Out of town. Out of state.
Mallory: I miss you already.
Jacqueline: I'll be back before you know it.
Mallory: Already know it.
Jacqueline: :(I love you.
Mallory: I love you too.
Jacqueline: I'll call you when we stop.
Mallory: k

~~~~~~~~~

Jacqueline had been driving for a little more than four hours when she stopped in Brunswick, Georgia. She pulled into a parking space, turned off the truck, and jumped down. As she stretched her back and legs, Elet awoke. "Where are we?"

"Brunswick."

"Brunswick?"

"South Georgia."

"Ah. What time is it?"

"Time to eat," she said and walked into tonight's fine dining establishment.

In a few minutes, the two emerged with two bags of fried items to be consumed on the road. She threw Elet the truck keys and climbed into the passenger's seat.

With a burger hanging out of his mouth, he cranked the truck, "Lemme show you how this is done."

She buckled her seatbelt and nibbled on her chicken. "I usually can't sleep in the car, but I think I'm gonna try to catch a little nap."

"Go, right ahead. We'll be in Myrtle Beach in no time."

"It's supposed to take another four hours."

"Says who?" he asked, chomping on fries. She held up her phone. "That's just an estimate. And, you were driving like you were scared of her."

"Only slightly." She had given up on eating. She rolled her bag closed and placed it on the floor board. She reclined the seat back and stared at him. "You know, I'm glad we're doing this."

"You are?"

"Yeah, aren't you?"

"I don't know. I could think of some other fun things we could have done instead."

"Like what?"

"Cancun? Bahamas? Denver? Fuck it, Brunswick?" They both laughed. Before he arrived at the next exit, she was asleep.

~~~~~~~~~

Her quick nap turned into hours. She slept in the passenger's seat like it was her bed. No dreams or thoughts filled her mind. She was at ease riding along in the dark with Elet behind the wheel. It's likely that she would have slept all night. If he had not known that she had made reservations at a hotel in Myrtle Beach, he could have just kept going towards Baltimore and she would have not been the wiser. Instead, she was welcomed back to the world with a slap on her chair and the sound of Elet's victory, "Made it in three hours and fifteen minutes." She stretched but didn't respond. Once on solid ground, she opened the back of the truck and removed their bags. Elet walked around to her side of the truck. Staring up at the hotel, he said, "What have you done?"

"What?" She was still groggy.

"We're only staying overnight. You booked us in an oceanfront resort like we're a couple on vacation."

Closing the doors, she said, "No, I didn't. If I had, it'd be a whole lot better." With bags over their shoulders, they entered the golf and spa resort that she had reserved for the evening. After checking them in and retrieving the keys, they located their elevators and headed up to their rooms. In the elevator, she asked, "Are you turning in?"

"Probably not. I'm gonna call Alex, but I doubt I'll turn in. It's like eight."

"Wanna meet back downstairs in the bar in ...like a half hour."

"Sure. But, don't you need to call Mallory back? She must've text a hundred times while you were sleeping." Jacqueline pulled her phone out of her pocket. She had not checked. Standing next to her, Elet could see the screen. "Holy shit. Is that Mallory?"

"No! It's not. Eyes forward."

"Who is that and why is she sending you pictures?"

"Just some girl from the past."

"Um. That's fucked up."

"I don't ask them to do it." She stepped forward as the doors opened to her floor.

As the doors closed, he said, "You don't tell them to stop."

~~~~~~~~~

Jacqueline entered her room and quickly called Mallory. The two spoke for a while, then Jacqueline explained that she was planning to meet Elet for dinner and she would call Mallory afterward. After a quick shower, Jacqueline returned to the downstairs bar. It was adorned with red velvet couches and wicker chairs. The wood paneling floors and low lights cast a warm glow. As she stood in the middle of the room searching for a table befitting two friends, she noticed that one side of the room exited to an oceanfront deck. She stepped to the bar to ask about service. The waitress directed her to take a menu and she would be right out there.

As she removed two menus from the serving side of the bar, she heard a voice say, "You gonna brave the deck?"

"Certainly."

"You aren't worried about it being too cold?"

"Hasn't anyone ever told you that the night air is good for the blood?" Jacqueline turned her head and stared in the face of her new friend. It was a round, full face on a slender frame. Jacqueline stared at it, not with interest, but with curiosity. She wondered if the new friend had once been overweight and her face was a sign of a recent transformation. As she cocked her head from side to side, she realized that her new friend might be getting the wrong idea. She had lingered too long for an easy extraction.

Before she could disappear onto the terrace, the new friend said, "I'm Sam. Samantha." Pointing to the stranger sitting next to her who Jacqueline had not noticed, she said, "This is my friend, Megan."

Leaning back from the bar to get a better view of Megan, Jacqueline was planning to introduce herself when Elet appeared in the bar. From across the room, she pointed to herself and said, "Hi. I'm Jacqueline and this is my friend, Elet." He waved.

"Elet?"

"Yup, Elet."

The curly headed brunette turned and caught a glimpse of the tall, sandy blonde man edging towards her with jeans and a t-shirt on. Then, she chose the line that he had heard a million times, "Elet. That's a great name."

Responding as he always did, "Thanks, but I can't take any credit. You'd have to talk to my mother about it." Then, he turned to Jacqueline, "Did you get us a table?"

"I was thinking that we'd sit on the deck. Waitress said she'd come out and take our order. You game?"

"Sure," he said.

Turning back towards the women, she said, "It was nice to meet you both. Now, we must brave the high seas." She placed the menus under her arm and pushed the door open that led to the deck. It was awkwardly warm. She was taken aback, but then she noticed the patio heaters. "This is nice," she said.

Pulling out a chair at a table in the far corner, Elet said, "I'm still not convinced you're not trying to seduce me."

As they laughed, they heard the familiar voices of strangers, "We decided to brave the winds with you. Is that okay?"

"Of course," Jacqueline said as she pushed back two chairs. Elet sighed and stood up to help them be seated.

"Oh, it's not cold at all. Did you know it was going to be warm?" Sam asked.

"No, I didn't. We were just as surprised as you were." The waitress appeared to get their orders. Jacqueline ordered a few appetizers and a drink. Elet ordered a beer. Then, she asked, "Would either of you like anything?"

Megan replied, "No, we've eaten."

"Are you sure? It's our treat." Jacqueline asked. Before she could finish the sentence, the girl ordered another pitcher of Mai Tais and some hot wings for her and her friend. Staring at Elet who had lifted his eyes in disbelief, Jacqueline said to the waitress, "Thanks. That should definitely do it."

Making conversation, Elet asked, "So, are you two from South Carolina?"

"No. We're just passing through." Megan responded. "We're personal assistants for two female golfers."

"Oh, is there a course nearby?"

They giggled. Sam responded, "You're at one."

"Shit, you are trying to get in my pants." He teased and hit Jacqueline with the napkin. The girls stared.

"Don't look at me that way. I'm not trying to get in his pants. He's getting married next month. We're heading to pick up his gift from me. It's in Baltimore. We're just staying the night and we're back on the road in the morning."

"Congratulations," they said almost in unison. Elet nodded his appreciation. There was silence for a while as they all stared out into the water.

"Aww, a Christmas wedding," Megan fawned over the idea.

"No, not that late. We're getting married on December fifth." Then, Jacqueline's phone buzzed. She removed it from her pocket and stared at it. As she began to type, Elet asked, "Mallory?"

Sighing, she said, "No, Clementine."

Jumping into the conversation, Sam asked, "So, you have multiple women?"

Jacqueline did not respond. The drinks and appetizers had come. As she reached to make herself a plate of appetizers, she tried to explain the confusion that was Clementine, "It's not like that. She's that person that you know, but you can't quite figure out. She's definitely not a romantic interest. Not on my part, but I'm not sure what she's after."

Drinking his beer and eating some of Megan's wings, Elet said, "Don't sound like that. You know what she wants."

"No, I don't."

"I think she's just lonely and she's just trying too hard. Remember that cat suit. Leather cat suits say I'm trying too hard." He slurped BBQ sauce from his fingers.

"Maybe."

"What'd she say in the text?"

"She said - how are things where you are. And, she sent a pic."

"Of herself?" he asked as he chewed.

"No, it's a pic of some girl."

"Tabs?"

"Not that I remember," and she handed him the phone.

"Oh shit." Elet face turned red and he squealed. "This girl has no sense of decency," but he continued to stare at the picture. He turned the phone around as if to be inspecting the picture from different angles. He held it to his face for so long that Megan was interested. She placed her hand on his arm and leaned into him in order to look.

She had been quiet for a long while before she said, "Oh my God, is that some girl's..."

Jacqueline cut her off, "Yeah, I'm pretty sure it is."

Megan said, "Was it forwarded to her or is she there taking that picture right now."

Sam had become interested, but she didn't walk over to Elet. Instead, she pleaded, "I wanna see."

"Be my guest," he responded and passed the phone to Megan who passed it to Sam.

"Humph," she said. "That's nothing." Without pause, Sam pushed back from the table, leaned forward, and through the glass top table, they saw Jacqueline's flash. "That should keep her quiet." Jacqueline and Megan laughed.

Elet glared. "I think I'm gonna take a walk down the beach to relax. Then, I'm gonna turn in." He stood up and took his beer from the waitress who was bringing another one. "Good night, ladies."

"Okay. What time do you want to leave in the morning?" Jacqueline asked as he passed by her.

Over his shoulder, he said, "Check out is at eleven. I'll meet you at the truck at eleven."

"You don't want to have breakfast?" She knew he was upset. She tried to keep him at the table as long as she could.

"Nope," was all he said as he headed off in the direction of the ocean.

Megan sprang up from the table and said, "Can I walk with you?"

He never turned around. Over his shoulder, he said, "It's a public beach." And, she went after him.

Alone now, Samantha said, "I'm sorry if I made him mad."

"He's fine."

"You two...you really aren't...together, right?"

"Elet and I?" She laughed and swigged her own beer. "No, he's definitely not my type. We've been friends for years. He's probably my best friend. But, it's soooo not romantic. Not even in our drunkest nights."

"Good." Jacqueline stared at her and wondered about her response, but she said nothing. She did not have to wait too long before Sam spoke again, "Do you want to join them on the beach?"

"We can."

"Walk me down to my room first. I should probably put on some...panties and shoes. We're on the first floor. It's just down the hall."

Jacqueline stood up. She felt a bit wobbly, but she pulled some cash from her wallet to leave for the waitress. Normally, she would not have exposed her wallet to a stranger, but tonight felt very abnormal. As she re-entered the bar, Samantha reached for her hand. Pulling her towards her room, Jacqueline followed.

As the room door opened, Jacqueline saw the tiniest hotel room that she'd ever seen. It seemed like it was intended to be a closet, but the mops had been placed out of sight. She sat on the edge of one of the full sized beds. Samantha went into the restroom. Looking around the room, there was no chair or desk. There was no flat panel television. There were two full size beds, a tube television, a large mirror, and a bathroom off in the corner. She was tipsy when she entered, but, quickly, she sobered as she stared at this room and wondered why it was never renovated. She wondered if Sam knew that there were better rooms in the hotel. She wondered if she should call the hotel manager on Sam's behalf. She was thinking all of this when Sam exited the bathroom. Naked.

Chapter 14

Driving in afternoon traffic with four female passengers is like hurtling through space in a ship full of puppies. It's loud, messy, and someone's going to be nipped at. As Josephine exited her sister's apartment complex in her black Yukon, it was near maximum capacity. Her sister, Alex, was sitting in the passenger's seat. As the bride-to-be, she saw the passenger's seat as her divine right. She had slid her feet out of her black heels and turned her body sideways in the seat, so that she could better face the rear of the cabin. In the row behind them, Paige and Mallory sat. All eyes faced the middle in SUVs. That was the prime location. The worst spot was inhabited by the maid-of-honor, Olive. She was in the final row. The row that was so unnecessary that most days it spent folded under the frame of the vehicle. But, for today's shopping extravaganza, Dom had excavated the seat from its dark cave, dusted off the crumbs, and made it presentable for the third most important member of the wedding party. Without regard for her poor seating, Olive leaned forward peering her head between Mallory and Paige. She was not to be denied any conversations, any opportunities to laugh, cry, yell, or guffaw.

Bumping across the land mines, Josephine asked, "So, Jacqueline and Elet left this afternoon, right?"

Far off outside her window, Mallory said, "Yup. After lunch."

Josephine remarked, "That's pretty exciting. The wedding's coming together."

Shouting from her rear seat, Olive said, "Hell, yeah. Now, all we need are dresses and suits."

Josephine responded, "Wait, how are we gonna pick out dresses if the guys don't have suits."

Rolling her eyes, Alex said, "Jo, we've gone over this. When we pick out your color, that will be their color. Elet doesn't even care. He's not even wearing that color, anyhow."

"Does he even know enough guys to fill the spots?" Olive asked.

"Remember he only needed three. Jacqueline is his best person." Alex reminded them. Mallory sighed.

Josephine said, "We're gonna have to make sure whatever color we pick is gonna look good on her, too. Mallory, what's a good color for her?" Mallory did not respond. "Mallory? Hello...Mallory?"

"Oh, sorry. Huh?" she asked as if she had not been there at all.

"What color looks good on Jacqueline?"

"Who knows," she said.

Staring at her with pursed lips, Alex said, "Alright, out with it. I can't have you ruining my night."

"Oh. It's nothing. It's just been a long day."

"My man is gone, too."

"Your man's gone, because his friend asked him to go."

"You know, it's only for a couple of days. Have you heard from her?" reminded Paige.

"Yeah, she sent me a couple of texts."

Trying to change the subject, Olive asked, "Where's Miss Zoe this afternoon?"

"She has cheer practice. My mom took her, so I could come dress shopping."

Paige said, "That's nice."

"Well, this isn't what I thought dress shopping would be like. I need you to liven up. We're shopping for dresses for my wedding." With arms folded, Alex reminded them.

"I know. I know. I'm sorry. It seems like there's always something wrong with me these days."

"Who are you telling?" Alex said under her breath.

Josephine reprimanded, "Don't say that."

"Someone needs to tell her not to be worried about everything all the time. It's like...all the time. We don't even talk about anything else except Jacqueline or Clementine."

"Oh, yeah. Whatever happened between you and Clementine, " Paige asked. "I overheard that you and she had words in my backyard, but no one ever told me what was going on."

Alex said, "It was nothing."

"Not true. Clementine rubbed Alex the wrong way at the party and she went off on her." Olive chirped. "I thought we were gonna throw down. I was ready to coldcock that girlfriend of hers." Olive swung jabs in the air. Mallory laughed.

Josephine said, "Yeah, I think little Miss Alex was a little bit jealous."

Alex always hated when her sister called her little Miss Alex. The very idea of it made her angry. "I wasn't jealous, Jo! I was helping out. Clementine is just a lonely bitch. She's finally made it and she doesn't know what to do with herself. Jacqueline isn't gonna tell her to chill the fuck out. And, she's obviously not really involved with that girl she brought to the party."

"They looked pretty involved to me," Mallory said.

"You've got to work on your gaydar. There's no way that that girl likes her. She didn't hang all over her. And, when I was cussin' Clementine out, that big bitch never said a word."

Punching her hand, Olive said, "I wish she woulda."

"Simmer down," Mallory giggled.

"I was ready," Olive said. "We ain't rumbled in years."

"Anyhow, Clementine could be cool as soon as she calms down and gets shit under control."

Paige asked, "So, how'd it end?"

"It really wasn't a thing. I just called her to the side of the house and told her that I knew about this little thing she had going on. She's just trying to be friends. She sees some people who are friends and she wants to be a part of it. But, I told her she's gotta get shit under control and get comfortable with who she really is and stop trying so hard to fit in. Then, we'll talk."

"Did she say anything?"

"Not really. She was stunned I said anything to her. She enjoys the attention she gets from making a scene."

"What attention?" Mallory said.

"Don't you see? She goes too far. It's not style. It's just a mess. I've seen her twice working two different styles. She doesn't know who she is. Poor little bitch is desperate for attention. She overdoes everything, so people will notice her."

"You're so wise," Josephine teased.

"But, why Jacqueline? I really think she likes her." Mallory said as she folded her arms.

"They farm the same pasture," Paige whispered.

"What?" Mallory screamed. The truck bellowed with laughter.

"She doesn't want to be with her. She doesn't like her. Not like that. You guys don't get it," Alex clarified.

"Enlighten us," Josephine said as they waited in traffic.

"Here's the deal. We've all got something that draws people in, right? Take Paige. She has that earthy mother thing. She's on your side. She soothes you. You go to her when you need someone. Then, there's Olive. Loyal. Fun. Friendly. She's your girl. She's up for whatever, whenever. She's the life of the party. Now, Josephine, she's a mix of worlds. She definitely has the mother thing, but she's got feisty street cred. She's gonna scream at you for getting into the fight, but she's gonna come get you from downtown, too. Mallory and I are the same. It's looks." The other women roared. "I mean it. Men. Well, and women, I guess. They look at us. We pull you in with our looks. We may keep you with something else, but it's definitely the look that's all ours all the time. Get it?" They grew silent listening. "I've known Jacqueline longer than any of you."

"You have not. I have known her longer than any of you," Paige said with her hand in the air.

With arms folded and a flash of arrogance, Mallory said, "But, I know her better."

"Are you all finished? She pulls people in with personality. She looks them in the face. She listens to their bullshit. She has something great to say to even the stupidest fuck. She makes everyone think they are worth listening to. That's why Clementine is desperate for her attention. She wants in her good graces. She wants to be her buddy. She likes how it makes her feel. She doesn't want to date her. She wants Jacqueline to take her to a gay club and use Jacqueline to get her cred. That's all this is about. She's hanging around in Jacqueline's old world living in her shadow." Josephine was nodding. Alex was thinking about what was said. The truck was silent.

Until Mallory asked, "Her old world?"

"Yeah, Elet overheard Clementine say that she's being going to Livewire."

"That swanky gay bar that Jacqueline used to go to?" Olive asked.

Leaning back in her seat with her arm stretched around the head rest, "That's the one," Alex said. "She wants Jacqueline to go there with her."

"What the hell! I'm gonna beat this girl's ass." Mallory was angry.

"Alright! That's what I'm talking about. Let's not be sad." Alex celebrated the change in mood.

"I see this bitch every day. She knows that we're dating and she's trying to get her to go out." Mallory was furious. "Don't I have enough problems without her fucking around with her head?"

"What about Drew?" Olive changed the subject. "What's his draw?"

"Drew? You know, I think he works, because he's this genuinely nice guy. You know, like Brett. Nothing has happened. He's not jaded. He went off to college. He's got college buddies and I think he's just happy go-lucky. Then, there's Dom. Everyone's big brother. The one that no one needs. The older brother who tortures you and picks on you and then when things get real he can't talk to you."

Laughing, Josephine said, "Yeah, that's my Dom."

Paige said, "Okay, what about Elet?"

"Elet Walden. He's a looker. Girls are always checking him out. He has that tall, tan white boy look. Close cut sandy blonde hair. A great smile.

Strong forearms. And, oddly, I think women like that he's barefoot in jeans. I think it drives them wild."

"Doesn't that bother you," Paige asked.

"Never. He never cares. He will stand there and talk to them for a second, but when things get too uncomfortable, he leaves. Either, he just disappears or finds his way to me."

"Aww, she does love him." Josephine said.

"Yeah, she's only ever gushed over one man more than that."

"What? Who?" Mallory said.

"Shut up, Olive."

But, Olive wouldn't be silenced, "Cooper. Her old high school boyfriend. He was a real charmer."

"First love," Paige swooned.

"Dumb love," Josephine said as they pulled into the parking lot of the dress shop. "I heard he was back in town. I wouldn't be surprised if he doesn't call you." As the women started to disembark, she finished with, "I'm just glad he didn't show up over the summer or we would really have something to worry about."

Alex smiled and held the door as the women walked inside. Then, she turned her phone on vibrate just to make sure any calls wouldn't be heard.

~~~~~~~~~

Mallory was shocked to find out that her mother and father had taken Zoe to her house rather just going to theirs. It had been a long day. She had dropped Zoe off to school at seven that morning. She had a tearful afternoon when Jacqueline left. Then, she searched for hours for the dress that Alex thought would be perfect. She was tired. Exhausted. All she wanted was to pick up Zoe, head to the penthouse, and relax in the tub until Jacqueline called her back. Standing on the porch of her own house, she whimpered like a teenager late for curfew. After a few minutes, she gathered her nerve and opened her door.

The smell of her mother's plumeria perfume made her sneeze. "Oh, Hi, baby," the sneeze queued her mother to greet her. "We've gotta find something to help with that sneezing." Barbara was a tall, thin older woman with a strong face. Her long, white hair was cut into a modern shag. Cradling her face, the ends of her hair swung about ears. Mallory's father sat on the couch reading magazines as if he was interested in what fashion trends were hot last season. After forty-two years of marriage to Barbara, he read anything. Barbara told people that he was a voracious reader. Mallory said that he read to avoid listening to her mother.

Mallory leaned forward and kissed the top of his balding head. The fringes of his salt and pepper hairs that remained tickled her nose as she said, "Hi, Dad."

"Hiya, Red." Richard had called his only daughter *Red* since the time he first noticed her sprigs of orange hair. His mother had been a redhead and his father had called her *Red*. He thought of it as a family tradition. He placed her magazine on the table and stood up to kiss her. "How was your night? Do we have a dress?" He clapped his spotted hands.

Too tired to engage in the antics that come with family, Mallory walked past him and sat on her couch. "After hours of looking, we have a dress."

Somehow, Barbara had vanished. She had passed through the living room and went to the kitchen without ever being seen, but she spoke as though she was with them, "You know, I saw Alex the other day. I was in town having my nails done and I saw her entering a restaurant with some black man. I almost didn't think it was her. But, I took a longer look and it was her. Well, I was gonna go and say hello, but they messed up my pinkie finger. By the time, I got it fixed she and the black man were gone. So, what do the dresses look like?"

"Wait a minute. Was it her or was it not her?" asked Mallory, wishing she could leave them in her house and go away.

"Oh, it was her. Her and some black man."

"Stop saying it like that. She's black. She knows black men. She's related to black men. She works with black men."

"Well, Mallory, I hope she doesn't know them all like that. But, your generation is so much touchier than we were in my time. Women only touched their husbands, not co-workers and friends. Anyhow, tell me about the dress."

Mallory was too distracted to give details. She was thinking about who this man might be. It seemed unlikely that it was Dom. She had no brothers or male cousins to Mallory's knowledge. She heard her mother say her name and quickly replied, "Oh. It's a nice, simple salmon slip dress that crisscrosses in the back. I can definitely wear it other places."

As she bagged up the trash, she asked, "So, the colors are salmon and what?"

"Elet's gonna wear a gray suit with a white shirt and a white tie. The groomsmen will be in gray suits and white shirts with salmon colored ties. Jacqueline'll wear gray suit pants and a salmon colored shirt but no tie. I think it's gonna be really nice."

"Good Lord. I forget that she's in the groom's party."

"Don't start, Mom." Mallory said. Richard surveyed the situation from over the top of the magazine.

"I'm not saying anything." She came from the kitchen and pretended to zip her mouth closed. She sat by Mallory on the couch. Stroking her daughter's hair, she said, "You know that your father and I support you. We're so proud of you. And, we trust your judgment. We just don't want you or our precious Zoe getting hurt anymore."

Mallory got up from the couch and gathered her things, "Mom, I know. You don't have to keep saying it. I know you love me and I know you support me. And, I know you don't want me to get hurt. But, I also know that you aren't excited about me dating a woman."

"We never said that. Did we, Richard? We never said that." Richard never looked up.

"You don't have to."

"Well, we were surprised. Men all your life, then poof, a woman. But, she's very nice. And, clearly, Zoe loves her. And, I'm guessing that you probably do, too." Mallory was rubbing her head. This was a conversation that they had had many times in the last few months.

"Everything's great, Mom."

"Where is she? Zoe says she's out of town. For work?"

"No, Mom. She and Elet went to pick up their wedding gift."

"They couldn't ship it?"

"It's a long story and it's been a long day. Can I tell you later?"

"Sure, darling. Zoe has been fed. I told her to take a bath, but she says you two are going to the penthouse."

"Yes, we're gonna stay over there."

"With Jacqueline out of town?"

"Yes."

"Is that safe?"

"Mom, she has a penthouse suite in a high-rise building overlooking the Bay with a doorman and security officers. I rent a two-bedroom house in Clearwater. Which one do you think is safer?"

"I know, I know. Zoe went on and on about it. Is it inheritance?"

"Nope. She bought it."

"All on her own?"

"Mom!"

"Fine. I just wanted to know what was going on in my only daughter's life. I worry about her."

"I'm fine. Zoe's fine. We're just gonna stay over there."

"Will you be moving in with her?"

"Mom, when I know, I'll let you know."

Richard had finished his article. He heaved himself from the depths of the couch and announced, "It's time to go, Barb. Zoe! Come and tell you old Grandpa goodnight." From around the corner, Zoe ran into the living room and into her grandfather's waiting arms. Holding her close, he said, "Pizza and a movie, tomorrow night?"

Unaware of what was happening tomorrow night, Mallory asked, "What's tomorrow night?"

"Mom, Grandma and Grandpa said I could stay tomorrow night. I don't have school and we could make a weekend of it. We can go to the zoo and the movies and everything. Can I? Can I?"

Overwhelmed, she said, "Yes, it's fine." She just wanted the madness to stop. She hugged her mother goodbye and watched as her mother hugged Zoe. "Zoe, go get your stuff together."

Walking her parents to the front door, her father turned in the entryway and said, "Red, we love ya. And, we want you to be with whomever makes you happy." Then, he kissed her on the forehead. Looking into her eyes, he said, "But, whoever it is better have plenty of stories to keep your mother entertained." He winked at her and headed outside to open the car door for his bride.

Waiting on Zoe to reappear, Mallory leaned against her loveseat and tapped her front tooth. She wondered who was that thin, balding man and how did he get stuck with Barb.

Chapter 15

Jacqueline awoke early enough that she thought that she might meet Elet for breakfast. She dressed quickly and headed downstairs. She looked around the breakfast area. She did not see him. She went to the sundries store to see if he might be there. He was not. She had failed to get his room number or she would have stopped by his room. Thinking that maybe he had overslept, she sent him a text. He did not respond. She began to wonder if he had spent the night with Megan, but she discarded that thought quickly. Deciding that he was either asleep or showering, she decided to collect some breakfast items from the buffet for him, return to her room, checkout, and wait for him at the truck.

After thirty minutes, all of that was complete. With her bags on her shoulder, she strode out of the hotel into the crisp morning air and headed towards the truck with pasties, coffee, sausage, toast, and a muffin. Much to her surprise, he was there.

"Good morning," she said.

"Hey."

"I tried to catch up with you for breakfast. Did you get anything?"

"Wasn't hungry."

"Well, I got you some stuff in case you were hungry."

"Thanks," he said as he took it from her open hands.

"Still tired?"

"Not really."

"Okay. Well, do you want me to take the first leg? You're definitely better than me at making up time."

"Sure," and he jumped into the passenger's side.

Thinking that he may have had a long night, she didn't say anything more. She eased the truck out of the parking lot and aimed back towards the interstate. She looked over at him and he had already curled up. This morning, the truck felt less cumbersome than it had yesterday. She was less apprehensive about how to handle it and felt more in command of its power and unexpected speed. Leaving the state roads behind, she was in complete command when she re-entered Interstate 95 north. She was passing slow traffic and making great time as she headed to Fayetteville. Since Elet was such a heavy sleeper, she was able to search the radio for songs she knew.

She was singing along when her phone rang. It was Mallory.

"Hey, honey."

"Hi, there. Sounds like you're having fun."

"I'm keeping myself awake."

"Elet asleep? He sleeps more than a newborn."

"Yeah, he does. So, you're heading off to have lunch with Alex?"

"Yes, Olive and I."

"No Paige?"

"She's got a meeting. It's just the three of us."

"Sorry that I'm missing that," Jacqueline said.

"Somehow, I don't think you are. But, anyhow, I wish you were heading home."

"Yeah, me too. I miss you, you know."

"I miss you, too. That bed's lonely without you in it."

"But, I bet you enjoyed being in the bathroom for hours without me interrupting you." She heard her laugh. "I miss that laugh."

"I've gotta get out of here and get back before the boss notices that I'm gone."

"You better. I hear she's a real slave driver."

"I love you."

"I love you, too. I'll talk to you later."

"Okay, baby." Mallory said as she hung up. Jacqueline smiled and placed the phone back in the cup holder.

With his back still to her, Elet spoke, "I don't even understand how you can talk when you're full of so much shit."

Shock came over Jacqueline. She wasn't sure if he was talking to her or talking in his sleep or talking about some text he received. All she could say was, "Elet?"

"I can't believe you. I really can't." He lifted his chair forward and turned to face her. His eyes were filled with rage.

"What are you talkin' about?"

Shaking his head with his arms crossed, he said, "It's all lies. All of it. And, she doesn't even know it."

"What's all lies?"

"All this love that you say that you have for her. It's all bullshit. Remember, I know the truth."

"I do love her. I wasn't lying."

"How can you love her and do what you did last night?"

"Man, that was crazy shit, wasn't it?" She started to laugh at thoughts of last night. "Oh, my God. I never saw any of that coming. Was Megan as crazy as Samantha was?"

"You're my best friend. We've been through all kinds of shit together. But, I can't do this with you right now. Now, right here. Not right now."

Finally realizing what he thought happened, she looked at him, "Wait, you think that I...and Samantha...Sam. Me and her?" He stared at her. "Hell, no. Absolutely not." He did not look as though he believed her. "Lemme tell you what happened. You left the table after the photo incident. Then, she said she wanted to get some...you know, underwear and flip flops and follow you two down the beach. So, I stumble back to her room and wait on her to get her shit. And, I'm staring at this tiny ass room when she comes out butt ass naked. I mean, I was on my way to drunk, but that sobered me up quick. I told her that it wasn't like that and apologized if she misunderstood and got out of there. I went back to my room and called Mallory." He did not look convinced. She said, "I swear. Look at my call log. Look!" She held it up to his face.

He glanced at it. "But, how'd you let yourself get into that situation?"

"How the hell was I supposed to know that things were gonna go like that? I thought they were gonna have a few drinks, eat a few wings, and everyone would have gone back to their rooms."

"Girls like that aren't interested in conversation and you know it," Elet lashed out.

"But, I swear that's all that I was interested in."

"Bullshit! You went in her room in the middle of the night knowing you had a girl back at home. This is the shit that pisses me off. You think that, because you don't say that you want more that you aren't wrong. This is the shit that you do! This is the shit that Alex does! I finally saw the shit that happens with my own eyes. You guys, go and hang out. You know that these guys and girls aren't interested in conversation and friendship. But, you think that it's all okay as long as that's all you say that you want. It's fucked up! It's fucked up for me! It's fucked up to Mallory! And, she doesn't even know that the shit's happening! It's fucked up to Megan and to Samantha who think that you want what they want. And, I never thought you were doing it." She stared at him. He was pounding on the dashboard. It had started to rain outside and the reflection of the rain on his face looked like angry tears. "We put ourselves on the line. I tell her that I love her, but I can't trust her to go to the fucking grocery store and not cheat on me! Fucking Mallory's sitting around waiting on you and your ass is out here flirting with some young kid! That damn girl was ready to sleep with you. She invited you to her room and you fucked with her head and walked out on her!" He was seething.

"Hang on, Elet. Hang on. We didn't pick up any girls. We left them at the bar to go eat on the patio. They followed us."

"Tell me you weren't flirting with them."

"I wasn't. I was just talking to them. They joined us."

"And the picture?"

"How the hell did I know that was going to happen? I passed you my phone. Megan was over your shoulder looking at it. She passed it to Sam. I had no idea she wasn't wearing panties or that she was going to use my phone to take a picture. No idea. We were both stunned. Now, you're right. I should not have gone to her room. But, she never made a move like she was going to seduce me. There was no handholding or whispering or seduction. Nothing. She said walk with me while I get some underwear and some flip flops. There's nothing sexy about that. And, when shit got real, I excused myself. I never touched her. I may have misled her and I may have hurt her feelings, but come on, nothing happened," Jacqueline declared.

"That's just what I mean. You put yourself in that situation and you don't even know it's wrong," Elet fumed.

"I did and I get what you're saying. That was a mistake. But, you can't believe that that shit happens to me every day anymore. Those days are long gone," trying to control her temper, Jacqueline said.

"I don't know. I just don't know. Last night, I felt like I was hovering over the moments right up to Alex's bad ideas. And, all I felt was anger that you had deceived me, too."

"Me?"

"Yes, I had always hoped with you there that I knew things were never too out of hand. That she may flirt or whatever, but you made sure that it was never too far gone."

"It never is. She may flirt. She may get a free drink or appetizer. She may have someone try to come to the table to talk, but he usually leaves in shame. Is it nice to those men? No. Is it good for you? Yes." That was the lie she had to tell, so that it would preface the newest truth. "But, all of that is ancient history. I've never seen her more focused on the wedding and your life together. Last night, we sat on the deck with two women while they went looking for bridesmaids' dresses. They've picked colors and clothes for us."

"Yeah, I know. She called me last night with the news."

"See?" She was trying to bring him back.

"It doesn't matter."

"What doesn't matter?"

"Yesterday. What about all the years? All the times? All the phone numbers who tried to call her? What about all the women who are still sending you fucking naked pictures? Why don't you two realize that we're worth more? Why should anyone put up with your fucking bullshit?" He was slamming his hands against the dash. She was staring at him. He did not hear any of her words and she did not pay attention to the road. They were heading over the Roanoke River. The interstate was less of a hundred feet past over the arms of the river. There were strips of wooded land to their right. Even on a sunny day, it would have been important to keep their eyes on the road, but on a cloudy, rainy day, it was all the more important. Neither of them saw that stray. Neither of them saw the road that was parallel to the highway, it was probably from where he came. But, when they felt the thud, they both had the same pang in their stomachs. The pang of fear and guilt that a person gets right after something that could've been avoided wasn't.

He stopped yelling. She stopped looking at him. They knew they had hit something. Each was looking at all the windows to see what it was. The tires weren't flat. The truck was still operational. They couldn't see anything outside, but without discussion, Jacqueline steered off the road. There was no one behind them. No one traveling on the other side. They were alone on the highway just south of the Virginia state line. They emerged from the truck. Jacqueline headed to the front and Elet headed to the back. It was not necessary to inspect the truck. It was fine. It hadn't suffered in damage, but a few yards back on the side of the road, they saw a heap and heard a moan they'd never heard before. He looked at her as she looked at him, then they raced towards the sound.

"Oh, my God. Oh, my God," he said as he saw the animal lying near the shoulder. Jacqueline stood over him as he took off his shirt and tried to apply pressure to the bleeding. As he pressed in one spot, the brown dog bled more. It's breathing was erratic and faint. Elet tried to straighten the animals bent torso. It moaned more.

Jacqueline screamed, "Stop, Elet. You're making it worse."

"I don't know what to do," as he continued to pull and tug on the dog's mangled frame.

"Elet, stop! Stop pulling on him! Don't you hear him?" she screamed.

"Jacqueline, we have to do something. We can't let him die."

"What are we going to do?"

"I don't know, but stop yelling at me and help me."

She bent down. She wasn't sure what his breed was. He was brown, medium sized. He had shaggy hair like a Collie her mom had when she was little, but his face looked more like a Lab. She could tell that his hind legs were broken, and there was something wrong with his back. His breathing was less steady and it appeared to cause him pain. He grumbled with each inhale. Elet pulled the dog close to his chest and rocked back and forth. She stroked his head and stared into his half-closed black eyes. As Elet rocked on his knees, his eyes were closed. She wondered if he was praying. Praying for the dog. Praying for her. Praying for himself. She wondered if he was praying to make the dog better, praying that it might get up, and return from where it came. She knew that that was not going to be the case. As the dog's breathing slowed even more and the blood poured from its mouth, she went back to the truck. From the backseat, she gathered Elet's pillow and blanket. From the glove box, she withdrew her holster. As she approached Elet, her prayers for strength had been answered. She knew she had to be strong for the animal and for Elet. She walked up behind Elet and, calmly, said, "He's suffering. We can't let it end this way."

With tears in his eyes, he was choking on his words when he said, "We caused this."

"I know, Elet. I know. And, now, we have to fix it. There's no one else."

"It's not right."

"Tell me the other options! He won't make it to a vet. Hell, we don't know where one is." She waved her arms in the air. "This is our fault. I know we caused it. I know we will have to live with it. But, all we can do now is try to not let him suffer. Look at him! He's suffering. Elet, we have to let him go. We have to give him some peace." His face was red with anguish and his chest and pants red with the dog's blood. But, he nodded. He knew what she said had been true. "You don't have to stand here and watch. You can go to the truck." He shook his head. He held the dog against his chest. She placed the blanket around it. Slowly, Elet stood with the dog in his arms. As he hoisted the animal up, she tucked the blanket around the dog.

Then, the two headed away from the interstate. They trudged along the muddy shoulder. Past fresh cut grass and low cut shrubs, Elet pressed towards the trees. The dog's snout stuck from under the gray blanket. She watched as he sniffed. His black nose wrinkling at the smell from the changing landscape. Elet was heading far from the interstate, but before reaching the local road behind the trees, they stopped walking. With rain pouring on their heads and tears pouring down their faces, they faced each other. Standing still staring into each other eyes, she nodded. He nodded in agreement. He placed the animal on the ground. It howled as its body rested against the cold, wet ground. Elet swallowed hard and covered it completely with the blanket. Its breaths were even fainter and more sporadic. Jacqueline walked over to the dog, crouched down, and placed the pillow over its head. He stopped her. He placed his hands on her hands. When she looked up at him expecting him to speak, she saw that his eyes were closed. She closed hers as well. They did not speak, but there on the shoulder of Interstate 95, each asked for forgiveness and prayed that this animal be spared. When he removed his hand, she opened her eyes. The rustling of the leaves let her know that he had stepped away from her. There was nothing to be said.

In the space of three long, deep breaths and pull of the trigger, it was over. The moaning stopped. The breaths went still. There was silence. They stood in the darkness for a while. Soaked, drained, bloody, they loomed silently staring up through the trees hoping the rain would wash away their sorrow and purge them of their sin. Then, Elet dropped to one knee next to the gray blanket. He placed his hand on the pillow and said, "We're sorry, fella. We're so sorry," in a near whisper.

Jacqueline placed her hand on his shoulder and said, "There wasn't anything else we could do."

He replied with, "Yup." Then, she watched him rise. He walked backwards for a few steps staring at the blanket, staring at the mound, staring at the animal. She had watched him while facing the road. She hadn't wanted to look back. When he, eventually, turned, the two walked side by side towards the light. With heads hung low, they trudged through the mud and silt. They climbed up the embankment that they didn't realize that they'd climbed down. They returned to the waiting truck. She returned the holster to the glove box and rose into the passenger's seat. He climbed behind the wheel. And, for some time, there they sat, without saying a word, without moving, with tears streaming down their faces.

~~~~~~~~~

As though time had stopped and restarted, traffic appeared on the interstate. The presence of other people jolted them back. Elet cranked the truck and headed north. In silence, he drove along the highway. He did not look in her direction and she did not look in his. They traveled along for miles saying nothing, listening to nothing, absorbed by their pain.

When he saw the sign for a truck stop, he did not ask if she wanted to stop. Instead, he pulled in a parking space and slid out of the truck as if he was depleted of strength. Once on his feet, he opened the back doors and located another shirt in his duffel bag. Closing the doors, he opened the hatch and began to pump gas. Without being asked, Jacqueline cleaned the blood from the bumper. Staring at her bloody hands, she dunked them in the windshield cleaner receptacle. Then, she spoke for the first time in over an hour, "Want something from inside?"

"Let's go grab a bite at the counter."

"Okay," she said. She climbed back into the truck, so they could drive it over to the truck stop counter.

In silence, they picked over burgers and fries. Neither of them ate or spoke. When they had played with their meals for long enough, Jacqueline left a twenty on the table and the two return to the truck. Once again, they headed north.

Chapter 16

Mallory met Olive on the corner across the street from Alex's office building. Prior to arriving, Mallory worried that she wouldn't be able to find Olive in the lunch crowd that had exited the plethora of offices to go in search of food. She was wrong. Standing on the corner with her hand in front of her eyes, she saw Olive approach from a nearby parking garage. She was wearing dark, skinny jeans, a blue plaid shirt that was tied at the bottom, and red sneakers. She smiled to herself. She wasn't embarrassed by the outfit. In fact, she thought how things could have been worse.

"Hey, girl," Olive said as she bounced towards her. She carved out space for herself in the midst of bustling office men and women and hugged Mallory.

Again, she was surprised by her emotional greetings and moaned as Olive released her, "Hey. Thanks for meeting me. I just get the feeling there's something up with Alex."

"Girl, there's always something up with Alex, but I'm glad you called." The two started to cross the intersection. Halfway to the other side, Olive said, "It's so cool to have girlfriends." Mallory threw her head back and laughed. Standing in the shadow of the glass building that housed *UpBeat* magazine, there was no need to block the sun. The glass skyscraper blocked all hope for light. Having never come to the building, the two were apprehensive that they would find Alex. As they stood off to the side of the building reading the directory of occupants and reviewing the posted map, Olive spotted Alex. She tugged against the scalloped sleeve for Mallory's white shirt.

"What?"

"Look over there."

"Is that Alex standing on the corner? Where's she going?"

"No, who's she waiting for?" Olive turned and walked to Alex who was standing curbside. "Hey, girl."

Shock covered Alex's face, "What're you doing here?"

"We came to surprise you for lunch."

"We?"

The busy lunch traffic had slowed Mallory. She didn't have Olive's skills of blazing a path for herself. Once she caught up, she said, "Surprise! We came to take you to lunch." Alex didn't say a word. She stood on the corner in a blue dress. It was high-waisted with a matching fabric belt and upturned collar. Alex looked like a housewife from a fifties television show. Mallory took her by the arm and started to walk away from the curb.

Resisting Alex said, "Wait. I can't go. I already have a lunch date."

"Oh, is it a business lunch?"

Alex was not nimble enough to dissuade Mallory. While she wanted to ease out of this conversation without upsetting them and without revealing the identity of her lunch date, she was not able to appropriately answer the question. Instead of saying yes, she said, "No, it's a friend."

"Well, that's great. It'd be great to meet your new work friends," Mallory saw the fear in her eyes. Looking for the person as well, "Is she getting her car? Is she picking you up? Where are we headed?"

Alex mumbled, "No."

Olive said, "Alex, what's wrong with you? Are you sick?"

"No. I went to the ...." She stopped speaking. Her eyes flashed from them standing on the street to the Cadillac sedan that pulled up to the sidewalk.

"Oh, a Cadillac. I like her already," Olive said as she reached for the door.

"Olive, you have to slide over when you open the door. Make room for me," Mallory added.

"Guys, you can't just invite yourself to lunch."

"Sure, we can. Just introduce us," Mallory said with her hand on Alex's shoulder.

Uncertain what had happened and how she could maneuver out of it now, Alex opened the passenger's door. She leaned her head inside and said, "Do you mind if a couple of my friends join us for lunch?" Mallory had her eyes fixated on Alex. Intently, she stared until she heard a man's voice say, "No problem, baby." Then, Mallory's blank stare became a smirk. Alex opened the door and sat down in the front seat.

Mallory was still standing outside of the car when she heard Olive say, "Well, well, well. Look who it is." Before her sentence was complete, Mallory was seated inside the car's cabin.

Alex said, "Mallory, this is Cooper. Cooper, I think you remember Olive."

Excited, he said, "Olive? How the hell are ya? Girl, I wanna get out and give you the biggest hug. I haven't seen you since..."

He was thinking of the year, or maybe the month, but Olive remembered the occasion. "Since we came home from the mall and caught you in bed with Ashley."

Without shame, he said, "Oh shit! I can't believe you went there. Damn, you're still messy." Regaining his composure, he looked quickly in Mallory's direction, "Mallory, is it? Mallory, don't listen to Olive. She's known me since I was a boy. She could probably tell you plenty of things she shouldn't. I'm Cooper."

His large hand was outstretched. He had extended it from the front seat back to her. She leaned forward and shook it. "Nice to meet you," she said. "Olive and I were planning to surprise Alex and take her lunch. We're sorry if we interrupted."

"Hell no. What kinda man would I be if I didn't want the company of three lovely ladies?" Driving now, he glanced over at Alex who sat in the far corner of the passenger's seat. She had her head in her hand and was staring out the window. He looked as if he wanted her to look at him. Aware of his glances, she would not make eye contact. He glanced at her, then the road, then her until he pulled the car in front of a well-recognized Italian restaurant, the place you would take a date for dinner, not a lunch date with an old friend. As the valet opened the doors, Mallory stood up and waited on Olive to emerge.

"So, this is what she was hiding." Mallory said.

"And, there's a damn good reason to hide Cooper."

"What is it? Obviously, they used to date."

"Yeah, he dated her and everyone else he could. Just wait, you'll figure him out."

As they headed into Martinelli's, there was the quiet hum of soft conversations. Mallory remembered when Jacqueline had brought her here.

She remembered the corner table, the laughs, the food, and how wonderful she felt sitting in a wonderful restaurant having a romantic dinner with the person she loved. Marveling in that memory, she flashed forward to Alex being taken here by a former boyfriend while Elet was out of town. "I really feel like Olive and I are interrupting something. I mean, Martinelli's."

"Nothing but the best for my baby doll."

Mallory lifted her eyebrows. She nudged Alex who had been silent all of this time, "You really should've told us that we were intruding on such an obviously special occasion."

"I had no idea we were coming here." Alex said. The maître d'hôtel pulled out the chairs of the women and handed each of them napkins and menus. The party listened as wines and specials were recollected by the waiter. Each ordered something to drink. Mallory asked for a few moments before making a lunch selection. When the waiter left, Alex provided her excuse, "I heard from Cooper only recently. He said he wanted to get together and have lunch and catch up while he was back in town."

"I'm sorry, Cooper. You're going to have to forgive me for asking so many questions, but I didn't know you don't live here?" Mallory asked.

"Oh, no. I grew up in Brandon with Alex and Olive, but I got the hell outta there as soon as I could." He laughed with such force that Mallory watched his burly frame rise and fall.

"Where do you live now?"

"Atl..."Alex started to say.

"I'm in between places right now," Cooper finished.

"Oh, are you thinking of returning to Brandon?" Mallory questioned. Her eyes had started to slim. She wanted to unpack what she felt was certain to be a lie. Cooper stopped speaking when the waiter returned. The waiter distributed the drinks and took their lunch orders. As the waiter was leaving,

Mallory returned to the inquisition. This time, she had a white wine spritzer to her lips and had crossed her legs. "So, you're relocating?"

"I would for the right reason," Cooper grinned.

"Wait a minute, I thought you were married," Olive asked.

"Separated," he said sharply.

"Any kids?" Mallory asked.

"Two boys, Dez and Marcus," he said and took a deep swallow of his rum and coke.

"You'd leave them behind?" Mallory asked. "I have a daughter and I couldn't imagine moving so far away that I couldn't be a part of my child's day to day life."

"I have relationships with all my kids regardless of where I was living."

"Oh, so there's kids from a previous marriage? How many do you have in total?"

"Five."

"Five!" Alex exclaimed.

"Five?" Mallory asked. "So, two with this wife and three with the previous one."

"It's not exactly like that," he chuckled as he took another sip of his drink.

"What's it like?" Alex had folded her arms.

"I've been a busy man. I've made a few relationship mistakes, but I love all my kids. I'm there for all of them. I pay my support. I see them when I can." He explained.

"So, where are the other kids?" Mallory asked as her foot dangled like a worm on a hook.

"Y'all remember Jeanine, don't you?" he asked as he swept his finger between Alex and Olive.

Before he could finish, Olive said, "That baby was yours? I knew it! Told ya, Alex!"

"You swore that you hadn't messed with her. You swore." Alex sounded confused and hurt.

"Listen, baby doll, I was a young man. I had hormones I couldn't explain. I was on the football team. All the girls wanted me. You know that. Tell her Olive."

Leaning towards Mallory, Olive said, "Jeanine was this nasty skank freak in high school. She got pregnant and said it was Cooper's. His dumb ass denied it, but the baby comes out and looks just like him. He was dating Alex when it happened. Supposedly, he wasn't messing around with anyone else. So, when Jeanine tried to tell Alex about all the girls he was messing with, Alex approached Cooper. He denied it. That girl left school." Turning to Cooper, "What happened to her?"

"She gave the boy to her parents and ran off."

"Where's she at now?" Alex asked.

He took a big swig of his drink and said, "Overdosed a few years ago."

"Oh my God. Where's the baby?" Alex asked.

"Jalen's a young man now. He lives with her parents in Brandon."

"But, you're his father. Why didn't you get custody of him when she left?" Mallory pressed.

"Shit. He didn't know me like that. He probably didn't want to leave them. It doesn't matter. He's good. They used to send me pictures and report cards and stuff. I guess that's what the money paid for." That sentence hung in the air as the waiter distributed the food. Alex stared at the salad that was placed in front of her. She was holding her full glass of water. Across from her, Olive began eating immediately. Salad fork in one hand and a breadstick, in the other hand, she hadn't lost her appetite.

Before the waiter left, Mallory ordered another white wine spritzer. Then, she said, "So, then you got married?"

"Yeah, my first wife was Nicole. She was gorgeous. She's the kinda woman who looks good up close and from a distance. She looks good in the morning and at night. She had that good hair, that good body, and that soft voice. But, she only looked good for a few years. I swear, my daughter ruined her. It was like NeNe sucked out all of her beauty. Nicole got angry. She got mean. She wanted to know where I was going and what I was doing. If I had to work late, she and the baby would show up and wait. If I went out of town, this bitch would leave the baby with her mama and check up on me. I'd come in from a conference and she'd be outside my hotel door. That shit was doomed." They watched as he used a breadstick to absorb the roux on his plate.

"Did you only have one daughter with her? NeNe, right?" Mallory inquired.

"Yeah. My NeNe is my only daughter. My baby girl. Her mother, Nicole, a monster." Then, he snarled his face and growled to Olive.

"That's two. And, two with your current wife. There's a kid unaccounted for," Mallory said.

"Devon. I didn't marry his mom. Technically, I was still married to Nicole."

"So, you had an affair?" Alex said.

"It is what he does," Olive said.

"Nah, used to do," he clarified.

"Wait, none of the kids are over eighteen. You're gonna have to pay child support on all of these kids. What do you do for a living?" Mallory asked.

"He's owns a couple of dental practices in Atlanta," Alex added.

"Oh, a dentist. Well, that's a good profession. People always need a dentist. What's the name of the practice? My dad has family up in Atlanta. Maybe, I can send some of them your way." Mallory's wheels were rolling, "Wait, are you selling the practice to relocate here? How does that work?"

"No, I'm not selling anything. I'll probably ask to just relocate to an office down here."

"Oh, so you don't own the practice? You work for a large practice," Mallory said.

"Right. Right. No Cavities Dental."

"I've seen them on TV. Didn't one of them get closed down for pill problems?" Olive asked.

"Yeah, I knew that guy, too. He was framed. Damn shame."

Alex interrupted, "Lemme get this right. You don't own the dental practice. You have got five kids from four women. You don't see most of them. And, soon you aren't gonna see any of them. What are you doing back here?"

"Baby doll, that's what I've been trying to tell you. I had to come here for business, but I knew when I got on that plane that I wasn't just coming here for business. I was coming home. And, when I was sitting there getting my tape up and I saw your article, the light flashed on. It's time to stop chasing all the wrong women and be with the woman of my dreams." He picked up her hand from the table and kissed it.

Alex frowned. Olive giggled. Mallory looked confused. "You do know that she's wearing an engagement ring, right?"

"That ain't nothing. That's just the mistake I'm here to prevent."

Olive laughed audibly. "You are still so full of shit. So, she dated you in high school and you cheated on her. She gave up her scholarship to follow your dumbass to the only college that would accept you. And, you cheated on her repeatedly there. Then, after two years, you just disappeared. No note. No card. You were just gone. We found out that you were kicked out of school for an indiscretion in the library. But, you don't even call to say goodbye. Your parents ship you off to Daytona to live with your grandparents. My dumbass used to drive her dumbass up there to see you and we found out you were engaged to some other girl. Then, you finally graduated and just disappeared to Atlanta. Now, you sit here with these same tired ass lines and your four hundred women and five hundred kids and tell her that she's once again the one baby doll of all baby dolls. That's funny as fuck."

"Olive, I never expected you to understand what we have. You've always been just hanging on her coattails."

"Enough, dammit! Don't you talk to her that way." Alex said as she leaned forward with her finger in his face.

"I'm sorry, baby doll. I was out of line. I'm sorry. But, your friends have put me through the ringer. I've been more than gentlemanly, but how can we expect them to understand the kinda love we have? The kinda love you feel no matter what people think. They just can't understand that."

Mallory laughed, "You have no idea how well I understand that." Alex swatted her with her napkin as Mallory and Olive cackled in unison.

"Baby doll, how are you gonna let them laugh at me? Tell them how much you love me. Tell them how you're gonna dump that punk ass white boy and we're gonna make all our dreams come true." Cooper had reached out for her.

"Andre," she had not called him by his first name in years. "Andre, you were the first man I ever loved. The one that I really thought I wanted. You were exciting. You were popular. The girls did want you. The boys wanted to hang with you. And, I was so happy when I thought that I was your everything. I tried to be your everything, but the truth is..." She paused. She had come to a revelation, "But, the truth is, you never wanted me. You never loved me. I was just one more thing. One more notch. One more girl. The one who took you back and forgave you. The one who was always there for you until you found someone else. Someone better, but, never again." She stood up from the table.

With her right index finger and right thumb holding her engagement ring, she continued, "When you texted me and said you were in town, I wanted to see you. I wanted to introduce you to my boyfriend." She smiled and corrected herself, "My fiancé. I wanted to see the two of you together, but he's out of town. He's gone to get the arch for our wedding, so, no, I'm not gonna dump him. I'm gonna marry him next month. And, I'll be sure to send your invitation to your parent's house." Then, she turned and walked away.

"You'll be back. You always come back," he said as she walked away.

Olive stood, smiled at him, and said, "It was great to see you, Cooper. Good luck."

Mallory stood from the table and reached for her purse. She removed her wallet and left fifty dollars on the table. "Dr. Andre Cooper. Cooper. Well, it's been a pleasure. If you come to the wedding, make sure you find me. I would love to introduce you to my girlfriend." And out she walked.

Outside, Alex was leaning against the glass of the restaurant. Olive and Mallory were celebrating as if they had won an Olympic medal. Eventually, they noticed Alex being supported by the side of a restaurant. Olive said, "Alex, are you okay?"

"Yeah, I just feel a little sick."

"Well, I'm sure that was pretty emotional."

"No, not from him. There really wasn't anything. I wanted to tell you guys that he had reached out to me, but I didn't think you'd believe me that I just wanted to see him, not sleep with him. I just wanted to see him. You know, I always wanted that fool to want me. I never figured out why he didn't. I spent years collecting other men's opinions. Plenty of other men have wanted me. Why didn't he ever?"

"Some people just aren't right for us," Mallory said as she shrugged her shoulders.

"Don't sweat it," Olive said as she perched beside her.

"He's really a loser, huh?"

Olive laughed, "Hell yeah, he is."

"Thanks for being there. Thanks. I'm really glad you forced lunch on me." She laughed.

"That's what we do," Mallory smiled.

As reality returned to her, Olive said, "Wait, he drove us here. How are we getting back to your work?"

Chapter 17

Jacqueline and Elet had spoken only briefly during the last leg of the drive. She was reclined in the passenger's seat, but she was not asleep. Her eyes stared blankly outside the passenger's side window. She had thought of trying to speak to Elet. She wanted to face him and say the things that had bubbled up in her mind these last few months; but after all that had happened today, she was not sure how or where to begin. Lying there, she thought of what a mess she had made. She thought of the things that were said, the accusations, but more importantly, she thought about the realizations. She had no idea how to undo the damage, but she knew she had no choice.

Elet had exited the interstate thirty minutes ago. He had not asked any navigational advice. He had not asked the name or the location of the hotel. He had turned this way and that way. He had steered through late evening traffic. He had commanded the truck to their destination without need for conversation or direction. Jacqueline had forgotten how independent and resourceful he was. In recent years, life had changed. He was no longer a press photographer just heading to the next story. His work has been selected by the AP wire enough that he was a freelance photographer. Now, he chose jobs, subjects, and locations based upon what interested him. He had won awards and prizes. He had had layouts in national and international magazines. He had written pieces for blogs and been interviewed on podcasts. At the same time, he'd continued exploring his hobbies. He had painted, sold graphic art designs, and matted and sold photos taken while working. It had paid off. His works were being recognized by the local studios and galleries. He had an upcoming multimedia show in Miami after the wedding. He had settled into new roles that allowed him to be more artistic and, in turn, he had become communicative, more engaging. She had forgotten that this had been a transformation. That he was once more introverted and isolated, but, now, he was an artist, a businessman, and a leader.

When he parked in the hotel parking lot, he leaned forward and gazed up at the building. Unlike the oceanfront structure in Myrtle Beach, this time they sat in a parking that looked like they had stepped back in time. He admired the palatial look of the hotel. He snatched his duffel bag from the back of the truck and went toward the hotel without her. Noticing that she was being left, she jumped from the truck and trotted to catch up to him. She dared not to speak. She enjoyed that after this long journey that he was enjoying staring up at the building. When they entered the lobby, he stopped and gazed around the building's entryway. It was dramatic. With marble columns lining the path from the doors to the hotel check-in desk, the entrance spoke of grandeur. He examined the ceiling. It had to be twenty feet high, maybe higher. It was adorned with stained glass and skylights. Allowing his eyes to travel back to eye level, he walked over and touched the sculpted relief on the walls. He noticed the glints of light upon them. Searching for the source, he admired the glass chandeliers that were overhead. She did not speak nor did she follow. She waited on him to turn around to her, to remember the closeness they'd shared.

And, he did. "This wasn't some building built to be a hotel. This was something else prior." He did not say this next to her. He was standing against the wall inspecting the ferns that sat in large marble pots between the columns.

"Yep, I read it was the headquarters of a railroad company. I think it was built in the early 1900s."

"Gilded Age."

"Yeah, I think that's what it said." She knew it was the Gilded Age. She had done her research about the hotel, but she was so happy that he was talking to her that she pretended to not know.

"The time when the captains of industry and commerce went to Europe and returned home to pay homage to their wealth by rebuilding the classics of the Western cultural heritage here. American architecture changed from being simplistic to ornate. Buildings weren't just functional, they were beautiful." She twisted her lips and cocked her head as if to thank him for the information. Proud of himself, he replied, "Bachelors in Architecture."

She smiled, "I remembered. I thought that you might like this."

He returned to her, "I do. I really do, but now, I know for sure that you're trying to get with me."

He laughed and she laughed. It was nice to just have laughter between them. The day had been so long. Things felt off kilter in both their lives. A laugh numbed the pain. She checked them in and they navigated to one of the two sweeping staircases rather than taking the elevator. From there, they meandered through the hotel staring out the floor to ceiling windows at the

Inner Harbor Waterfront. It was almost eight in the evening. As she passed the glimpses of the outside world, her mind traveled back and she thought she could see the gas lights that would have lined the harbor in the early twentieth century. After a few minutes, they came upon a corridor and were forced to take the elevator.

With the doors closed, she asked, "I'd like for you to meet me, and only me, back downstairs in a half hour. Will you?"

"I'm hungry. I was going to meet you anyways, but that was a really good line. You should save it for someone you've got a chance with." She laughed and the elevator doors opened. Based on the arrows, her room and his room were at opposite ends of the floor. Each turned and went in search of their room.

Having been the one to reserve the rooms, she wondered what he thought of his. Her room was not going to be a surprise. It was the Mediterranean Suite. It had rich dark colors with appropriately matching rich, dark fabrics. At almost six hundred feet, it was a huge expanse for one night, but she had wanted them to each enjoy the night. The marble bathroom had a separate walk-in shower from its soaking tub. When she opened the door, she was delighted to see clean linens and open space. She unpacked a few things and jumped in for a quick shower. Desperately, she tried to wash away all of her emotions, but they clung to her like the steam hung in the air. Looking at her clothes, dirty and blood-stained, she balled them up and placed them in the trash can. There was no need to save them, to take them home, and think that they could ever be clean again.

As she redressed, she put on a shirt that Mallory had bought for her while they were on Seaborn Island over the summer. Smiling, she sent her a text,

Jacqueline: The little stuff reminds me of you. Isn't that funny?

Mallory: No. Everything reminds me of you.

Jacqueline: Just checked into the hotel in Baltimore. Took a quick shower.

Mallory: Alone?

Jacqueline: Of course. I'm going to run downstairs and eat dinner with Elet. Then, come back up to the room and talk to you until you doze off. Okay?

Mallory: Okay, baby.

~~~~~~~~

Then, quickly, she headed downstairs to meet him, but, this time, he beat her. The bar was decorated with plush couches of different prints. The walls were adorned in sheets of gold relief. There was a fireplace flickering in the center. He sat in a dark table far off in the corner. "I'm glad you found me. I was wondering if I should text." He leaned back in his chair. "This place is amazing. My room has this dark blue blanket. It's super thick. I wanted to curl up in it and tell you I wasn't coming down."

Chuckling, she said, "Well, I didn't expect that."

"I went ahead and ordered a couple of drinks and a couple of appetizers."

"Cool." She was uncomfortable tonight. She was never uncomfortable with him, but, after everything that happened, it was to be expected. She just didn't like how it felt. She had to say something. She had to clear her mind or she was going to erupt. "Let me say something and don't interrupt me." She held her hand up as if it could stop words from coming out of his mouth. "I knew you first. You are my best friend. Now and always. And, when I'm out with Alex, I always respect your relationship. I do my best to help her steer clear of trouble, because when I am with her, I do think of you. Now, I know that last night you wondered if that was true, but it is. It really is. Your worst fears haven't been realized. It's not wild orgy where anything goes." She stopped speaking as the food and drinks came.

He was quiet for a bit as the waitress placed the food in front of them. While making himself a plate, he said, "I know. And, you are my best friend and you shouldn't have to be on watch like that. I have to trust her. I can't expect for her to travel with a guardian." He stopped talking to eat a potato skin. Chewing, he went on, "And, I shouldn't have lost my temper like that. I'm sorry. I mean, I can't believe what happened today. I can't get it out of my mind." She waved him off. "Hear me out. I love her. I've loved her even when everyone tells me to break it off with her. There's no argument. They aren't changing my mind. This isn't up for a vote. Despite everything, I still want to marry her. When we're together, I feel like we're the only two people alive. But, there's no reason to lie. When she leaves me I wonder if I'm enough, if my love's enough."

"You're more than enough. Her need for attention is just that. It has nothing to do with you."

"But, it could. It could. What if one day someone else's attention is better than mine?"

"There's no answer for that for anyone of us." She sat back in her seat and thought about what she had said. After a few minutes of silence, she elaborated, "I don't know. I guess it's a gamble. It takes constant work, constant attention, and it's still out of your control. But, when it's good, there's nothing better."

"You're probably right," he said and chomped on his jerky. "But, listen, I gotta ask you something." He wiped his hands and cleaned his face on this napkin. Then, leaning back in his chair, with his foot on her chair, he asked, "Jacqueline, what're we doing here?"

"What? I thought you liked it."

"I love the hotel, but why're we here? We left home to drive to Baltimore to pick up a wedding arch that you coulda had transported to Tampa. What are you running from?"

"I'm not running from anything."

"We've been friends for a long time. I've told you crazy shit through the years. And, you've blown me away with some of your shit. So, talk to me. What's going on? Are you over this thing with Mallory?"

"No. No, I'm not."

"Then, you're being an asshole." He removed his foot from her chair and went back to eating. "She's given up everything to be with you. She's changed her entire life. And, it can't have been easy. I mean, I don't know what it's like to have to tell your friends and family that you're in love with someone who is the same sex as you, but I damn sure know what it's like to say that you love a girl who is another race than you. I don't care what people say." There was Ranch dressing on his fingertips and he was licking it off. "It takes people some time to get used to new stuff. Even if, the new thing is something that's always all around them. My mom was always okay. Silas made it all a joke, but Reese had a hard time with it." He filled his mouth with pizza, but he went on, "Now, I know things have changed for you, too. And, it looks like you're thriving in it, but, from what I hear, your secretive shit is driving her crazy. But, I know you. There's always a plan. You're always thinking something. So, here we are. It's time to fess up. What the hell is going on?"

She took a slice of his flatbread pizza. Chewing it slowly and sipping her drink, she huffed. "Things have changed for me, too."

"I know."

"I've shared my world with them. All of it."

"It's not the penthouse or the Laredo that she wants shared with her. You keep people at arm's length. You're around them. You're in the room." He encircled the room with his greasy fingertips. "They think they know you, but there's so much about you that they've got no idea about. I don't know how I got to know as much as I do, but you better tell her something or you're gonna lose her. There's a woman and her kid waiting on you to stop fucking around."

She slammed the table, but then, spoke in an angry whispered tone, "I'm not fucking around! I'm with them every night. I haven't gone anywhere."

"Yeah, you're with them. You're with them the way you are with everyone else. You make them feel okay without really saying anything. And, when they ask you a question about something real, you clam up, make a joke, or just push away. They think it's because you don't care. Do you realize that? Do you realize that most people think that you're avoiding real shit, because you don't care?" His words stayed in the space between them. She looked at him and breathed loudly and deeply. Instantly, she discredited what he had said in her mind, then his glaring eyes kept repeating it over and over until she started to think about it. Just when she was ready to fold, he finished his thought, "And, now, you've gone and left. You've been right there with them until shit got thick. Then, you up and hauled ass. You and I left and went to Baltimore for four days," he said. "I'm not saying you don't love her. I think you do. I've never seen you this way, but what I don't understand is why don't you talk to her?"

"I dunno. It feels like...boasting." He laughed. "I'm serious. You're telling me that Alex knows all about your college years? Time in the Peace Corps? Where you went? What you've seen? She knows about field work?

She knows about the photographs? The awards? The money? You've told her everything?"

Haughtily, he said, "I've told her most of it."

"Well, then, you're better than me. I haven't told her anything. I'm scared to sit down and tell her everything. I'm scared. Is that okay?

"Scared of what? Scared that she'll know you've got a mini-fortune? Scared you've got a plan for a future you could make happen?"

"Scared of plenty of stuff. People always think nothing scares me, that nothing bothers me anymore. But, that's ridiculous. Of course, I'm still scared of things, worried about things. I don't want to seem over the top. I don't want to seem like it's too much. My life is complicated."

Chuckling, he said, "Bullshit. You've lived up in that secret lair for too long by yourself. Your life isn't complicated. You've pushed everything out. Some of those girls weren't bad. You just didn't want to invest in them. And, hell, that's okay, but this girl is in. You hear me?" He smashed the tip of his pointing finger against the tabletop. "She's already in. You let her come in. You wanted her in. Your secret lair is crumbling. You can either push her out and rebuild your walls or you can open that shit up."

"It's not a secret lair," she uttered.

"Is, too. It has its own elevator. A secret elevator." He laughed. She laughed, too. "I know you have something to lose. Don't we all?" Shaking his head, he said, "I swear you've got a lot more to lose if you just watch her walk away. You've got more with her than you have ever had in your whole pathetic life." He knew when to pause and let her digest. He sat back in his chair and drank some of his beer. Peeling her back, slowly, he asked, "Does she know about your five-year plan?"

"No, does Alex know yours?"

"Can we just make it to the altar first?" He quipped. Turning his head to wipe his mouth, he glanced outside. Rain had caught up to them in Maryland. He thought of the dog. He shook his head to push the image from his mind. Looking at the falling rain, he spoke to her, "What's it, again? Hit your magical number and you disappear. Are you still going to resign? Or, did all of that change now that they've come into your life? I think you want them to be a part of your life, a part of your future. If I'm right, then she has to know what you'd like to do. You can't just plan shit in a vacuum and think she'll always be cool with it. You've gotta tell her where you want to head and see if she wants to go, too."

"What if she doesn't?"

"Then, the two of you figure it out together or you walk away from her." Jacqueline looked up at him in shock. "That looks says you don't want to lose her."

"You still nervous about Alex?" she changed the subject.

"Every day," he said quietly as he watched the rain fall.

"What are you gonna do?"

He looked at her. He cracked his own neck. He was looking at her, but looking past her. As if he was talking to himself, he whimpered, "I'm gonna have to talk to her. Just like you're gonna have to talk to Mallory."

"Then, what?" she asked him. She wanted his answer as much as she was searching for her own answer.

"Then," he took another long swig of his beer. "We," pointed to her and then back to himself, "are gonna give it every fucking thing we've got."

"And, if it doesn't work out?"

He looked around the room. He stared at the fabric lined walls. He closed his eyes and listened to the fireplace. He looked at the men and women who had filled the bar but sat quietly among themselves without intrusion. He smiled back at her and said, "If it doesn't work out, we'll relocate to Baltimore."

She smiled. Half-knowing, he was teasing, but half-calmed in the notion that he had a plan. They did not speak on the subject of relationships anymore that evening. They sat in the bar and enjoyed talking. Talking about house renovations. Talking about traveling. Talking about the honeymoon and the wedding gift he'd picked out for Alex. The elephant had left the room. And, life at that bar, in that moment, was fine. That was all the goodness she could desire.

Chapter 18

Elet stumbled down the hallway and back into his room. He would have passed out across the bed, but his phone beckoned. It was a text message from Reese asking how the trip was going. He had hoped it was Alex. Realizing that they'd spoken only briefly, he called her. The phone rang and rang. Waiting, he started to become angry thinking that she was not going to answer. He feared that his call would go to voicemail. It did not; right before the last ring before voicemail triggered, she answered.

"Hey, sexy," she said.

"Hey, you," Elet was tired and slightly drunk. The day was weighing on him.

"Are you okay?" she asked.

"Of course, I'm always okay. I'm Okay Elet. You should start calling me that."

"Sounds like someone has been drinking," she said.

"Not that much."

"Doesn't take much anymore."

He grinned, "I remember when we first met. Do you?"

"Of course, I do."

"Jacqueline and I had gone out. I had been out of town on a project. We went out to catch up. Who goes to a bar to catch up?" He posed the question, but answered before she could reply. "Stupid us. That's who. We were sitting at a bar having some food and a few drinks. What the hell was the name of that place?"

"Hooligans."

"Yeah, that was it. It was an Irish place. We should go back there."

"We can't. They went out of business."

"Aw, Really? We should've gone the last night they were open. We could have had one more night there." Then, he was silent.

"Honey?" she thought he might have passed out.

He hadn't passed out. He was thinking of the restaurant. He was remembering the dark bar and the fluorescent signs. "Oh. Yeah. Jacqueline was sitting on one end of the corner and I was sitting on the other. I saw her looking over my head at someone coming towards us. I assumed it was some girl she was interested in. I told her something. Something funny, but she didn't laugh. So, I got pissed off, because I knew that she wasn't listening. But, I went on anyways. I kept telling her about this date that I had been on a few days before."

"I didn't know you were talking about some other girl the night we met."

"Yeah, people find me attractive."

"I know they do, baby."

"So, she's not listening. So, I look to see who she's looking at. And, there's this woman heading our way. The woman's looking down at her nails. She's wearing a white dress with a big, brown belt and really thick shoes."

"It was a sash and I was wearing wedges."

"Whatever. And, I'm thinking this girl is gorgeous. She's just whizzing through the crowd. People are moving outta her way. She's touching people as she passes by them. They're just parting the way for her to pass by them and checking her out after she goes by. Now, I'm staring at her. Then, I think Jacqueline is also staring at her. Well, shit, we'd never had that problem before. Rarely. I mean, we never really wanted to talk to the same girl. So, I was deciding if I wanted to talk to the girl first or if I was gonna let Jacqueline try and if she failed, I thought I'd take a chance at it."

"Never be runner-up, baby."

"So, I turn to Jacqueline and I say, 'she's not even your type.' And, she laughs and says that the girl isn't her type and that she'll be my wingman and get the girl to notice me. So, I sit up tall on the stool." He sat up tall in his bed. "I ran my fingers through my hair. Remember, it was longer back then. I check out my teeth in the mirror over the bar. I turn around on the stool just in time to make eye contact with the girl. I look at her and smile. She looks back and me and winks, but she doesn't stop. She rounds the bar towards Jacqueline. Jacqueline speaks and the girl speaks back. She knows Jacqueline. And, I'm excited on the inside. Jacqueline introduces me to the girl. She says something like, 'This is my buddy, Elet. Keep him company while I run to the restroom.' She stands up and gives the girl her stool. And, I think that I should have done that."

"Then, she heads to the bathroom, but she never comes back. She left us there to talk."

"And, we talked all night. We laughed and joked. We played pool. You told me that you just started working at the paper with her. I told you that I used to work there. As the bar started to close, I asked for your number and you take a napkin off the table and get a pen from your purse and write down your number. The lights come on and the jukebox goes off. And, you're just standing there smiling at me. And, you said 'What now' and I said, 'I'll take you home and call you tomorrow.' You said, you had your car. Then, I laughed and had to admit I rode with Jacqueline who had just left me stranded. And you said..."

"I think she did it on purpose," she interrupted.

"Yeah. That's what you said. And, you took me home."

"You called me the next morning. And, the rest is history," she said.

"I loved you. Right then. You were smart and funny. You could hold a really good conversation. You were great."

"I was?" she teased.

"Still are. I know why all the other men want to talk to you. They see what I saw that night. I know why they want to get your number and keep talking to you. They want to feel like I did when you answered my call the next day. I really do understand." Silence, he stopped talking and she said nothing. "I'm not saying I don't understand. But, I've been thinking. I've been driving up to Baltimore to get a wedding arch for our wedding. It's in a couple of weeks, now. When I'm standing there promising a bunch of things to you, I just want you to promise me one thing."

She started to shake. Scared of what he was going to say, she gathered her courage and asked, "What's that?"

"Promise me I'll be the only man in your life."

"You are," she said quietly.

"I'm not. They're everywhere. Everywhere. And, you like that, but I don't. I mean, I'm proud when men stop to stare at my girlfriend. I am."

"I like when girls look at my boyfriend."

"But, I don't even know they're there. I'm looking for you and I see you looking at some other man. You don't send them away. You like the attention, but it kills me. Do you know how many people tell me not to marry you? They think you're cheating on me. They think I could do better. They tell me I deserve better. It goes on and on."

"Do you think I'm cheating on you?" He chuckled and it infuriated her. "What's funny?"

"That's an interesting question, isn't it? Cheating on me. Are you having sex with someone else? Are you confiding in someone else? Are leading other guys on? Are you acting in ways when I'm not around that you wouldn't act if I was? Are you thinking of being with someone else? Aren't all of those cheatin'?"

"Elet, what are you asking me?"

"Fuck if I know. All I know is I feel like all of you have confused my love for weakness. And, I'm not weak."

"I know that you aren't weak. You're the strongest, most interesting person..."

"Don't compliment me. Listen to me. I'm a man. I'm not some fool. I'm a human fuckin' being..." His voice trailed off. "I know you're out there flirting. I know men give you their numbers. I don't know what you do with them. We're like a month from getting married. I got a house for us to live in together as a couple. I want to spend the rest of my life with you. I don't want you to change who you are. I don't want you to dress different or change your job or change your personality. I want you to be the woman I met in Hooligans bar that night, but I won't marry you if I'm not enough to keep you."

"Oh, Elet, you're more than enough for me."

"But, I'm not," he wanted to say more, but he felt his heart in his throat. His eyes and head felt full. He was starting to heat up.

"You are. You're all that I need and I'm sorry if I ever let you feel any other way. I want to marry you. Only you. I'm serious. I know I've made mistakes along the way. I know I've been selfish, but you've got nothing to worry about. I'll be a perfect wife."

"I don't need perfect. I just need...faithful," he barely squeezed those words out.

"I'm sorry you feel like you've gotta say all of this to me. I'm sorry, it's not a given. But, I'll make damn sure you start feeling it. Okay?"

Sitting up on the edge of his bed, he cleared his throat. With his head in his hands, he sniffled and said, "Okay." He glanced around the room. Walking to the window to look out at the harbor, he muttered, "I wish you were here. It's an incredible room. I mean, really."

"Is it?" she was holding back her own tears.

"Yeah, I'm standing here staring at the Baltimore Harbor. In a room with a big tub and a separate shower. It's amazing. You'd love this place." He stopped talking and watched a couple outside their window. The man walked beside the woman, but each was staring at their cellphones. Neither looked at each other or the harbor or the hotel. "You should come."

"You want me to come to Baltimore?"

"Can you?"

"Maybe. Do you really want me to just come up there for the day or two?"

"More than anything."

She rubbed her head. "Okay, baby. I'll be there. I'll figure it out. Are you okay? Are we okay?"

"Yeah. It'll all be fine, right?"

"Of course, it will. Why don't you get some rest? I need to make some reservations."

"Then, you're gonna go to bed?"

"Probably. I might call Mallory, first, but I'll be going to bed soon."

"Okay. Sleep well. I love you," and he hung up the phone.

Still holding her phone, she noticed that he had hung up, but she breathed, "We love you, too," and then, she wept.

~~~~~~~~~

When Jacqueline entered her room, she went straight to the restroom. Standing in front of the oversized mirror under the fluorescent lights, she thought of Mallory. She thought of what Elet had said to her today and the things that he had been saying over these last few weeks. It made sense. It all made sense. She was avoiding having conversations with Mallory about the future, but everyone was wrong. It was never that she did not want a relationship with her. It was the fear of being wrong. She stared at herself. She stared at her closely cropped black hair that was slowly graying. She stared at her face and the start of the lines. She snickered when she wondered if this is what Alex did alone in her bathroom. She shook off her emotions and headed into the shower.

She stood under the running water hoping to get away from all that haunted her, but her thoughts followed her. She thought back over the last few months. She thought of all that had changed in her life and how it could never be as it was. She did not want it to be. As usual, she exited the shower with more resolve than when she entered it. Quickly, she dressed and reached for her phone.

"Hi, there," she said with eagerness in her voice.

Unfortunately, she found a tired girlfriend answered, "Hi, yourself. You sound like you're having fun."

"Actually, today was a horrible day. I was thinking of you in the shower and I was excited when you picked up."

"Perv," Mallory said and exhaled.

"What's wrong?"

"Nothing, it's been a long day. Zoe got sick at school, so my mom..."

"What? What happened? Why didn't you call me?"

"Call you?"

"Yes! Why didn't you call me?"

"Well, you're in Baltimore." Left hook to Jacqueline's stomach. It hurt so bad that she straightened up in the chair waiting to hear more information. "She's fine. She threw up, again."

"Maybe, we should take her to a doctor. A specialist. We need to get to the bottom of this."

Mallory giggled. "No need. Turns out little Zoe has a stash of candy in her backpack. She's been taking it off the secretary's desk and eating it whenever she pleased."

"Geez."

"She's fine. My mom picked her up. She was gonna spend the weekend with my folks, anyhow. There's no school til Tuesday."

"This isn't a holiday."

"It's a holiday for the teachers. Anyhow, I'm over here getting clothes to take to my parent's house."

"They hate me..." She mumbled.

"They don't hate you. They're just worried about me."

"Worried? Am I a monster?"

"Nope, you're not a monster. You're just not tied down."

Zing! The uppercut to the chin hurt Jacqueline worse than the left hook. "I'm not tied down?"

"You know, no kids. No long-term relationships."

Straight jab to the eye. She leaned back. The world went dark. She thought of putting her head between her knees. Mallory had no idea how this hurt her. "Well." She could not think of anything else to say.

"Well?"

"Is that how you feel, too?" There was silence. Jacqueline could no longer hear her stirring about in the room. She could not hear the drawers opening and closing. She could not sense any movement at all. "Mallory, did I lose you? Are you there?"

"I'm here."

"Did you hear what I said?"

"Yes," Mallory said.

"And?"

"And, what?"

Jacqueline pressed, "Do you think I'm unreliable and unstable?"

"No."

"Then, what took you so long to answer me?"

"Do we have to get into this?" Mallory was rubbing her forehead.

"Into what?"

"I can't play this game with you tonight. It's been a long day. I still have to drive to my parents, and, then figure out where I'm gonna sleep tonight. I don't want to try to have a conversation with you that leaves me in tears and you telling me that everything's going great."

And, that was it. The knockout blow. Those where her own words. That is what she had been saying whenever there appeared to be the need for a real conversation. As Mallory repeated her words back to her, they felt hollow; she felt hollow. She had not really meant them. She was uncertain where the conversation was headed and so, she always deflected it with that line. Then, she held Mallory close and soothed her. Soothed her. Soothed her. Jacqueline thought about that over and over again. "I'm sorry."

"About what?"

"Nothing." She bit her lip. "Do you have plans for the weekend?"

"Nope," she sighed again. "It'll just be me and a good book. I think I may get together with Alex and Olive, but I don't know."

"Why don't you dump them and come to Baltimore? I think we need to talk and I'd rather not do this over the phone." Silence again. Jacqueline moved her eyes from one side of her head to the other as if she could see Mallory if she strained them far enough. "Mallory? Honey?"

Deep breath, "I'm here. You want me to come to Baltimore, so we can talk?"

"Yes."

"And, you only decided that after I told you that Zoe was at my parents through Tuesday?"

"Kinda. I mean, it's the kinda thing we shouldn't talk about in front of her."

"Yeah. Well, I'm sure I could get an afternoon or late morning flight out."

"I'm already checking. Looks like there's a flight that'd get you here about two thirty. Want me to book it?"

"You know, I can reserve my own flight. I can pay for my own flight. I make money. And, I have a job."

"I know. I was..."

"You were what?"

"I don't know. I was just gonna reserve it for you."

"And pay for it? And pay for Elet's hotel and his food and gas? How much has all of this been?"

"I didn't pay for all the gas and food. And, I prearranged the hotel. I made him come up here. And, you're my girlfriend and I asked you to come up here, so it seemed like the least I could do."

"You want me to come up there, so we can talk. I'll reserve it and pay for it myself."

"Wait. Don't be upset. I wasn't beckoning you. I wanted to see you. I wanted you to come up here. I wanted us to be alone, so we could talk about things."

"Okay, but I'll still pay my own way."

"If it'll make you feel better," Jacqueline relented.

"It will. I need to get off the phone. I have a bunch of things to do. I will see you tomorrow."

"I love you. I will be there to get you. Just let me know when."

"I love you, too. I'll reserve the two thirty. Thank you," then, she hung up and cried.

Chapter 19

Early the next morning, Elet awoke. Tired and hungover, he drug himself into the bathroom and stared at his unshaved face. He thought, *I should shave before Alex arrives.* Then, the night came back to him. *Did I give her an ultimatum? Did she agree? Was I drunk? Did I ask her to come up here? Did I tell Jacqueline?* All at once, those questions flooded into his pounding head. They were supported by a chorus of *Fuck, Fuck, Fuck.* He went in search of his cellphone. It was tangled in the covers where he had been lying. Alex had text in the night.

Alex: I hope you're asleep. You sounded pretty out of it. I wonder if you'll even remember we spoke. Or what we spoke about. You told me about how I've hurt you and how ppl think you shouldn't marry me. I'm sorry for all the pain I've caused. I really am, but I wont let it happen anymore. Please don't listen to them. You're the only man I want. I swear and I'll spend the rest of my life proving that to you. I got a flight. I get there at 230. Don't leave me at the airport. I luv you.

He called Jacqueline.

"Elet, it's like eight." Jacqueline said as she rubbed her eyes. "We said we'd go to the port later and check out the arch. Did you forget?"

"No, I didn't forget. Alex's comin'."

"Coming here?" She was awake, now.

"Yeah, here! I called her last night."

"While you were drunk?" She sat upright in the bed. As she reached for her glasses, she asked, "Oh, shit, Elet. What'd you say?"

"Apparently, I said it all."

"What all?"

"Everythin' I've been thinkin',"

"And, she's still coming?"

"Yeah, it must've worked. Listen to this text she sent me," and he read it to her.

"Well, that sounds good. What're you worried about?"

"What if I didn't mean it? What if I was mean to her? What if I hurt her or said something I shouldn't have?"

"Elet," she sighed. "I don't think that's in you. I'm sure you spoke from your heart." He did not respond, so she continued, "If you had upset her, the text would've been worse, right?"

"Right," he agreed.

"Right. Maybe, you've turned a corner." He was silent. She thought she'd change the subject. She admitted, "I talked to Mallory, too."

"How'd it go?"

"I'm not so sure."

"What?" She sensed that he had sat up in his bed.

"Yeah, I called last night to talk to her and found out that Zoe got sick at school. Do you know she didn't even bother to tell me? I guess I'm not such a good catch after all." And, with a sigh, she fell back upon the bed.

"She said that?"

"Not to me, but her parents said it. And, the way she sounded, I bet she didn't disagree."

"That doesn't sound like her at all..." He tried to reassure her.

Interrupting him, she went on, "So, I tried to talk to her, but she didn't want to talk. She said she was busy getting clothes for Zoe to spend the weekend with her parents. I figured that since Zoe would be out of town and she had no plans, then she should come up here, so we could talk..."

"Yeah," he paused, "that kinda sounds like you wanna breakup."

"Yeah, she definitely took it that way. I tried to explain that wasn't what I meant, but I don't think she believed me."

"Who would, Captain Secrets?"

"So, I don't even know what to say or do." She rustled around in the bed. With the phone to her face, she rolled from one side to the other. Then defeated, she told him, "Elet, I don't want to lose her."

"Then, it's time to open up. It's time to tell her anything and everything. It's time to talk about the five-year plan, relationships, and what you want."

"Yeah, I know."

"That didn't sound convincing. Don't you know what you want?"

"I know what I want."

"Then, why'd you sound like that?"

"I dunno. I've been thinking about what I want a lot. I think about it all the time. When we are driving places or talking to people or hanging out, I think. I'm always thinking about our future together. Then, last night, I realized I never tell her. She doesn't even know, so what if she doesn't want it?"

"Dammit! You've gotta be kidding me. She's out on a limb with her kid waiting on you. She wants it. She thinks you don't."

"But I do. But, what if I get it and one of us don't want it? I mean, what if it doesn't last?"

"What if me and Alex don't last?" Neither of them said anything. Then, Elet said, "'member last night?"

"Yeah." Last night was a blur, but she thought she should agree.

"If it doesn't work out, then we move to Baltimore. We sell it all and just come here. We start over."

"Deal," she said. She remembered that conversation. Lying on her back in bed, replaying the prior night's conversation in her head made her smile. Then, she remembered, "Mallory gets in at two thirty. When does Alex get here?"

"Same time. I bet they're on the same flight. Do you think they know it?"

"Absolutely. They've all talked about us by now. Alex to Olive. Olive to Mallory. Mallory to Paige. Paige to Alex. Alex to Mallory. Olive to Paige."

"Don't forget Jo. She's in there somewhere."

Getting out of bed, she said, "Let's go to the port at one, and then, we'll swing by and pick them up."

"Can you patch things up by dinnertime? Maybe, we can all go out. My treat."

"I hope there's nothing to patch up."

"Oh, you're gonna have some patching and a lot of talking to do. A lot of talkin'. You've been hiding for too long."

"Gees," she said and hung up the phone. She spent the rest of the morning in her room, biting her nails, and trying to plan the biggest conversation of her life.

~~~~~~~~

The Port of Baltimore was only five minutes southeast of the hotel. They could've ridden public transit if they weren't heading to the airport afterward. Getting to the Port was simple, navigating around the Port in search of their terminal proved to be quite the challenge. After half an hour of searching on their own, then another forty-five minutes following the advice of twelve people, they found Dundalk Marine Terminal and the Ports America Packaging. Having called for directions so often, Frank, the Equipment Control Manager, was walking to the truck before Elet turned it off. As they parked and exited the truck, he stopped and waited.

"Thanks for sending us a selfie," Jacqueline said.

"No problem, folks. Glad we gotcha here. Let's go see your baby." Wearing a gray and yellow zippered suit and a yellow hard hat, Frank led them through a maze of containers.

Walking through the rows and rows of containers, Jacqueline felt lost. Left then right then straight then left then right. She wondered if they were lost. "How do you know which one is ours?"

"That's my job," Frank rifled off. From behind, his frame seemed thin, but when he turned to face them, there was a sizable stomach. As he walked ahead of them, Elet wobbled from side to side mocking Frank. Trying to hold her laughter, Jacqueline slapped him on his back.

"Almost there, Frank?" Elet asked after following him for fifteen minutes.

"Right around this corner." When they turned the corner, there was a clearing. In front of them sat half of a container, there was no metal top like all the others. Instead, there was a combination of pulleys and ropes that held a thick, black plastic in place. Frank held his arm out like a mother holding her children in the car when braking, and said, "Hang back a second while my guys open 'er up."

First, the bungees were released. They fell to the ground with such force that tiny pieces of gravel and dust floated into the air. Then, the pulleys were removed. With a clank, they swung down against the sides of the container. Then, one of the men in gray jumpsuits drove over a machine. With a claw on its end, it lifted off the plastic. There, in the maze of containers in the Baltimore port, there was an unveiling. Before they could see wood, they could smell wood. Crafted from koa wood on the Big Island of Hawaii and shipped to Maryland, it smelled of moisture, of soil, of Hawaii. It stood within its structure and radiated in its natural array of colors when fully exposed. The workmen who had unveiled it stopped and stared. They walked around its exterior, stood up against the container, and looked up at the slats overhead.

"Damn it, man. I thought it's was gonna be a two post arch. Four posts tops, but this thing's not an arch at all. This is like a damn gazebo," Elet said.

"More of an arched pergola," Frank corrected.

Concerned, Jacqueline said, "Do you like it?"

"I... love it. I don't know how I could ever..."

"You just did," she said as she blinked away her tears.

"This thing's a gift?" Frank asked.

"Yes, he's my best friend and he and his bride will get married underneath it next month."

"You're a helluva friend," Frank said.

"Not always," she responded.

"How the hell am I gonna get this thing home?" Elet walked toward it for a closer inspection.

Frank and Jacqueline followed. "Don't worry, son. It disassembles. We'll show you how to dissemble and reassemble it. You can do it yourself if you've got some friends. It's not hard." Elet stood next to one of the posts. Jacqueline stood across from him. Each ran their hand along it. It was smooth and cool to the touch. Jacqueline was pointing out the different patterns when Frank spoke. "The spirit of the volcano."

"Excuse me," Jacqueline had not understood him but knew he'd said something.

"Koa wood comes in the largest variety of colors and patterns. This one's called a curly pattern. They say the patterns and the color spectrum exist, because the volcano's spirit is in the tree which, of course, translates into the lumber."

"I like the sound of that," Elet said. As he walked around the structure, the workmen began to show him documents and features. They opened the container and the men stepped inside. Elet stood under the structure with a smile on his face. He rubbed against the posts. He pushed against them. He inspected the construction and lightning.

Jacqueline left Elet to discuss the construction with the workmen. She walked closer to Frank. Standing further away, she smiled and thought of home. Her bed and her front doors were made of the same koa but of the curved pattern. She thought of having bedroom furniture made, but her mind halted and her thoughts filled with one word, *Mallory.* She laughed.

"What was that about?" Frank asked.

"Sorry, I was just thinking."

"Oh, don't let me forget." He went to the container and extracted a large metal box. It had been harnessed inside the container. He unlocked the box and pushed it to where she was standing. He removed a key from his key chain and used a code on the invoice to open the electronic panel that was on the side of the metal box. Once the code was entered, the box beeped. Frank opened the door. Jacqueline peered into the open box only to see a smaller box inside. It was a simple lock box. "I think you have the code for this one."

"I do?"

"Yes, you should have an email with a code on it. It's the code for this."

She pulled out her phone and searched for her order. As she skimmed over it, she said, "Sure is a lot of security."

"I'd think you'd want something like this to be as secure as you could get it."

"You know what's in there?"

"Yes, ma'am. There can't be any secrets at the Port. I read the manifest and all items get x-rayed. I know what's in here. I thought it was for him, but, now I know it's not."

Looking up at him, she said, "No, it's not for him. He doesn't even know I have it."

"Thought he was your best friend?" Frank nodded in Elet's direction.

"Found it," she said and ignored his comment. Frank passed her lock box to her. She took a deep breath and entered 3-3-6-0-6.

"Push the button and pull the handle," Frank advised. When she did, the box opened and inside was a smaller box. It was also made of koa. As she held it in her hands, she bit her lip. "May I look inside?" Frank asked.

"For a safety check?" she asked.

"No, I just want to admire the work." She passed the box to him, He opened it and said, "They're beautiful." He rotated the box in his hands as if to get a better look. He was turning the box to face her.

She halted him. "No! Don't!"

"You don't want to see them?" he asked.

"No, I think I'll wait."

He closed the box and smiled at her. "Love's scary. Prolly s'pose to be. Keeps you honest." He closed the box and held it out to her in his upturned palm. As she removed it from his hand, the sun reflected off his wedding ring. Speaking to the workman, he said, "Cover 'er up." Then, he yelled to Elet, "We'll be around all day every day. You leave 'er here and come get 'er when you're ready to head back south. We'll load 'er up and remind ya how to reassemble. Okay, boss?"

"Okay," Elet said with the same smile on his face as it he had had since he saw the arch.

"Can y'all make it back to the truck?" Frank asked.

With an overabundance of confidence, Elet said, "Sure."

"All right, then. Have a good one. Call me when you're ready." Jacqueline thanked Frank and waited for Elet to catch up to her.

"That's the best thing ever," Elet said placing his arm around her. He kissed her on the cheek. "I love you so much."

"Now, who's trying to bed who," she responded with a laugh.

Then, they walked around for another half hour trying to find their way back to the truck.

~~~~~~~~~

They arrived at the airport only a few minutes before the plane touched down. Elet emerged from the truck, but he did not proceed inside of the terminal. Instead, he gathered cups, wrappers, and various other articles of trash. Jacqueline stood back and surveyed what was happening rather than help. Then, his faraway actions became quite obvious. He did not want Alex to see the truck in this condition. She opened the back door and collected debris in the back. She folded his sweatshirt and brushed out crumbs. She returned his phone charger to the glove compartment and used paper towels to wipe off the dash. Once it looked presentable, he stepped away and gave it the once over. After removing a few chewing gum wrappers, he nodded to her. She nodded back. The truck was ready.

Jacqueline had wanted to walk inside and be at the gate when Mallory emerged from the tunnel. Of course, that was no longer allowed. There was an atrium for people to await members of their party. She and Elet waited there. Neither sat. They paced about staring at the Arrivals sign for information. The ten minutes they waited felt like hours. Then, they saw them - a redhead in a white sweater, jeans, and black boots walking next to a black girl with natural hair who was wearing a red dress, black tights and black boots. Jacqueline and Elet left the atrium, pressing their bodies through the other people who were waiting, and headed straight to them.

"Hey, baby," Elet said. Alex did not respond. Gently, she kissed him.

"Hi, there," Jacqueline said, "I'm glad you're here." She hugged Mallory and kissed her cheek. While entangled, she took her bag from her hands.

"Maybe, we should stay away more often if we're gonna get these kinda receptions," Mallory teased.

"Do we need to go to baggage claim?" Elet said.

"No, we both just did a carry on," Alex answered. Taking her bag, they proceeded out of the terminal. No one said much of anything. As they snaked through the terminal, the two couples split from a party of four into two parties of two. Jacqueline and Mallory lagged behind Elet and Alex who were more determined to exit the airport. In their more leisurely pace, Jacqueline felt the awkwardness and wondered if Mallory had cried all night. Her face had more color than usual. She had felt bad about the conversation and kept looking at Mallory, hoping to meet her eyes. She never did. Mallory was focused on the exit, but her nonchalant pace reflected her apprehension.

When Elet and Alex reached the doors, he yelled back to Jacqueline, "Meet us at the truck."

She agreed, then she tried to talk to Mallory, "How was the flight?" She asked the classic traveler question.

"The turbulence was horrible. Alex threw up. It was crazy."

"Sorry, baby, I know how you hate that."

"I was so happy when we finally landed."

"You look tired. Elet wants to have dinner tonight, but why don't we hang out in the room some before we go?" Looking at her watch, she said, "It's still early. You and Alex could probably both use the rest."

"And, it seems that we all need to talk."

"What?"

"Nothing."

They stepped outside into the brisk October breeze of the Mid-Atlantic. Jacqueline saw Mallory shudder, so she removed her coat. Placing it on her shoulders, she said, "I want you to stop saying 'nothing' and 'nevermind' to me. I want you to just say what you feel or think."

Pulling Jacqueline's jacket tight around her, she asked "Sure about that?" and scurried across the parking lot to the truck. Jacqueline did not reply. This was not the place nor the time, but it was coming. It was coming very, very quickly.

~~~~~~~~~

When they reached the hotel, Alex and Mallory spoke even less than they had when they arrived. They walked into the hotel and stared at its detail. They walked to the stairs and let their eyes wander upwards at the double winding staircase of marble that was three floors overhead. Alex touched the brown and gold walls noticing that the gold was relief.

Realizing that there was no reason to wait on them, Jacqueline spoke to Elet. "What time do you want to get together?"

"I'll text you with a time in a bit," he responded.

She said, "Okay."

As she headed toward Mallory, she heard him say, "It's okay to be honest." She nodded to let him know that she had heard him and followed Mallory up the winding stairs.

Elet returned to Alex who was admiring the paintings between the elevators, "Do you want to ride up to the room or walk up those stairs?"

"Let's ride." He pressed the button. Once inside, he selected their floor. "Are you okay?"

"Yeah, it was a rough ride."

"Wanna take a nap?"

"Nah, I just wanna sit down somewhere that isn't moving."

As the elevator doors opened, she leaned forward and looked out. Walking ahead of her, he said, "Come on, the room's down here."

"Why did you two get such a nice hotel?"

"I had nothing to do with this. You know me. I'da had us sleepin' in the truck. Jacqueline reserved these rooms." He swiped the door card and pushed the door open for Alex. "Welcome home," he said.

"Oh my God! Were you two planning on staying the whole weekend the entire time? This is not a one night stay kinda room."

Elet laughed. "I know, right? I've been asking her that since we left." He plopped down on the blue velvet couch. "She went downstairs today and changed the reservations through Monday. She had these rooms reserved for just one day. It's crazy, isn't it?"

Taking her bag into the bedroom, she said, "No, it's Jacqueline." Elet arose from the couch and came into the room to help her. He lifted the bag, placed it on the bed, and opened it. "We should just go ahead and get married. Screw the Club, the invitations, the flowers, the food, the band. Let's just elope. We already have a honeymoon suite."

"Hmm, we could do that. Go down to the courthouse, get married, and go back home like nothing happened. Fuck 'em all," he agreed.

Alex had undressed. She removed her yoga pants and his t-shirt from her bag. She was putting them on as she said, "What about all the non-refundable deposits?"

Elet snapped his fingers. "Fuck, I forgot about those. Well, I guess we better go through with it. But, we could go ahead and get married here. No one would know."

She stroked his face, "You're brilliant, Elet Thomas Walden." String into his eyes, her smile faded. After a deep breath, she said, "I love you, you know?"

"I know. And, I love you, too."

"Do you really know?"

"I really know."

"I haven't always been fair to you. I know that. In fact, I've spent most of my life being selfish. Being self-centered. I'm not saying I can fix it overnight, but I am saying I'm working on it and have been."

Kissing her hands, he said, "Things've been better than they ever were. I'm sorry about last night. I was outta line."

"No, you weren't. You shoulda said that and so much worse to me. You shoulda said it years ago." She pulled her hands from his mouth and walked into the living room area. She sat on the velvet couch and patted for him to join her. "I wanna be an open book. I want you to ask me whatever you want to ask me. I want to tell you whatever you want to know, so you know that there's nothing between us." He didn't say anything. "Come on, Elet. You have to have questions." Still, he said nothing. "Why haven't I moved in?" she posed her own question. "That apartment was the first place I ever got on my own. It's dumb and selfish, but I was so proud of that. My sister lives in my grandmother's house. My parents live in a house that my uncle used to own. I've got something of my own. None of them do. I was the first one to do something on my own and I liked that. I didn't realize until last night how dumb that was."

"Nah, it's not dumb, but I do want that to be our house. Not yours and not mine. Ours. You know, your name is on it. It doesn't belong to just me. That's why I haven't moved into it. We'll move in together. You aren't coming to stay with me and I'm not coming to stay with you. We're moving in to a new place together."

"I like the sound of that. And, no one gave it to us," she was thinking aloud.

"Hell, no. We got a thirty-year mortgage on that thing," he teased.

"Don't tease. Ask me something. Don't avoid it. What am I doing at night? Do I have any other men's phone numbers? Have I slept with...?"

"I don't need to know all of that."

"Don't you wonder?"

"If I did, I couldn't sit here on this couch with you right now. I'm sure I've imagined worse than what you've done. Somehow, I've forgiven you for my worst nightmares. So, it doesn't matter what you really did. I'm over it. What I want is a wonderful future."

"Oh, but, Elet, I want you to know I've always been yours. I mean, there's been a shit ton of dumbness, but I've always been yours."

"I know."

"Last week, I found out that Cooper was in town. Remember me telling you about him?"

"Your first real boyfriend?"

"Right, I wanted you to meet him. That was my first thought. I wanted you to meet him."

"Why? Why would you want your boyfriend to meet your first boyfriend?"

"Fiancé." She corrected him as she tied her hair up. "I have no idea. I just did. It was like I wanted you two to sit across from each other, so I could see where I came from and where I was heading. Crazy, huh?"

"Did you see him?"

She folded her legs underneath her. He faced her from the other end. She began, "Aha, a question," she hit him with the pillow. "Yes, he, Olive, Mallory, and I had lunch. Oh my God, they were all over him. Turns out he's had like five kids from four women or four kids and five women. It's some crazy bullshit. So, he's telling them about how great things were when we dated and Olive's reminding him that she and I walked in him in bed with our other roommate. And, get this, the girl who said she was pregnant with his baby in high school, really was pregnant with his baby! And, she's dead and he didn't go get the boy. I mean, he's so fuckin' shady. I was sitting at the table stunned. Stunned. I mean, this guy destroyed me. He never seemed to want me. He'd string me along and I'd run behind him. Then, he'd dump me and disappear. I used to chase after him like some fool," her voice started to drift off. "It happened for years," she became quieter. "But, then yesterday, I was like I gotta get outta here. I didn't want to know why he didn't want me. It didn't matter. Like for the first time, ever, none of it mattered. Yesterday, he was just some jackass and I just couldn't listen to it anymore." Regaining her strength, she straightened out her legs until they almost touched him and said, "Oh my God, baby, I was looking around like I was running from a fire."

Laughing, he said, "So, what'd you do?"

"I don't even remember what I said. I pushed away from the table and said that I had to go. I told him goodbye and walked out of the restaurant." They both laughed.

"You didn't? You left your friends at the table and walked out?"

Laughing, she said, "Olive must've left next, because she was the first one to meet me outside. Mallory didn't show up for a few minutes. Knowing her, she gave him a piece of her mind. I don't even think we paid." They were both laughing. She slid down in the couch and put her feet in his lap. "What's worse is we rode with him. We got outside and realized we needed a cab." And, they erupted in laughter.

After a few minutes, he wiped the tears from his eyes and, "You know, he's the problem, right?"

"What?"

"He rejected you. He disappeared. He made you feel like you were unattractive, undesirable. He's why you do what you do. Jacqueline's right.

You don't want the men. You want to collect the compliments. You just want to know you're desirable."

Alex didn't say anything. She thought about what he said for a while. She wanted to deny it but thought against it. "That might've been true, but it's all in the past, now. I only need one man to think I'm attractive."

Elet looked from side to side. He leaned forward and looked into the bedroom area. Then, he said, "Who the fuck is he? I'll fuck him up." And, she giggled and hit him with the pillow that had been under her head.

Chapter 20

"What were you planning?" Mallory asked as Jacqueline opened the hotel room door for her.

"What?"

"You got this room for a one-night stay?"

"Yeah," Jacqueline said. "I thought it should be like a mini-celebration." She closed the door as Mallory entered. She tried to ignore the rest of her comments about the room. Rather than refute them, Jacqueline laid across the bed.

"Were you planning on coming back?" Mallory asked while seated on the toilet.

"Of course. You know you've asked me that before. What makes you think I'd just disappear like that?"

She was washing her hands. "I don't know it seems like you could."

"I wouldn't." Jacqueline rolled onto her side and made room for Mallory to lie beside her. "Come here."

"You wanna talk now? Not on Sunday?" Mallory was standing in the bathroom. She was facing Jacqueline, but she was resting against the sink. She had her arms folded.

Jacqueline knew that the stance meant. She got off the bed, slipped her feet out of her loafers, and walked to the bathroom doorway. With her hands on the door frame, she sighed, "Why do you think I wanted you to come here?"

"I'm scared to speculate," She bowed her head.

"Me, too," she agreed and returned to the bed. "A few months ago, it seemed like we were on top of the world, but in the last few weeks, it seems most conversations are steps away from an international event. I wanted to know what's wrong."

Mallory relented her ground and entered the bedroom. She sat on the edge of the bed with her back to Jacqueline and removed her boots. "Nothing's wrong. Not really. Everything's just right."

"Then, what are we dancing around?"

"Nothin..."

"Don't say it. That's all you ever say to my questions. Don't say 'nothing' when there's obviously something going on."

"I don't want to come here and cry. I don't want to hear I'm overreacting. I'm tired of everyone telling me that everything's perfect when it doesn't feel perfect."

Jacqueline lifted off the bed and ran her hand along Mallory's back. "Could it be perfect?"

"Yeah, I think it can," she replied with her hand on her forehead.

Jacqueline slid next to her in the bed. Softly, she said, "Then, let's do what it takes to be perfect." Brushing her bangs from the front of her face, she asked, "Why aren't you telling me what you're telling everyone else?"

"I don't want to push you away. I don't want to ask so many questions that our relationship becomes any harder on you," Mallory had begun to sniffle.

"Am I having a difficult time?"

"I dunno. Are you? You don't tell me." Jacqueline stood up. She left the room. Fearing the worst, Mallory asked, "Where are you going?"

She reappeared with the chair from the desk that had been in the other room. She rolled it in front of Mallory and sat down in it. "Okay, let's do this. Let's have all of the conversations you want to have. We're gonna sit here all night if we have to, but we're gonna talk about everything you want to talk about. No dodging. No bullshitting. Whatever you want to know you ask." Mallory stared at her. "I mean it. I'm not lying to you. I called you up here, because I realized that I've been holding back. And, it's driving us both crazy. And, I don't want that. I'm gonna work harder at being open, but it's hard for me."

"Why? Why can't you tell me anything?"

"A bunch of reasons. I guess I've never had anyone to tell. I've told Elet all kinds of things through the years, but I still hold a lot back. Sometimes, I feel like I'm boasting. Sometimes, I think no one cares. I dunno. I'm just not used to talking about me. I'm good at letting other people talk about themselves, you know?"

"But, I wanna know," Mallory said and reached out and touched her hands. "I wanna know all the things you're thinking of and dreaming of. I see you spaced out and I wonder where you are."

"Just ask me."

"I'm scared you're thinking how'd I get trapped with them."

Jacqueline shot out of the chair and returned to her side on the bed. "I never ever think that. Never." She kissed her.

Jacqueline was returning to her office chair, but Mallory said, "Lie beside me. Hold me close just in case I don't like what I hear." Jacqueline reclined onto her back. Mallory nestled in close and put her head on her shoulder. "Why do you buy everything for everyone?"

"That's your first question?" Jacqueline had not expected to be asked that. She did not have an answer. "Hmm, let's see. First of all, I don't. Yes, I paid for the hotel rooms, but I haven't paid for every meal or all the gas. We've split it for the most part. I covered the rooms, because I made him come. This wasn't his idea and we're driving his truck. The rooms seemed like the least I could do."

"This isn't all you pay for. If we go out to dinner, you try to pick up the check."

"Depends on the crowd. Depends on the situation. I don't always, but I get it. I do it. I guess I've been very lucky and I think it's the least I can do."

"I don't want you to feel like money is all you have to offer. I don't want you to think your money is what I want from you. Hell, I don't even know how much you have or where it all came from or whatever."

"I never thought of you just wanting me for money. I never have. I guess you and Zoe are different. I mean, you have access to every other part of me, so why not the money? I don't know. It seems like that's what a fam... Nevermind."

Mallory lifted her head. Staring at her, she said, "Family? Why didn't you say it?"

Jacqueline bit her lip. "I have a lot to lose as well."

"What?"

"Everyone thinks I don't talk about the future with you, because I'm not thinking of one. Everyone thinks you aren't talking about the future with me, because I may hurt you. No one ever considered what I fear that you may not want the future that I want."

"Are you scared I'll hurt you?"

"Not on purpose, but what if you don't want what I want? I mean, you were married before and it didn't work out. What if you never wanted things to progress past where we already are. No one ever thinks I could be protecting myself. You and Zoe are my family. I don't want to lose that."

Mallory sat up completely. Her legs were folded beneath her. Jacqueline raised up and balanced her weight on her arm and elbow. "We aren't going anywhere unless you tell me that you want us out. Which by the way is exactly what I thought you wanted to tell me."

"Never," Jacqueline leaned forward and put her head in her lap.

"So, what do you want?" Mallory asked stroking her face.

"All of it," Jacqueline said quietly.

"All of it?"

"*All* of it. What am I thinking and dreaming of? A future together. A real one. You have a key to my place and the Jeep. I have a key to your place and the car. You have the passcode to the alarm. You've redecorated. You can sign into the computer and see all of my information. Financial. Personal. All of it."

"I wouldn't do that."

"You can, though."

"I leave the mail on the counter when I come home. There's nothing stopping you from looking in it. There aren't any secrets. There are just questions you haven't asked or papers you haven't read."

"I would never just look. That's an invasion of your privacy."

"I don't have any left from you. Especially now." There was silence. "On the desk in the office is an envelope. Inside the envelope are your cards."

"My cards? What cards?"

"I added you to my credit cards. Yours are in the office. I hadn't figured how to tell you."

"This is what I'm talking about. I don't need your cards."

"I know. But, it's not about need. That's the thing. I'm not trying to own you or possess you. That's what I couldn't tell you." She got off the bed. Her mind was working fast. She had to move around the room. "It's not about need. It's about what I want. I want you to have what I have. I want us to be a family in every way. I know I need to learn to talk to you about things first and not just act. I'm not used to that, but I can do that. I did it today. When they unveiled the arch, I thought I gotta ask Mallory if we should have a dresser and chest of drawers made to match the bed. See, I didn't just order it. My mind thought to run it by you." Mallory smiled at her. "I know you don't need me. I don't want you to need me. I want you to want to share your life with me and let me share mine with you."

"I want that, too," Mallory said. She got from the bed and walked to her. "I do. I don't want to not know where we're sleeping every night. I don't want clothes in two places."

"I don't want you to feel like you need that place, so you can entertain your friends or Zoe's friends, or your family."

"Uh, what?"

"Well, you never have people over to the penthouse?"

Mallory frowned, "Do you think I'm having parties at my house with my other friends on the few nights I get mad and sleep there without you."

"Yes?" Jacqueline hesitated.

Mallory laughed, "No, it's me and Zoe alone. I'm angry with you and Zoe's angry with me."

"Well, why do you keep it? A place? A place for just you and Zoe?"

"I keep it, because you haven't been ready for us to be together all the time." Mallory returned to the bed.

Jacqueline followed her, "I never said that."

"You never said different. I've been keeping it, because I didn't know what was gonna happen between us."

"When's the lease up?"

"It was up two months ago. I've been paying month to month. Paige said that she thought you'd come around in less than another year. So, I've just been waiting."

"Well, Fuck," Jacqueline was surprised, then a memory struck. "You know how I said I wanted it all and you know how I said I'm learning to talk to you about everything now. Learning is the key word."

"What else have you done?"

"I talked to Victoria," Jacqueline admitted.

"Who's Victoria? Wait, did you ever sleep with her?"

"She's my happily married real estate attorney and agent."

"First, why do you have a real estate attorney and agent? Second, what'd you talk to her about?"

"First, it's we. Why do we have a real estate attorney and agent?"

"Fine, Jax, why do we have a real estate attorney?"

"We've been driving around. We go to people's houses. I drive through subdivisions and neighborhoods. And, I don't know. I just think it might be time to think about selling the penthouse, so I contacted Victoria. Nothing is final. I realized we should probably talk about it."

"You think! This is exactly the kinda stuff we have to talk about. We can't talk about moving in together without talking about you selling the place we are moving into."

"First things first, we could sell it and live at your place. We could sign for another year and we could move into your house. We could offer to buy it. I'm open to all options."

"Who the hell moves into the two bedroom in Clearwater when the other option is a bayfront penthouse?"

"I just wanted you to have the option. Listen, I want it all. And, I guess I realized how that penthouse doesn't say family. It says single life. I want a place that's home for us all. A new place that we decorate and make a life in together. I don't want a place that you're scared to let Zoe and her friends enjoy. That balcony freaks you out. And, you hate walking across the parking lot with groceries or bags. Part of my all of it might be a new place."

"I'm not opposed to any of that, but we need to talk about it. I don't want you to feel like you have to pay all of the bills."

"I don't want a partner or a roommate. I want a joint bank account from which the bills are paid for the life we lead. I don't need to be on the loan for your car, but I do want joint stuff."

"Like?"

"Bank account. Insurance. Stuff. The deed for the property. I want us to share everything."

"You know what you're talking about?"

"I know. Are you okay with that?"

Mallory fidgeted. She played with her hands, "I am, but are you?"

Jacqueline rolled to face her, "It was my idea."

Mallory stroked her face, "You've only been trying this for five months."

"How long do I need? Is there a written grace period? I know right now. I've known. I've tried to add you to my bank accounts and the bank won't let me without your signature. But, they let me start a college fund for Zoe."

"What?"

"Did you have one?"

"Well, no. But, we definitely should've talked about that."

"I thought about mentioning that, but I decided that even if you rejected me, I'll still love Zoe. And, there should be money around for her dreams."

"Wait. Before we go any further, we need to talk about the details. I need to know things."

"Like what?"

"How much are the bills? And how much do you make?"

Jacqueline responded sarcastically, "How much do you make and how much are your bills?"

Nonchalantly, Mallory answered, "As you know, I recently got a big promotion. Now, I make seventy thousand a year. With the new raise, I make enough to put money into a 401K. I've been putting about three percent a check, so I could get the company match. I just got a new car. It's like five hundred a month. I'm paying eleven hundred for rent on a house we stay out once or twice a week."

"Ouch. We gotta do something about that."

"Let me finish. Let' see. I pay electricity, water, sewage, and cable over there, too. That's not too bad. I mean, we aren't there so the electric, water, and sewage are about a hundred bucks a month. The cable is about one-fifty since you pay that even if no one watches it. Then, there's car insurance, gas, a couple of credit cards. I don't ever really buy any food. My girlfriend does most of the cooking and keeps both houses well stocked, but I have a daughter. She's almost eight. Her extended day and extracurricular activities are a killer. But, all in all I spend about three five hundred dollars a month. It used to be all I could do to make ends meet, but now, that I have this new job, things are a lot easier. I put about six hundred dollars into savings every month. How 'bout you?" With a welcoming smile on her face, Mallory looked at Jacqueline and awaited her response.

Nervously, she ran her hand through her hair and said, "Well, I wish I could explain things as easily as that."

"Start at the beginning. What's the mortgage?"

"God, I hate talking about finances. It scares people off."

"I wasn't scared until you said that. But, go ahead. Let's do this. How much is the mortgage?"

"It's about three thousand."

Mallory gasped. "Maybe, we should back up. How much was the penthouse when you first bought it?"

"The mortgage or the total cost?"

Looking uncomfortable, Mallory said, "Both."

"Total cost was a little over a million, but the mortgage was for five hundred thousand."

"Wait, it's a new building. It wasn't an inheritance. How'd the mortgage get down to half?"

Jacqueline sat up. "That's what it was when I got it. It's not what it is now." She returned to pacing, "This is a long story."

"I'm listening."

"Before we go any further, I haven't shared these kinda details of my life with anyone. Not all of this. Not what I make. Not what I pay. Not how I got all the money. Elet knows some of it, but no one knows all of it. If we go any further..."

"I know, you'll have to kill me."

"I'm serious. I don't want anyone to know. This is between us."

"I know, honey. This is our business and no one else's."

Jacqueline liked the sound of that, but she was nervous to share the intimate details with Mallory just the same. However, she had to go on. "There was this woman named Sheryl who dropped out of school in her senior year to join a band and go on the road. Well, a funk group. It was the seventies. Anyhow, she was a backup singer. The band didn't make loads of money or have huge commercial success, but they had a few hits. More importantly, she fell in love with the lead percussionist, Dexter. Well, the two got married, one thing lead to another, and before Sheryl knew it, she was pregnant. She and Dexter had a little girl. They loved their daughter, but they couldn't raise a child on the road. So, they shipped the baby off to live with his mother. Well, his lack of a serious commitment and the absence of the baby caused friction between them. So, as music styles started changing, Sheryl left the band. She wanted him to leave, too. She begged him to go, but he wouldn't. He wanted to make it big. His dream of fame was bigger than the dream of family. So, she left him, picked up her baby from her ex-husband's mother, and returned to Florida. She put herself through school and got a good job. Eventually, she met a man, got married, had some other kids, and gave them all a pretty good life. All the while, Dexter chased his dream. He went from percussionist to songwriter to accompanist to film composer. He and his family kept a relationship with his only child until he passed away about eight years ago."

"Okay, so your father died and left you money?"

"Something like that. My father died and left me a life insurance policy, a house in LA, some stocks, an overseas account, several cars, and royalties from record and film companies. Big Jack had Jack set me up with their financial adviser after the estate was dispersed. I needed to solidify my assets so, I bought the penthouse. I used all of the life insurance money on it."

"You were in your early twenties. Who gave you a half a million-dollar mortgage?"

"Any bank I wanted. I had half a million-dollar check, guaranteed royalties, and assets. I sold all the vehicles. All of them except the vehicle I learned to drive in. I'll never sell it."

"The Laredo," she touched her chest.

"I used the first royalty checks to furnish the penthouse. In the beginning, I was just paying for electricity and the mortgage. Just sliding by. Then, I went from staff writer to head writer to editorials to department lead to Managing Editor. But, my bills didn't really increase, but my pay has."

"Do you still get royalty checks?"

"Yeah, I never touch them. They're just direct deposited.

"How much are they?"

"It varies. They can be a couple of thousand if someone samples the hook of a song or it can be tens of thousands if people play one of the movies. I never cashed in the stocks. They just ride the market. And, I still own his house. Elet and I talked about going out there and hiring some people to renovate it, but I don't know what to do with it."

"Does it have a mortgage?"

"No, it's paid off. It has electricity, water, security system. I pay the taxes, but it just sits in the Santa Monica canyons. Waiting on me. It's beautiful, but you don't need a summer home in California, if you live in Florida. And, you don't need a house in the canyon if you live on water. But, it was my dad's house. I love it. It has so many memories. Anyhow, you see my problem."

"Were you close to him?"

"He didn't want my mom, but he loved me. I flew to be with him all the time. At the house in California or movie sets or on vacation or with his friends."

"Well, it's good you were close. He never had any other kids?"

She laughed and said, "None have turned up."

Mallory reached out for her to stop pacing, "I'm sorry. How'd he die?"

Returning to her, Jacqueline said, "He had a stroke in the middle of the night. He must've been working. They found him with sheet music still in his lap. I kept it. It's back at the house."

"He's the reason you play the violin?" Mallory was almost talking to herself.

"No, actually, it was my grandmother. She thought it was important to play an instrument. She had made him play as a boy. When I was old enough, she made me play an instrument as well."

"I assume she's dead as well?"

"Just months before him," she said quietly.

"Oh, I'm so sorry, honey." Mallory pulled Jacqueline down to the bed. "Do you want to go on? Or, is this enough? I don't want you to feel..."

"No, this is about us. We've gotta do this. Once it's out in the open, then it'll be easier to have all the side conversations."

Mallory was deep in thought. "Okay." With a sigh, she proceeded, "That explains the money. What do you make now? What's your total monthly bills?"

"Jack gave me a raise. Do you remember? I overheard Alex talking about it. I'm sure Mrs. Pennington told Evelyn who told Alex."

"Sure, there was lots of gossip, but no one knows how much or, even, it was true."

287

"I make half a mil a year."

"Fuck," Mallory looked nauseous.

"Well, don't say that. You'll mess me up. I've gotta say it all in one move or I'm not gonna be able to do it."

"Okay," she looked faint. "I guess you should go on."

"I get a fifty-thousand dollar bonus in profitable years. I put a quarter of my regular check and all of my bonus into my 401K. My bills are about eight thousand a month." Jacqueline was looking up at the ceiling. It was obvious that she'd practiced this speech. "After all of my deductions, I get almost twenty thousand a month. Then, I pay electricity, water, and sewage for both places, cable at the penthouse, cellphone, credit cards, food, food, and more food, gas. Oh, I pay six thousand on the mortgage these days rather than the three thousand that's due. And, I pay my mom's mortgage. When it's all said and done, I put about twelve thousand in my savings each month. "

Mallory didn't speak. She sat on the bed as though she was blowing in the wind. Jacqueline had wondered if she had heard what she said. "Well, that was a lot. I don't know if I got all of that. I think I need a minute." Then, she stood from the bed and began to pace.

"Sorry."

"I never thought...I mean, it's a good kinda problem to have. I just need to wrap my mind around what you've said. There's a lot of money. And, you've been saving most of it."

Jacqueline sighed, "Yeah, I had this plan."

"What plan?"

"There was this plan. I've been saving for years. Once I hit a number, I was gonna sell the penthouse and move."

"To where?"

"Any European market that'd have me," she was embarrassed to tell Mallory this story.

"What?"

"Only Elet knew this. When I had two million saved, between my 401K and my saving account, I was going to sell the penthouse and go to London or Paris and start over." She chuckled. "I know it's stupid. But, I was willing to start over. I'd be a features writer again if I could just work for an overseas conglomerate. Something big." Mallory stopped, turned to her, and smiled. "I know it's stupid."

"Actually, it's pretty amazing. No one would have ever believed this about you."

"Yeah, I know," she rolled on her side to face the wall.

Sitting on the bed, beside her, Mallory asked, "How close are you?"

"About five years to go," she mumbled.

With her hand on her side, "Zoe would be almost twelve by then. What preteen wouldn't want to live in Europe?"

Quickly, Jacqueline faced her, "It's okay. I mean, having you in my life is worth more that this dumb plan."

"Why? There's nothing stopping us." Jacqueline looked confused. Mallory elaborated, "I want to be with you. I want to go where you go. We're a family now. I never imagined I'd be where I am right now, so I'm open to anything." Mallory leaned into her face and said, "Don't be scared of what I might say. You might just be surprised at my response." She kissed her tenderly.

"I don't want you to just decide that my plan works for us. I mean, we should come up with our own five-year plan. If Europe works, fine, but we may need to stay here until Zoe graduates."

"We'll figure it all out together. Nothing's off the table." Mallory got off the bed. Jacqueline leaned from the bed and saw her enter the living room and retrieve her purse. "Okay, let's make a list of things to do in the short term."

Jacqueline smiled and sat up. "Okay. Let's go."

"Why do you pay your mother's mortgage?"

"She had some lean months when she retired, so I helped her out. Then, I just never stopped."

"Can we?"

"We?"

"Yes, we."

"We'd need to talk to her."

"You never talk about her. Do you two have a bad relationship?"

"No, not really. I think I felt like a constant reminder of my father. I think I felt like she'd rather not have to explain me. I don't know. I never really fit in. I mean, I'm an oddball everywhere I go."

"Not with me," Mallory mumbled and wrote meet, J's mom, and talk about mortgage. When she finished writing, she said, "Check. Next item. How much do you owe on the penthouse?"

"Lemme check. I have an email from Vicki."

"She's Vicki, now?"

Jacqueline snickered and scrolled through her phone. "I owe three hundred eighty-eight thousand dollars."

"Wow! You've paid a ton. What's it worth?"

Scrolling through the email, Jacqueline said, "Vicki says the cost of properties in the building have skyrocketed since the building was built. The last sale of a penthouse was five million and it was on the fourth floor. She says she'll list it at ten million when I'm ready to put it on the market." Jacqueline looked up. "I don't know that it'll get ten million."

"What does Vicki think?"

"Realtors never think less."

"What are we willing to take for it?" Jacqueline shrugged her shoulders. Mallory pressed, "Throw out a number."

Hesitantly, Jacqueline said, "Eight."

"I can't believe I was scared to tell you the Mercedes was six hundred a month. And, here we are talking about eight million dollars like it's nothing."

"You said the car was five hundred." Jacqueline teased. "Listen, even at eight, we'd have enough to pay off your car, buy a new place, pay off the miscellaneous credit cards, redecorate the new place, and try to save two million."

Mallory laughed. "Wait, how much do we owe on the penthouse?"

"Three hundred eighty-eight thousand."

Jacqueline watched as she calculated. "If it sold for eight million dollars, we'd still have over seven and a half million. If we put two million away, that's still five and a half million. We aren't spending all of that. A new place doesn't have to cost us an arm and a leg."

"No, I guess not. I don't want too much house. I was thinking of nothing more than a million."

"Then, what's the other four and a half million dollars going towards?"

"I don't know. Your credit cards, your car, and furniture."

Mallory chuckled. "I don't know what you're thinking. I've got like three thousand dollars of credit card debt. Which, I might add, I felt horrible about until about twenty minutes ago. But, shit! And, that car was about forty thousand or so. Which also used to upset me. We aren't hiring a decorator. We're going to regular stores and buying regular stuff. It won't take four million to furnish any place we live in together. Okay?"

"Okay. So, you think we'll have enough?"

"How much is your credit card debt?"

"That Black card doesn't have a limit. And, I think the other one has a ten thousand limit."

Mallory gulped. "What's the balance on them?"

"The Black card has the hotel rooms on it. It'll be paid off on Monday. And, the other card probably has a thousand on it."

Relieved, Mallory said, "Oh, well, that's nothing. Who knew you had a Black card?"

"You do, too. It's on the desk."

Mallory stared at her. "Yeah, I forgot about that. Well, do we want to sell the penthouse?"

"What do you want?"

"I want us to be together, but you seem ready to go."

"I just think it might be time. I think I want something else for us. Do you want to keep it? Rent it? Live in it?"

"I love the penthouse, but I hear your head churning. I want to be with you wherever you'll be happy. We're already well beyond what I'm used to. Have you already looked for us a new place?"

Jacqueline lowered her head. "What's the right answer?"

"Go ahead and tell me."

"I've looked at a few places. In Apollo Beach. I considered you and Zoe in what a new place needed to have. Ample space. Two offices. Swimming pool. Access to a dock or marina. Large kitchen. Place for entertaining. Place for Zoe to play. Space for kids to come over. I told Vicki all about you both. She wants to meet you." Lowering her head, she said, "but, then we had the arch blow up and I've ceased all activity."

"Apollo Beach is further away."

"Kinda, but not really. It's south instead of west, but they have A schools."

Mallory smiled, "You checked the schools?"

"Well, yeah. We've got an eight-year-old. I mean, the schools around the penthouse aren't great and the one she goes to in Clearwater isn't either. So, it seemed like if we were gonna sell, then we should only look in places where the schools are better. But, are we selling?"

"Maybe. We'll see. We'll look at the two houses and some others and see if we find something we love. I love the penthouse, but I would love for us to pick something out that was just for the three of us. Okay, LA house. What do you want to do?"

"I don't know. I can't decide."

"Let's make some time to go out there and look at it. I don't know that I can be much help until I've been there."

"New Years in LA?"

"Oh, that would be nice. Zoe'll be with her dad," Mallory swooned. "Shopping in Beverly Hills." As she danced, she continued to add to her list. "Okay, I got that. I can add the Laredo to my car insurance and I'll add you to my credit cards. You can add me to your cell plan. End the lease at my place?"

"I'd like that," Jacqueline said. Mallory continued with things to do. She was merging their lives together in a methodical, dispassionate way. Jacqueline was feeling distressed.

Noticing her distance, Mallory asked, "Are you okay with all of this?"

"Yeah, it's all technicalities. I guess I want to know if this is what you want."

Leaving the paper and pencil behind, Mallory crawled across the bed to Jacqueline and said, "This is what I've always wanted. I want a life with you. Together. We can merge all the odds and ends together and then, we can go be happy. Day in and day out."

"I love you." Jacqueline said. Worried, she continued to speak before Mallory could respond, "Do you know what I've been talking about? Do you understand?"

Mallory looked confused. "I think I do. You want me forever."

"I do, but I don't like the term girlfriend." She stood up and walked around to the other side of the bed. She had her right hand in her pocket. Her fingers were wrapped tight around the box that Frank had given her hours earlier at the Port. She stared down into Mallory's sea green eyes. She was ready. Ready to make the biggest move her life.

Then, there was a knock at the door.

Chapter 21

Before Jacqueline opened the door, she could hear Elet and Alex outside. They were giggling. For a second, she thought of not opening it, of pretending to not hear them, but she knew Mallory would never play along. Instead, she became irritated when she opened it to find their giggling faces.

"I'm glad you opened the door. I didn't want to call and tell you this. This is so great I had to come tell you in person," Elet said all at once. Alex walked around him, entered the room, and sat on the couch. Mallory came out of the room and joined her.

"Uh, we were kinda in the middle of something," Jacqueline said.

"I'm sorry, but you're gonna wanna know what I got."

"Can't I hear it in a few minutes?" she tried to plead with him. Her hand was still in her pocket. Her fingers were still wrapped around the box. She was lifting her eyebrows hoping he would get the hint.

"I couldn't be happier with the trip and the arch. I mean, you've been my very best friend forever and I was thinking I'd never be able to repay you for all you've done for me."

"You don't have to. I... We don't expect any repayment."

Alex said, "Oh, so we've made some progress. Are we a we now?"

Mallory mumbled to her, "We've always been a we. I guess I didn't know." The girls snickered on the couch. This would have pleased Jacqueline if she didn't want Alex and Elet to get out.

"Listen, we can talk about that later. We don't have a lot of time."

"I thought we were going to dinner later," Jacqueline gave up and went and leaned against the desk. She was rubbing her face and hoping that if she just let him finish that they'd go away.

"We aren't going to dinner. We've got tickets to game six of the World Series!! The car'll be here soon to take us to Nats Park! And, it just so happens Silas is gonna meet us there!"

"What? Are you serious? This is the best." Jacqueline sprang from the desk and wrapped her arms around his neck. "You didn't have to try to repay me, but I'm sure glad you wanted to with tickets to the World Series."

"I'm sorry. It's not in an American League park."

"Who cares," she screamed. "Is Silas gonna come sit with us? Did he get to come since he's part of the Cards affiliate?"

"Nope. Even better. He'll be playing in the outfield. He got called up."

Mallory said, "That's amazing."

Alex said, "You two better go get changed. We've gotta go soon."

~~~~~~~

Jacqueline headed to the bedroom behind Mallory. As she closed the door, she asked her, "What were you gonna say before they came in?"

"Now's not the time." Jacqueline said changing clothes.

"Maybe later?"

"Definitely later. When the time's right." As Mallory went to the restroom, Jacqueline placed the box back in the room safe.

When she exited the bathroom, she said, "Are you sure you're okay with all of this?"

"What? All of what?"

"You've got so much. I don' t know why..."

"I have got nothing without you and Zoe. All the money in the world wouldn't matter without you," She pulled Mallory close and started to kiss her. After only a few seconds, the door opened.

Alex stuck her head into the room and said, "Stop making out. Get dressed. We've gotta go." Then, she closed the door behind her.

Jacqueline couldn't finish her kiss. Mallory was laughing. She said, "I may kill her."

~~~~~~~~

As they walked into the stadium, Jacqueline reached down and held Mallory's hand. Over the buzz of the crowd, she said, "I'm glad we talked."

"I am, too. I'm glad you see a future for us."

"I can't remember the past without you."

"Me either," Mallory snuggled into her side.

After they located their seats, Jacqueline and Elet headed back up the stairs for snacks.

Waiting to be alone, Alex turned to Mallory and began her line of questioning, "Okay, they're gone. Spill it."

Mallory moved closer, "We talked and talked and talked. She was scared. She wasn't sure what I wanted. I think she wants more."

"What do you mean?"

"I mean, I think she's trying to figure out how to ask me to marry her."

Alex leaned away, "Shut the front door. Are you serious? Already? Do you want that?"

"I never thought she'd want to. I mean, I thought the best possible outcome was just living together. But, I always wanted to marry her. I never thought about a wedding or anything like that, but I really did always imagine us married. I don't even know why. After I got divorced, I said I'd never get married, again. I think I've told everyone that." Alex nodded in agreement. "But, I don't know. I've felt like a dumb teenager. I've imagined being married to her."

"Well, at least, you can stop paying on that tiny ass house in Clearwater and move into a penthouse." Then, she hummed the theme to the Jeffersons.

"Stop that," Mallory swatted at her. "It doesn't matter. We may sell it and move to another place that's all ours."

"Who does that? It's a penthouse on Tampa Bay! It's huge. Everyone wants to live there."

"Exactly! Turns out she paid less than what it's worth. She could make a ton."

"Oh, hell yeah. Let's go get that mansion," Alex yelled.

"She wants to live in Apollo Beach."

"She's already been looking? What am I saying? Jacqueline probably already has an offer on a few places."

"We talked about that, too. No more sudden moves. No serious purchases without talking first."

"You know, she just isn't used to having to ask or talk before she does stuff. That's all."

"I know. I think she'll get better about it."

"Does she really have a house in mind?"

"She said she looked at two." Mallory said.

"She looked at twelve and drilled down to two. Girl, if she's gonna sell that penthouse that she loves and is already looking for new places, she has a ring. Just wait. I guarantee it."

"You think?"

"Hell! I know so. I'm so excited for you." Alex hugged her as they sat side by side.

"Shut up. It hasn't happened yet. Don't jinx me. What happened with you and Elet? Are things okay?"

"You know, I think they're really good. I told him about Cooper."

"You did?" Mallory was shocked.

"Yup. And, you know what, we laughed about it. He didn't want to know what I've done or how bad it'd been. He just wants things to be on the up and up now."

"Are they?"

"Absolutely. I've been straight since the summer. I saw Cooper, but it was always on the up and up. But, I'm so glad you guys were there to help me get my head straight about that fool. Girl, it was time to close that door once and for all."

~~~~~~~~~

In line for snacks and drinks, Elet asked, "How'd the talk go?"

"Good, I think."

"You don't know?"

"I think I do, but I'm not sure."

"Well, how are you gonna find out?"

"I was about to find out for sure when you knocked."

Elet kicked the gravel, "Oops. My bad. Things look good."

299

"I told her that I wanted it all. All of it."

"What does that mean?"

"That's what I'm scared of. We did talk specifically about moving in and selling the penthouse."

"What the fuck? Um, you didn't run that by me."

"Was I supposed to?"

"You can't just sell your place and move in with someone you've dated for like five months."

"Why not?"

"Well, it's not been long enough."

"Too late now."

"Wait a minute." Doing air quotes, he asked, "by 'all the way,' do you mean marriage? How the hell did you go from flirting with two girls yesterday to marriage today? We didn't talk about that either. What the fuck is going on?" With his hands in his pockets, he looked as though he might jump up and down.

"I love her," Jacqueline explained quietly. "And, everything you've been telling me was right."

Elet quieted. "Does she love you, too?"

"She says she does."

"Do you have a ring?"

"Maybe."

"When are you gonna do it?"

"I got no idea, now."

"It's gotta be memorable."

"It's already memorable. I mean, how many times was she really gonna get a black girl to propose?"

Elet laughed. "How'd we get here?"

300

"She's the one, man."

"She is. She is. Did you tell her everything?"

"I think so."

"Dead father?"

"Check."

"Five-year plan?"

"Check, but I think I'm scraping it."

"Really? I mean, I guess you have to."

"She said she wasn't opposed to it. But, it seems like it's too much to ask. I mean, I could sell the penthouse and go. I wouldn't need five more years, but that's not fair to her. I mean, she's got a good thing at work and she's worked damn hard to get it. And, Zoe's little. She needs cheerleading and sleepovers and elementary school and all that shit. I can't expect them to give up everything to let me fulfill some dream.

"Good. Good." He shook his head. "I'm so proud of you for seeing it like that. On one hand, I would go wherever Alex needed to go to make her dreams come true, but, on the other hand, I would give up my dreams for her. Just don't decide for her. Just talk it through. I don't want to see you go to London or whatever, but I don't want you to be all miserable around here."

"But, I'm not miserable. I'm good. I'm really good. And, I don't know if I could go. Who'd I have to straighten me out?" She gave him a crooked smile.

"I couldn't do this without you." Then, he returned to his list, "Let's see. What about Tabs?"

"Do I have to tell her about that?"

"What are gonna do about Clementine?"

"I think Alex wrangled her in for me."

301

"That's my girl. But, you got pictures while we've been gone. You may have to do something."

"Yeah, I know. But, what? She knows I'm in a relationship. She knows I don't go to Livewire anymore. She's just crazy."

"You may have to out crazy her crazy."

"Fuck. I really wanted her to catch a hint."

"She's not the type to do that."

She ran her hand through her hair. "We may have to have an honest conversation, too. We aren't really friends, but I think I need to lay some shit on the line with her."

"Might work. Maybe, she needs to hear it from you, not your posse." The two came up next to order. As they stood to the side to wait, Elet said, "So, you told her that you wanted her to move in. You hinted at marriage. You talked about selling the penthouse. You're scraping the five-year plan. You talked about why you've got problems talking about shit. Hmm, I think you did it all. I'm so fuckin' proud of you." Jacqueline beamed.

The food was ready. As they got napkins and condiments, she gave the order a once over. Then, she said, "You didn't get Alex a drink."

"I got her water in my pocket."

"She didn't want a drink drink?"

"Nope. Just a water's what she said. She was kinda out of it in the room, too. Maybe, she's gettin' sick."

"How'd things go between you and her?"

"You know, it's all good. She told me that dude, Cooper, came to town. Turns out she and Mallory and Olive had lunch with him."

"That had to be eventful," Jacqueline said."

"I didn't even have to ask. I don't know. Things felt good. I didn't wonder where she'd been or what she'd been up to. She just told me."

302

"That's great, man."

"Maybe, I just need to tell her how what she was doing made me feel. Maybe, I needed to come clean, so she'd open up. I guess she's more like you than I realize."

They walked the steep stairs back to the seats. Mallory and Alex had decided to sit together on the inside with Elet and Jacqueline on the outside. As they entered the row, Alex stood up and screamed, "Silas!" He was playing left field and from their seats he was only a few yards away from them. He leaned over and waved his cap. "Look at him. He's made it."

They noticed that he was walking from left field to the stands, so they walked down to talk to him. "What's up, little brother?" Elet asked as he shook his brother's hand.

Wearing his Cardinals uniform, he looked taller and thinner than he really was. "Hey, Elet. I'm glad you were in town. That's great fuckin' luck, isn't it?"

"Save some of that luck for the game," Alex said.

"Don't worry. I got plenty."

"Silas, when you hit your second home run tonight, I want the ball," Jacqueline said.

"The first one is for me. The second one is for them, but you can have the third."

"Okay. I'll take it."

"Be safe out here tonight. It's cold and dark. Keep your eyes on the ball." Mallory warned him.

"Okay, Mom," he teased.

Elet's face became serious. "Did you call Mom? Did you tell her, DeeDee, and Reese to watch?"

"Yeah, I called Mom. I sent a text to DeeDee and Reese. Reese called me back. I spoke to everyone. Even Pam. She told me not to screw up."

"I'm gonna fuck her up one day. Just wait," Alex said.

"Simmer down, sis. I think she'll be gone soon." Alex liked the way he called her sis. She liked the idea of being his sister, of them all being family.

"I doubt that. I think Reese loves her." Mallory said.

Silas looked around, "Looks like that's going 'round."

"What about you? When're you gonna settle down?" Mallory asked.

As he started to run back into position, he said, "Don't worry. When I get a pro contract, I'll marry a Playboy centerfold like the other guys. It'll give Alex someone to hate more than Pam." Watching him go, Elet stared at the Walden name bobbing up and down on his little brother's Cardinal's jersey. Alex and Mallory had started to return to their seats when Jacqueline walked over to him.

"He's all grown up," she said.

"Yeah, he is. Look at him. I remember when he said he wanted to play ball and no one believed him. Now, look at him."

"You look like a proud father."

"I kinda feel like one. Since Dad died, I've felt like their father."

"I know. You did good."

"All right. Enough of this. There's girls up there waiting."

When they returned to their seats, Mallory slipped her hand into Jacqueline's. They were looking around the stadium, talking about the seats, trying the various snacks they'd bought when Jacqueline's phone rang. She felt it buzz in her pocket. The night was so near perfect. It was so wonderful that she didn't want to ruin it by answering the call of some long gone life she wanted to forget. So, she didn't answer. She just let it ring and ring and ring. Praying it would end soon, she kept her head down until finally it stopped. When it did, she relaxed and slouched in her seat. Then, there was a long buzz. She thought, *Fuck a text.* Fearing that it would continue, she pulled the phone out of her pocket. She was going to block the number.

Mallory felt her remove the phone and groaned instantly. Jacqueline leaned over and said, "When I get back to town, I'll get a new phone. A new number. A fresh start. I promise."

Mallory smiled and kissed her. "Thank you, honey." She looked over her shoulder to see what the person had said or sent. Recognizing the number instantly, she said, "Wait, that's my dad's cellphone number. Read the message."

Jacqueline read it to her, "It says. Hi, is everything okay?"

"My dad doesn't text. That has to be Zoe," Mallory shook her head and said, "That kid's all yours."

Jacqueline: Hi, Zoe?

Zoe: My iPad is dead. I left my charger at home. Grandpa said I could use his phone to talk 2 u.

Jacqueline: Okay. Just as long as he gave you permission.

Zoe: He did. What's going on?

Jacqueline: We're at a baseball game. Silas is playing. You can see it on TV.

Zoe: R things ok

Jacqueline: Yes, why wouldn't they be?

Zoe: Mom was crying. I was scared u didn't want us anymore.

Jacqueline: Adults can have disagreements and still love each other.

Zoe: u luv mom?

Jacqueline: Yes, of course, I do. Very much. And, you too.

Zoe: I was scared u weren't coming back.

Jacqueline: Of course, I'm coming back. We're a family. We always come back to each other.

Zoe: When will u be back?

Jacqueline: She'll be home on Sunday. I should be there by Monday night. Tuesday when you're back home, we need to have a family meeting.

Zoe: About what?

Jacqueline: All kinds of stuff

Zoe: Is it bad

Jacqueline: No, it's all good stuff.

Zoe: Cross your heart

Jacqueline: Cross my heart.

ABOUT THE AUTHOR

To those who are genuinely curious, K L Finalley was born in Florida in the seventies. In an effort to avoid the starvation of herself and her family, she has maintained steady employment while writing. In those rare moments when she is not working or writing, she enjoys baseball and vodka – in unison when available.

For more information, visit the below:

www.klfinalley.com

www.facebook.com/klfinalley

ALSO BY K L FINALLEY

EMERSON NOVELS

Cross Your Fingers

Cross Your Heart